NOT QUITE OVER YOU

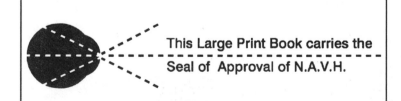

This Large Print Book carries the
Seal of Approval of N.A.V.H.

NOT QUITE OVER YOU

SUSAN MALLERY

WHEELER PUBLISHING
A part of Gale, a Cengage Company

Farmington Hills, Mich • San Francisco • New York • Waterville, Maine
Meriden, Conn • Mason, Ohio • Chicago

Copyright © 2018 by Susan Mallery, Inc.
Happily Inc.
Wheeler Publishing, a part of Gale, a Cengage Company.

Wheeler Publishing Large Print Hardcover.
The text of this Large Print edition is unabridged.
Other aspects of the book may vary from the original edition.
Set in 16 pt. Plantin.

LIBRARY OF CONGRESS CIP DATA ON FILE.
CATALOGUING IN PUBLICATION FOR THIS BOOK
IS AVAILABLE FROM THE LIBRARY OF CONGRESS

ISBN-13: 978-1-4328-5788-2 (hardcover)

Published in 2018 by arrangement with Harlequin Books S.A.

Printed in the United States of America
1 2 3 4 5 6 7 22 21 20 19 18

To Shari — you are a delight
and an unexpected bonus in my life.
Thank you for being so kind and
generous and just plain fun to be
around. This one is for you. Well,
honestly, you're going to have to share
Mr. Whiskers with the whole group,
but the rest of it is yours!!

CHAPTER ONE

Love at first sight was never a wise decision, but Silver Tesdal couldn't help herself. Sure, the Airstream was a few years old, with a couple of exterior dents and a messed-up interior in need of complete refurbishing, but still, the lines, the space. It was everything she'd wished for. She would need a three-quarter-ton truck to tow it and more staff, but she could make that happen — at least in her dreams.

There was a second, smaller Airstream in even worse condition, but the twenty-three-foot length would be perfect for low-key affairs. She could already picture what the two would look like refurbished and sporting her AlcoHaul company logo.

She leaned back in her desk chair and smiled. Right now her "company" had exactly one full-time employee — her. She hired any staff she needed on a per-job basis. But, she thought longingly as she looked at the For Sale listings on her computer, with the Airstreams, all that would change. She would need someone to run each of the new trailers, which meant a second and third employee, and hey, the money to meet payroll.

But first she had to buy the trailers, fix them up, get a couple of trucks to tow them from venue to venue and make sure she had enough bookings to make it all worthwhile. She'd run the numbers and she could do it and still turn a profit . . . In time. As for making it all happen now, when the trailers were available, for that she needed a loan. And while she loved her some Airstreams, she was less excited about dealing with banks.

Silver shut down her browser and picked up the slim, black leather briefcase she'd bought for eight dollars at an estate sale a couple of years ago. She wasn't the briefcase type, but since starting her business, she'd realized there were times she had to fit in with the conventional world. The briefcase helped her fool those who would otherwise judge.

She slipped in her wallet and her phone, then smoothed the front of her black pencil skirt before heading to the door to her loft. Today and today only, she'd traded in jeans and a tank top for a skirt, silk shell and cropped black blazer. She had applied conservative makeup and had pulled her long blond hair back into a French braid. Faux gold studs and black pumps with three-inch heels completed her transformation. She felt stupid, but knew appearances mattered. Dumb but true.

Ten minutes later, she pulled her truck into the parking lot of California First Savings and Loan. She had already been turned down by three other banks. If California First didn't give her a loan, then she was screwed.

"Not screwed," she murmured to herself. "If I don't get the loan, I will go on as before. I'm doing great and whatever the outcome, I'm going to be completely and totally fine."

Only she wanted the Airstreams. She wanted to grow her business and be more than anyone had assumed was possible. She was just a nobody from the wrong side of the tracks who had made a lot of stupid decisions along the way. Being able to expand her business meant proving to herself that she'd left all that behind. And yes, there might be a bit of *neenerneener* to those who had told her she would never amount to anything, but that was just a bonus.

She walked into the bank and headed directly to the executive offices. Her appointment was with Libby Saunders, the vice president in charge of commercial lending. Silver had met with her once before, when she'd applied for the loan, and today they were to discuss the outcome of the loan committee meeting. Despite Libby being the mother of one of Silver's closest friends, the thirty minutes with Libby had been tense and awkward.

Libby couldn't have made it more clear she disapproved of Silver, of her business and the viability of her business plan. Silver had been determined to defy the odds. She'd rerun the numbers, had lowered the amount she'd wanted to borrow and had instructed all her friends to pray, burn sage or sacrifice to create good karma.

She knocked once on Libby's open office door. The older woman looked up from her computer.

Libby was in her fifties and nearly a caricature of what people assumed a woman in banking management should look like. She wore dark suits, pearls and always had her hair up in a tight bun. She looked disapproving, with a perpetual almost-frown knitting her eyebrows together. Silver tried to remember if she'd ever seen Libby smile and couldn't. Not that she was around her that much, but on the surface, the banker was not a happy person.

"Silver," she said, the corners of her mouth nearly but not quite lifting in a smile. "How nice of you to be on time." She motioned to the chair opposite her desk.

"Libby."

Silver sat down and did her best to look confident and professional. She set her briefcase where Libby could see it and be impressed.

The other woman barely glanced at her estate sale find. "You did an excellent job revising your business plan. The numbers look good."

Silver allowed herself an internal fist bump, but kept her expression neutral.

"Having said that, I'm sorry to tell you that we won't be giving you the loan. You were right on the edge of being approved, but given the nature of your business — with the potential for liability and lack of steady customers — the committee simply couldn't come to an agreement."

A committee of one, Silver thought, determined not to let her disappointment and bitterness show. Libby had been her last hope. Okay, not Libby but the bank. Silver had already been to every other one in town. There was no point in trying out of the area. Happily Inc was a quirky destination wedding town. Things here moved to their own rhythm. Explaining to a banker outside Happily Inc that she wanted to buy trailers to fix up to be traveling bars for weddings would make her sound like an idiot — despite her excellent business plan.

"I am sorry," Libby added, her eyes bright with something that looked a whole lot more like satisfaction than regret.

She should have known, Silver told herself. There was no escaping her past — not in this town. Not with people like Libby around.

Silver knew the polite thing to do was to thank the other woman or offer to shake her hand or something socially acceptable. But she couldn't do it. Instead, she nodded before standing and made her way out of the suddenly too-warm office.

She felt ridiculous in her business clothes, as if she were a child at Halloween. No one was fooled. She was who she had always been — wild Silver Tesdal, the woman who owned a bar and didn't give a damn about what anyone thought of her.

She held on to her stupid briefcase as she

crossed the lobby, her heels clicking on the marble floor.

"Silver?"

The voice came from behind her. She didn't have to turn around to know who was calling her name. She did her best not to hunch like a cat in the rain, even as she faked a smile.

"Drew. Fancy seeing you here."

She didn't express surprise at seeing him — Drew also worked at the bank. He was, in fact, heir apparent to the glory that was California First Savings and Loan. A fact that was no doubt thrilling to him, annoying to her and completely irrelevant when it came to her loan.

His dark gaze swept over her, taking in the skirt, the heels and the briefcase. "What are you doing here?"

"Visiting an old friend."

"You don't have any friends here," he told her.

"Yes, I'm aware of that." More so now than ever.

Unfortunately, Drew wasn't an idiot. He looked from her back to the executive offices.

"You had a meeting with Libby."

"She *is* in charge of commercial loans." She began walking toward the exit.

All she had to do was get in her truck, then get home. She would go for a four-mile run, take a shower, scream into a pillow, and then mask her disappointment with a bottle of red wine and a burger. Tomorrow she would be strong and determined, but tonight there would be wine.

"Your loan application for the Airstreams," he said, as if putting the pieces together. "The loan committee isn't supposed to meet until tomorrow."

"They decided to meet early."

She could see the glass door leading to the parking lot, could almost touch it. Freedom was just. So. Close.

He stepped between her and the door. "She turned you down."

Not a question and not anything she wanted to talk about.

Sarcasm would be easy. There were a thousand choices, each of them more biting than the one before. Sarcasm could be a weapon, as were lies and the act of simply ignoring him and walking away. They were also proof that she felt the need to protect herself, as if Drew could still hurt her. Twelve years after the fact, shouldn't she not care in the least? Wouldn't that be the real victory?

She summoned a genuine smile. One that

made her seem smart and confident and more than capable — or so she hoped. Because to her at least, the truth was just so obvious.

"Drew, there was no way Libby was going to be anything but a long shot. I did my best and I wouldn't change anything." *Not even falling in love with you all those years ago. Even if you were an immature jerk who didn't know what he'd lost until it was too late.*

Okay, that last bit might have taken away her claim to the high ground, but at least she'd only thought it rather than saying it.

"Let me talk to her," he began.

"No. It's done. Let it go. I'm going to."

Even if letting it go meant not having two beautiful Airstreams to remodel. There would be other used trailers when she could save enough cash to buy them, refurbish them and gift them with trucks to tow them. She hadn't done the math, but she would guess her time frame would be two years. Maybe three.

The thought of waiting all that time was too depressing for words, but hey, that was why there was going to be wine later.

"It's not right," he told her. "I saw your business plan. You're an excellent risk."

"According to Libby, I was right on the margin. Hardly an excellent risk."

His gaze flickered. *Ah,* she thought. Some things never changed. Drew had never been a very good liar.

"We're done," she said, heading for the door.

Not just with the loan process, she thought, but with whatever had ever been between them all those years ago. She'd processed the anger, hurt, sadness, resentment and nearly every emotion in between. Facing him like this in a moment of disappointment and shame, she was happy to admit she felt almost nothing. Finally. Finally Drew was just some guy she used to know. Talk about a miracle.

She reached her truck, slid onto the seat and reviewed her plan. A run, a shower, wine and a burger. Celebrating the loan would have been a whole lot better, but that hadn't happened so she'd earned a night to mourn. First thing tomorrow, she would get her butt in gear and start a new plan. One that didn't involve banks or loans. She would be self-sufficient, she would be victorious and, truth be told, she would probably be a little hung over. But no matter what, she would be fine.

Drew Lovato took a couple of days to consider his options. Calling a special meeting of the commercial loan committee was one, only he'd checked the records of the last meeting and Silver's loan application had been shot down 7–2. He doubted any impassioned plea on his part would make a difference. Libby had made her case first, and apparently it had been a good one. A single swing vote he could probably manage, but finding three people willing to vote yes instead of no seemed unlikely.

He didn't know what his aunt had against Silver, but there was something, he thought grimly. Regardless, Silver still needed the money to expand her business.

Soon, he promised himself. When his grandfather retired and Drew took over the bank, policies would change. He wanted to support local businesses and help the community grow. That meant loaning money to entrepreneurs like Silver.

His second thought had been to set up a fake loan through the bank — using his own money. However, violating federal banking statutes was never a good idea. He doubted he would enjoy prison.

He could simply give her what she needed to buy the trailers. He smiled as he imagined how *that* conversation would go. Would she tear him a new one before or after she backed her truck over him? Silver was many

17

things — beautiful, smart, determined. She was also proud as hell, highly verbal and occasionally impulsive. The combination made life with her interesting, to say the least, and sometimes it came with an unexpected thrown object.

Alternatively, he could offer to loan her the money, using the same terms as the banks. Whatever risk the loan committee might have worried about wouldn't exist for him. He knew she would sell a kidney before defaulting on him of all people. Which meant she would probably say no. Or several versions of no, some of which would question his masculinity, his humanity and his relationship with everyone's mother.

The last option, and to be honest, the one he liked the best, was for him to buy into her business as a minority partner. He would supply cash and together they would grow the business.

There were several advantages on his end. While he'd thought he was over Silver, in the past few months, he'd found himself thinking about her more than was healthy. There was something about her — some combination of determination and sass — that he found difficult to ignore.

He knew he would enjoy spending time

with her and even if close proximity didn't lead to them rekindling their attraction, he liked the idea of adding value to her small company. He was a banker by birth and by trade — his world was a happier place when those who depended on him did well. Improving the community was part of his job description, so he would start with Silver. The question was how to convince her?

After discarding the idea of asking her friends to help with an intervention, which they would all likely refuse, and drugging her and forcing her to sign the paperwork — a little too much like a Jasper Dembenski novel for a guy who basically worked in a bank — he came up with what he thought was the perfect solution. He would use Silver's pride against her.

Smug in his brilliance, Drew purchased the two Airstreams and arranged to have them transported to Silver. He knew she kept her current trailer in the huge, fenced lot behind the graphic design and printing store. On the morning of, the trucker dropping off the trailers texted Silver that her delivery was thirty minutes out. He also gave Drew a heads-up. Drew arrived just as the delivery did and told himself the fireworks would be worth it. That or he would be dead, and hey, then he wouldn't care.

Silver stood in the middle of the paved lot, frowning mightily, with her hands on her hips. Drew pulled up just as she started explaining to the delivery guy that she hadn't bought the trailers.

"I wanted to," she said, looking adorably confused. "I've been by to look at them a half-dozen times, but I never . . ."

Her voice trailed off when she spotted Drew walking toward her. He figured confusion would quickly spiral into good, old-fashioned rage any second now. Three, two . . .

"Did you have something to do with this?" she demanded, glaring at him. "What is going on? Why are you here? Why do I have trailers? Dammit, Drew, what have you done?"

He motioned to the delivery driver, who was surreptitiously inching backward toward the safety of his cab.

"Sign the paperwork, Silver."

"I will not. These are not my trailers." She folded her arms across her chest. "And you can't make me."

Drew told himself he would admire the way she looked in tight jeans and tank top, with her long blond hair pulled back in a ponytail, later. After all this was settled, he would try to figure out if the tattoo on her left arm was new, because he sure didn't remember it and he'd seen every inch of her.

"I can't make you? That's mature." He motioned for the driver to give him the clipboard. "I'll sign for them. Let's get them unloaded."

"No," Silver said forcefully. "I will not let you put them here. This is my property." She hesitated. "I rent this space."

"I really have a schedule to keep," the driver said, looking anxious.

"Leave 'em by the curb." Drew grinned. "There's plenty of room and that's public property."

"The Happily Inc police department won't let you park them there indefinitely," Silver told him. "It's a violation of code."

"Or so you hope."

Drew wasn't concerned. There was no way Silver would leave her precious trailers unprotected for more than a day or two. She might take a while to come around but he was confident she would see the beauty of his plan. And if she didn't, well, he could take a nice long trip and see the country in one of his two Airstreams.

The trailers were unhitched and backed into place in a matter of minutes. Drew pocketed a copy of the paperwork and the driver took off, nearly burning rubber in his haste to get away. Silver waited until he was gone before approaching Drew. Her pale blue eyes filled with icy rage while her whole body stiffened, as if she were doing her best not to kill him.

"Whatever you've done, I don't want any part of it," she said, poking him in the chest hard enough to bruise. "You think you're so slick and that you can manipulate me, but you're wrong. I don't care why you did this or what you think is going to happen, but you are the wrongest kind of wrong there is. You don't get to dictate my life."

He'd been hoping they'd moved past politely acknowledging each other to being something closer to friends, but based on her behavior, he'd been a little too optimistic. Or maybe her anger was about something else, he thought. Maybe it was about not being sure what he expected from her in return. Maybe she was worried he was dangling an Airstream-sized carrot and she was going to have to make a choice she wouldn't like to get it.

He had assumed enough time had passed for her to think better of him, but now he wasn't sure. As to the trailers, he was simply going to wait her out.

"I'm not dictating anything," he told her, careful to keep his voice neutral. "I have an idea I hope you'll find interesting. When you're ready to talk."

The glare turned into a glower. "I'll never be ready to talk to you."

With that, she turned her back on him and walked away. Drew took a few minutes to inspect the interiors before locking up both trailers. He'd taken the day off work, so didn't have to worry about getting back to the bank. He would run some errands, grab a couple of sandwiches for lunch, then return to the trailers and wait. He had a feeling it wouldn't take long to lure out Silver.

As he walked to his car, he wondered if he'd made a massive miscalculation. Maybe she wouldn't come around. Maybe she really did hate him. Regardless, he had to try. Doing the right thing was part of his DNA and how he tried to live his life. Whenever he'd stepped away from that path, he'd been overwhelmed with regrets. Maybe not at the time, but later and permanently. Not marrying Silver Tesdal when she'd been pregnant with their child was the biggest regret of all.

CHAPTER TWO

"Either talk to him or I'm calling the police," Wynn said as she checked a printed wedding invitation against the approved proof.

"He's not breaking the law." Silver did her best to look out the window without being seen by anyone outside the building — namely a tall, possibly good-looking guy sitting in an Airstream.

"Drew's not the one I'm going to have arrested," her friend murmured without looking up. She held her long, dark curly hair out of her way as she turned her head to study the invitation from every angle.

"You wouldn't!"

Wynn looked up from the proof. "I wouldn't," she agreed, "but you are starting to get on my nerves. Come on, Silver. This isn't like you. Grow a pair and deal with Drew or take a baseball bat to his head, but don't *dither.* It's freaking me out."

"I don't know what to do," Silver admitted.

"You know exactly what to do. The problem is much more that you don't want to do it." Wynn nodded at her assistant. "They're perfect. Print them. The bride wants two hundred. Let's do a run of two-fifty, just in case."

"You got it, boss."

Wynn returned her attention to Silver. "You need trailers — he has trailers. Yes, he's going to want something in exchange. So go find out what it is." She shrugged. "I doubt it's sex. No sex is worth two of those." She pointed toward the trailers. "Not even sex with you."

"Maybe I'm amazing."

"No one is that amazing."

Silver had to agree with her. The trailers were so wonderful. She was desperate to go explore them, to touch every surface and imagine the possibilities, only she couldn't give in. Whatever Drew had planned, it was going to be bad for her.

"He's trying to lure me," Silver said, looking out the window again.

"And it's working. Now get on out there and find out what he wants. I think Hunter left some sports equipment in the back room. You can go see if there's a baseball bat for you to borrow if that makes you feel better."

"I don't need a baseball bat."

Maybe a little courage and some backbone, she thought as she straightened her shoulders. Dammit, why did this always happen? In every other situation in life she was strong and powerful, but when it came to Drew she was little more than a whimpering mess.

"Okay, I'm going out there to confront him."

"Good luck."

Silver nodded. She could do this, she told herself. She'd handled much-tougher situations when it came to Drew. For ninety-one magical days the summer she'd turned eighteen, she'd loved him with every fiber of her being. She'd given herself to him, heart and soul, and then she'd pretended she was totally fine when he went off to college. She'd even had the smarts to break up with him so that he could go live his life without her. She'd told him that they were never meant to be and that he should simply move on.

She'd done the right thing and she could always be proud of herself for that. But it had been so incredibly hard. She'd loved him more than she'd thought it was possible to love anyone. She'd loved him knowing that loving a man turned a woman into a fool. She'd been a willing fool and she'd gotten her heart ripped out and chopped with a meat cleaver.

"All in the past," she whispered to herself as she crossed the sidewalk. "All in the past."

The door to the largest trailer was open, as if in invitation. She felt herself starting to hunch again, then forced herself to stand tall. Lured or not, she would walk in proud and strong. Whatever was going on, she could handle it. She'd been through a whole lot worse with Drew.

She stepped into the trailer. Drew sat at the long sofa, an e-reader in his hands. He glanced up and smiled.

"Hi. How's it going?"

She ignored his questions and asked one of her own. "What are you doing here?"

"Waiting for you. I have lunch, if you're hungry."

He motioned to the built-in table and benches, as if expecting her to sit down. What was with him having *lunch* ready for the two of them? This wasn't a social visit. *Ack,* she should have taken Wynn up on her offer of a baseball bat.

Silver sank onto the padded bench. She put her hands on the table, then shoved them onto her lap only to put them back on the table. Everything about this felt weird and awkward and just plain uncomfortable. She wanted to run and scream, only before she could do either, she couldn't help noticing the perfect lines of the trailer. The size was just right and with a little refurbishing, there could be so much storage. She would have room for a long bar and beer on tap and —

"Turkey okay?" he asked, holding out two sandwiches. "Or ham?"

"Turkey."

He passed it over, then grabbed them each a can of diet soda along with a pile of napkins before sitting across from her. He nodded at the interior of the trailer.

"Needs a lot of work, but I see the potential."

"*You* see it?" She rolled her eyes. "You have no idea what this could be. To you it's just some old trailer, but to me, it's the next phase of my business. I've put thought into what I'm doing, Drew. I didn't just write a check."

"Contempt for the very money you wanted to borrow for yourself." His tone was mild, his expression more amused than offended. He took a bite of his sandwich. "Without the check you're so willing to deride, there would be no trailers. At least not now."

He had a point, which really annoyed her.

"Fine," she grumbled as she unwrapped her sandwich. "Why are you here?"

"I'm living the dream. Why are you here?"

She wondered if it would be wrong to kick him right in the shin. *So much violence,* she thought with a sigh. Her visceral reaction to Drew was because she knew he had all the power and she had none. Not a situation she enjoyed, ever.

Instead of answering, she started eating her sandwich. He continued with his and they had lunch in complete silence. He finished first. He opened a bag of chips, offered it to her, then spoke.

"So here's the thing," he began. "My grandfather is thinking of retiring."

"Okay." Hardly news. Grandpa Frank wasn't a young man. He was charming and vibrant but well past the age of retirement.

"There are complications," he continued. "Namely who is going to be chairman of the board when that happens."

"Why is there a question? You're the heir apparent, aren't you?" Drew had been the firstborn of the firstborn. With great power and all that. He had been destined to run the bank since before he'd started kindergarten. Back when they'd been dating, he'd talked about his future with excitement and anticipation. Drew had actually *liked* the idea of being in banking. Crazy, but that was Drew.

"Libby wants to throw her hat in the ring."

"I wish you'd told me that before I ate my sandwich," she said, pushing away the second half. "Why is she even in contention?"

"Technically anyone can throw his or her hat in the ring. I'm the obvious choice, but that doesn't mean the bank is my only interest."

"I thought that was all you'd been trained to do. Isn't that the point of your entire existence? You love the bank. Don't tell me you don't want to be the bank king right here in town. As if."

He smiled at her. "Silver, we all grow and change. I have. Every now and then I like to do something unexpected, just to see who's paying attention."

"I have no idea what that means."

"Me either but it sounds good." He leaned back against the bench. "So here's the thing. I have these two trailers."

She'd just started to relax, she thought as her entire body stiffened. She had no idea what was going on, but she had a bad feeling this might be a game to him. A cruel game with her as the target.

She remembered when they'd played different types of games, when their sport had been about pleasing each other. They'd been so desperately in love — or at least she had been. She was less sure about him. Despite his protestations at the time, in the end, he'd left her without a backward glance.

Not anything she needed to deal with right now, she told herself. She had to focus on the problem at hand — namely what did he want in return for the two Airstreams?

He put his large hands on the table and leaned toward her. "I'd appreciate it if you'd just listen to what I have to say, and then we'll discuss it."

She had no idea what "it" was, nor did she want to promise to not interrupt, or scream or hit him with something. But if she did anything but nod, he would suspect she was more upset than she should be.

"Fine," she said. "Talk."

"I want to buy into your business as a minority partner."

"What? Are you insane? Did you fall and hit your head? A minority partner? A *partner*? Of my business? The one I conceived of and saved for and started and have made successful all on my own?" She glared at him. "By. My. Self. There's only been me, Drew. Just me. A partner. Are you on crack?"

He smiled. "As long as you're willing to listen."

She leaned back and crossed her arms over her chest. "Go ahead."

"I want to start building my personal portfolio. I've been thinking of buying into several businesses around town. If that works out, I'll expand my empire, so to speak, and look for opportunities in Palm Springs, maybe Riverside or San Diego. When Libby turned down your loan I realized that I had a chance to act." One shoulder rose. "I'll admit I was impulsive, buying the trailers, but I could see what you wanted to do. I like your business plan. You've thought it all through."

She told herself the compliment didn't matter. She didn't need or want his approval. He was giving her an opportunity to expand — that was what was important.

"How do you see this working?" she asked, relaxing only slightly.

"I would want to be a real partner. I'd want to help with future planning and really be involved. Obviously I have a full-time job, but I could help out when you're shorthanded. Your work is mostly on the weekends, when I'm off."

She snorted. "You'd work parties?"

"Why not?"

"Gee, I don't know. Have you ever been a professional bartender? Or even an amateur one? Do you have the slightest idea what it's like to serve drinks to two or three hundred people in a very short period of time? Do you have a bartender's license? Do you know the difference between a mojito and a margarita?"

"Tequila." He chuckled. "Okay, I'd have to learn to be a bartender. I'm saying I'm willing to do that. I want to do that. I want to be more than the guy with a check. I want to be invested."

Her stomach clenched. *Nerves,* she told herself. *Just nerves and a dose of apprehension.* "Are you going to bartending school?"

"I was hoping I could learn some online and you'd teach me the rest. Silver, I'm a hard worker, I'm available nights and weekends and I'm not going to run off with the tip money."

"You couldn't just loan me the money to buy the trailers?" she asked before she could stop herself. While she never thought she would even think the question, let alone say it, the truth was owing him money would

33

be way better than giving up part of her business.

"I could, but I'd rather do this."

Typical. Men wanted what they wanted and the rest of the world didn't matter at all. "Maybe the hardware store in town would like a buy-in."

"Maybe they would, but your business is more fun."

"Oh, I don't know. All those power tools, the lumber section. It's a man's playhouse." She pressed her lips together. "How minority of a partner would you want to be?" Ninety-ten would be great, she thought. Wishful thinking but still great.

"Fifty-two–forty-eight."

She tried not to wince. That was nearly as close to fifty-fifty as they could get.

"I'm buying in with two trailers," he pointed out, as if he could read her mind. "I'll also invest twenty grand to cover refurbishing them. Hopefully there will be a few dollars left to put toward the trucks to tow them."

"I have savings," she said, trying to do the math in her head. "Enough to cover the trucks." Especially if she didn't have to buy the trailers or pay for refurbishing them. In fact there would be enough left over for her to explore some other ideas she had.

Agreeing to his deal meant she could move forward with her plans. AlcoHaul could grow and she could stop turning down business every week. But that came at a hefty price — working closely with Drew. Could she do that?

"I just don't know," she admitted. "I'm not sure we can work together."

"We always did fine together before."

"We were dating, and then we broke up."

"But we got along. Besides, I'm more mature now."

"Oh please."

"I'm saying I think we'd be good together."

In business, she reminded herself. He was talking business and only business. If she wanted anything else, she was a complete fool. And she wasn't ever going to be a fool for a man again — certainly not for Drew.

"I need to think about this," she told him. "Give me a few days to consider the offer, and then we'll talk."

"Sure." He looked at the print shop. "Is Wynn going to be okay with the trailers parked out here?"

He was manipulating her, she told herself. Trying to get her to offer to store them in the lot with her other trailer, knowing full well if she took that much ownership it

35

would be harder to walk away.

"I'll talk to her," she said instead. "Wynn's pretty easygoing and if these are parked on a side street, I doubt she'll care." She flashed him a smile. "I think your bigger concern is the police. I'm fairly sure there are zoning laws and you're violating them."

"I'll take my chances."

Why wouldn't he? Given his family connections, he would likely get special consideration from most city officials, including the police.

She stood and picked up the rest of her sandwich. "Thanks for lunch. I'll be in touch."

"I'll be waiting."

He stood, as well. In the small trailer, that put them far too close together. She could see the flecks of gold in his dark irises and the faint scar by the corner of his mouth. He wasn't the only one invading her space — the past was there as well, threatening to overwhelm her.

"Silver, I hope you'll agree to this. You've done really well with your business. With a little help, I think you can take things to the next level."

She wanted to ask if he ever had regrets about how things had ended. She wanted to know how long it had taken him to forget her and move on to the next woman and the next. She was desperate to find out if he ever thought of the child they'd made, then had given away.

What she said instead was, "Let me think about it."

"You know where to find me."

"I always have."

Drew watched carefully as Jasper stepped close. His friend moved as fast as a snake, striking out when Drew least expected it. He'd learned the hard way not to relax when Jasper spun away. More times than not, he came back harder, faster and ready to win.

The workout room was silent except for the sound of their breathing and the crack of the sticks connecting. Usually music pounded but not when they worked with fighting sticks. Concentration was required.

A couple of years ago, Jasper had wanted to use fighting sticks in one of his novels. He'd hired a trainer to spend a week in Happily Inc, teaching him. His friends had been invited to the intense classes, as had a few of the local fitness trainers. As far as Drew knew, the book was finished and sent off to the publisher, but Jasper continued to train with sticks because he liked it.

Drew's cousin Cade sat on the mat, out of range of their combat, calling out advice, praise and slurs.

"Duck, Drew. Watch that left arm of his. Jasper, my mama hits harder than that. Oh, good one. Get 'em."

Jasper advanced, forcing Drew to retreat. Drew sidestepped, faked a slash, then came in hard. Jasper slipped on the mat and went down on one knee just as the timer dinged.

"Well done," Cade called as he scrambled to his feet. "We got off lucky today. Only a handful of bruises and no broken bones."

The sticks were solid wood and struck hard. Getting hurt came with the territory. None of them had more than bruises, but they were often impressive and took a while to heal.

Jasper tossed Drew a towel, then took one for himself. They all walked to the stools in the corner. On the way, they grabbed water from the refrigerator against the wall.

Jasper's house was high enough in the mountains to be surrounded by trees. In the summer, the temperature was a good twenty or thirty degrees cooler than in town, and every now and then there was winter snow.

His place had started as a two-room cabin maybe eighty years ago. It had been added onto at least a dozen times. The house was a hodgepodge of styles and materials. Some of the rooms were large and stately and others were oddly shaped and poorly constructed.

When Jasper had bought the house, he'd built an office and the workout room. The latter had the traditional array of equipment found in a home gym, along with a big open area and a wall of mirrors. From what Drew could tell, Jasper was a "method" writer. He liked to physically work through any action scenes. He often had friends over to block out fight scenes and a couple of summers ago, he'd spent six weeks getting familiar with a hunting bow.

When they were seated, Cade unscrewed the top on his water. "So, Drew. Buying trailers?"

Jasper raised his eyebrows. "You bought trailers?"

"They're not for me."

"He's trying to bribe Silver into sleeping with him," Cade said with a chuckle. "I'm not sure that's the best way to get her attention, but if you don't have the goods personally then hey, whatever works."

"Shut up." Drew's tone was mild. He was used to his cousin's teasing. They'd been tight since birth.

"Why trailers?" Jasper asked. "And you did use the plural version of the word so there's more than one?"

"I want to buy into her business." He thought about mentioning the trouble with the bank loan but not only was the information personal, Libby was Cade's mother. The two weren't close but he doubted Cade would appreciate him dissing his mom.

He also wasn't going tell them that he'd flat-out lied to Silver. Yes, he wanted to be involved in her business, but not because he was "building his personal portfolio" or whatever other crap he'd told her. He was a bank guy, through and through. He had no more interest in buying into other businesses than sprouting wings, but the fib had been necessary to get her to agree.

As to the why — as in why was he working so hard? — that was harder to define. He just couldn't get her out of his head. Given their past, simply asking her out seemed fraught with peril. But this way, he could get to know her again while doing something interesting. Should things work out, then great. Should they not, he would loan her the money to buy him out — no harm done.

"The trailers were for sale, so I bought them. I'm hoping Silver lets me be a minority partner."

"She strikes me as the kind of person who prefers to be in charge." Jasper chugged more water. "Why that business?"

"Silver and I go way back. I'm helping an old friend."

Cade snorted. "Is that what we're calling it?" He turned to Jasper. "Drew and Silver have a past. The summer before Drew here took off for college, he and Silver had a thing. It was a hell of a summer. I still remember that party before Labor Day."

"Silver and I threw a big party by the falls," Drew explained to Jasper. "Underage teens, a lot of drinking."

Cade touched his water bottle to Drew's. "My first time getting drunk. I paid for it the next day, but the party was killer." He chuckled.

Jasper studied Drew. "So you and Silver were an item? Then what?"

"I went off to college." He hesitated. "Silver insisted we break up before I left. I didn't want to, but she was determined."

"She can be stubborn that way," Cade told him.

"She can. Then I left." There was more. So much more. Before he could decide what he should and shouldn't say, he found himself blurting, "She was pregnant."

Both Cade and Jasper stared at him.

"Seriously?" Cade asked. "What happened?"

"She came to visit me at college. I was well into my freshman year and had moved on. I didn't want to believe her, but I knew what we'd been doing. I proposed, she said no. We agreed to give up the baby for adoption."

Jasper and Cade exchanged a look.

"So you have a kid out there," Jasper said. "How old is he? Or she?"

"Nearly twelve. I never asked what she had. I assumed a boy." He'd always pictured a son, one who looked just like him. Ego, he supposed. And a lack of any other input. Of course, if they'd had a girl, he would have assumed she looked exactly like Silver.

"A kid," Cade said quietly. "Bethany and I want kids. The sooner the better, but you beat us all."

"We were young and foolish." They'd been passionately in love, he thought. That part had been about as real as it got.

"Is the baby why you want to go into business with her?" Jasper asked. "Out of guilt?"

"I don't feel guilty." Drew paused. "We were kids ourselves. We couldn't have been decent parents. I want to invest in Silver's company because I think it's the smart thing to do. I've run the numbers. She works hard, makes a good profit and is turning business away every week. It's a sound business decision."

"Uh-huh." Jasper didn't look convinced. "What did she say?"

"I think the real question is what did she hit you with when you told her what you'd done?" Cade chuckled.

"She's thinking about it." Drew grinned. "She was fine with it."

"Liar."

"Okay, but she really did listen."

Jasper finished his water and tossed the bottle into the recycling bin in the corner. "So you're going to invest in Silver's company, and then what? Are you going to help her manage the other trailers?"

"We're still discussing the details."

"The bank getting to you?" Cade sounded sympathetic. "I don't know how you stand it, being there all day. It's like a big, brick trap."

Drew knew the bank wasn't a trap — it was a living, breathing creature tied to the community. The bank was possibilities and he had a million ideas about how he was going to make it better.

"The bank is the least of it," he said, avoiding the question.

Cade shook his head. "Your folks still on you?" He turned to Jasper. "Drew's parents are . . . unusual. Happily Inc was never big enough for them. They always wanted to be somewhere else, doing something else. Howard, Drew's dad, got involved politically and got an ambassadorship when Drew was still in school. Where was it again?"

"Andorra," Drew said, remembering the thrill of having his parents leave town while he was in high school. He'd moved in with Grandpa Frank and life had gotten a whole lot easier. "It's near Spain."

"Never heard of it," Jasper said. "Maybe I should do some research and set a book there."

Cade grinned. "You should. Anyway, Howard had a couple more ambassadorships after that, then left the diplomatic corps to join a lobbying firm."

"They're still there," Drew admitted grimly. "Growing the company and making room for their firstborn."

Their only born, he added silently. Nothing would make his parents — mostly his mother — happier than having him take over the family bank for a couple of years, and then join his parents' lobbying firm. While he was all over the first half, he had no interest in being a lobbyist.

"Not your dream job?" Jasper asked.

"Not even close."

Jasper grinned at Cade. "Too bad they're not your parents. Imagine how happy they'd be to know their son was marrying a genuine princess."

"I don't know where to start with that," Cade admitted, then looked at Drew. "Have you told your mom about the engagement?"

"No, and I don't plan to. The last thing any of us want is my mother camping out in town so she can go to your wedding or whatever it turns out to be."

Cade had bought a stallion from the king of El Bahar. The "stable girl" who had delivered the stallion had turned out to be a royal princess in disguise. Cade and Bethany had fallen in love and were getting married. While the details hadn't been worked out, there would be some kind of event or celebration locally, complete with the royal family attending.

"Your mom is going to find out."

"Not from me." Drew wouldn't do that to someone he didn't like, let alone a cousin.

"Have you two decided on your wedding plans?" Jasper asked. "You could always elope."

Cade grimaced. "We've talked about it,

but Bethany doesn't want to disappoint her parents. We're definitely holding the ceremony in El Bahar, but we're going to do something here, too. The details are being worked out."

Drew supposed that the logistics of marrying into a royal family put his life questions in perspective.

"Let me know if there's going to be a party," Jasper told him. "I'm heading to New York in a couple of weeks. I can rearrange things if it means hanging out with royals."

Cade didn't look convinced. "You're like Drew. You don't care anything about someone being royal or important."

Jasper grinned. "That is true, but I'm always looking for ideas for the next book. Plus, you're a friend. Someone has to be around to keep the crazies off your back."

Drew nodded. "Jasper will handle them and I'll run interference with my mother if she shows up."

Cade winced. "Thanks, Drew. You're a good friend."

"You know it."

CHAPTER THREE

Silver lay on the carpet, her feet propped up on the sofa. She rested her cell phone on her stomach and adjusted her earbuds.

Leigh was due to call in about three minutes and her friend was nothing if not prompt. While she waited, Silver thought about all that had happened in the past few days and wondered if she had an answer to the obvious question — what was she going to do about the trailers?

She was tempted. Very tempted. They were exactly what she wanted and with them she would have a chance to expand her business. Between the extra twenty grand Drew was throwing in on top of her own savings, she could refurbish both of them, buy the trucks needed to pull them, have enough left over for an emergency fund *and* have some work done downstairs.

Her second-floor loft apartment sat above retail space. Currently, Silver used the downstairs as a showroom, with large posters showing her trailer at a variety of venues and a couple of tables set up like a party. There was a place to go over drinks menus and discuss specifics. But she kept thinking she should do something to monetize the square footage. Right now it was just deadweight.

Again, with Drew's help, all that could change. The price would be both working with him and having to share the profits. He wasn't buying into her business for the thrill of it. She had so much to think about.

She picked up her phone and smiled. One minute to go. While she was waiting, she touched the screen to display her photos. She went right to the folder that held the pictures of Autumn, then scrolled through a half dozen.

Autumn was eleven, with dark hair and deep blue eyes and looked a lot like her dad. She was smart, pretty and kind. Okay, and yes, she had a bit of the devil in her, but she wasn't mean — just adventurous.

Silver studied the child she and Drew had created and knew that at some point she was going to have to come clean. Especially if they were going to work together. Not that she'd done anything wrong. She'd gotten pregnant and she'd told Drew. They'd agreed on adoption and Silver had returned home to find the right family.

What Drew didn't know was that while pregnant, Silver had gotten close to the adopting couple. That she'd ended up living with them the last few months of her pregnancy and that she and Leigh had formed a tight bond that still existed today. Drew didn't know that after Autumn's birth, when Silver had felt confused and uncertain about her future, she'd gone back to Los Angeles and had lived with Leigh and her husband. Although the two of them had eventually divorced, Silver, Leigh and Autumn were family. They talked all the time, visited a lot, and Silver regularly took Autumn for a weekend or two every year.

The familiar guilt returned. Silver pushed it away, telling herself that it wasn't as if she'd lied to Drew. He'd never once asked. For all he knew, she could have lost the baby. For him, once the decision had been made, he'd totally forgotten about the pregnancy, while she'd had to live it for the next six months. And beyond.

Her phone rang. She pushed the talk button and smiled. "Hey, you."

"Hey, yourself."

Leigh's voice was happy and filled with affection. They were only twelve years apart in age, so more like sisters than mother and daughter.

"I got your text about the trailers," Leigh continued. "What are you going to do?"

"I'm still thinking."

"It seems like a good opportunity."

"You think I should work with Drew?"

"If he's going to be a minority partner, then why not? You get the trailers, you don't have to worry about a bank loan and you can grow the business how you want to."

"But it's Drew."

"At least you know him and he has a strong business background."

"Maybe knowing him is the problem," she grumbled. "I don't know if we can work together or not."

At one time, she'd been wildly in love with him, but they'd both been young and that was so different from a business relationship.

"Could you trust him?" Leigh asked. "Because without trust, there isn't anything."

"I have to think about that, too," Silver told her. "I would need to get to know him again."

Leigh laughed. "Good thing he's already committed to the trailers. It means he's stuck with your timetable."

"I hadn't thought about it that way, but you're right. So what's new with you?"

"I do have some exciting news. At least I hope you'll think it's exciting."

"Yes?"

"Denton has decided he really wants a wedding."

Silver smiled. Leigh's fiancé had been all in on a big wedding, then had wanted an elopement and was, apparently, back on with a wedding.

"That man. He needs to make up his mind."

"I agree. The thing is, I told him it doesn't matter to me, but I'd really prefer a wedding. Some for me but mostly for Autumn. She is desperate to be a bridesmaid."

Silver felt her chest tighten a little at the thought of Autumn in a beautiful dress, walking down the aisle in front of her mother.

"Have you two figured out when? Or where, for that matter? Just say the word and I'll clear my calendar."

Silver would be at the wedding, but just as important, she would stay with Autumn while Leigh and Denton went off on their honeymoon.

"It's funny you should ask that. We have set the date. It's in a couple of months."

"Oh?" Silver swung her feet to the ground and sat up. "Won't Autumn be in school? Are you going to delay your honeymoon?"

"I know, I know. So many details. And here's the thing." Leigh hesitated. "Gosh, I hope you're going to be okay with this."

Silver frowned. What wouldn't she understand? "You're marrying a great guy. Of course I'm good with it."

"It's not the who — it's the where. Now hear me out. Once Denton said he wanted a wedding rather than us just eloping or getting it done at City Hall, things kind of snowballed. We were talking locations and on a whim, I called around in Happily Inc. You'll never guess!"

Silver felt her breath catch in her throat. Happily Inc, as in the town where she lived? Where *Drew* lived?

"Tell me," she said, hoping she didn't sound the least bit worried.

"I spoke to this wonderful woman — Pallas. Do you know her?"

Silver told herself to stay totally calm. That everything was going to be fine. "Uh-huh. She owns Weddings Out of the Box."

"Yes, that's her. She'd just had a cancellation for a theme wedding. The bride and groom couldn't stand waiting and eloped, but everything had already been ordered, so it was just there if I wanted to claim it. I'd never thought about doing anything like that, but it's a *Great Gatsby* theme. The time period is so fun and the ideas they had were just charming. My dress is going to work and I've been looking online and I've found the best dress for you and another one for Autumn and well, Denton and I want to get married in Happily Inc and then have Autumn stay with you while we go on our honeymoon. Is that okay?"

Silver was grateful to be sitting on the floor so she didn't have to worry about freaking out and fainting. Autumn here? Leigh getting married *here*? No. No! They couldn't. She couldn't. There was no way to keep Drew from finding out about their daughter if Autumn was in town for a week or two.

"I could take care of Autumn at your place," Silver offered, thinking that if she limited the amount of Happily Inc time then . . .

"Funny story." Leigh laughed. "You know Denton and I each listed our condos and we're building a house together?"

"Uh-huh."

"Well, our condos have sold and are closing right before the wedding, but we can't get into our new place until after the honeymoon. We're moving everything into storage. I guess technically we're between homes. Or we will be."

Silver pulled her legs to her chest and rested her head on her knees. She told herself to breathe, that everything would be just fine.

"Silver? Is this okay?"

"Of course it is," she lied. "Yes, and yes. I'm thrilled you're getting married here, and of course Autumn can stay with me while you and Denton are on your honeymoon. It will be fun."

She hoped she sounded perfectly happy and excited and did she mention happy? "What about Autumn's schoolwork?"

"I've taken care of that. Her teachers are giving her the assignments ahead of time. There's a home-schooling kind of internet lab in town and I've already checked with them. Autumn will be there for six hours a day, Monday through Friday, just like regular school." Leigh laughed. "It's all coming together, just like it was meant to be."

"Just like." Silver's voice was faint.

She was well and truly trapped. She loved Leigh and couldn't be anything but happy for her. Being with Autumn was always fun and she looked forward to their one-on-one girl time. The only problem was, of course, Drew. There was no way Silver could explain away a kid who looked like him, who was the exact age their child would have been. He wasn't stupid — he would put the pieces together. And not just him. Anyone who saw Autumn and Drew within twenty feet of each other would have questions.

"I'm going to have to come clean with him," Silver said. "Tell Drew about Autumn."

"There is that." Leigh's voice softened. "I'm a little worried about it. Am I pushing you?"

"No, of course not. You're getting married and I'm so happy. I'll get together with Pallas and talk to her about how things are going. You're going to love how she handles things. I'll create the perfect signature cocktail for your reception. Leigh, this is going to be the wedding of your dreams."

"Oh, sweetie, thank you. I appreciate what you're saying so much. Autumn is super excited about everything. Okay, I need to run but we'll talk soon."

"Of course. I love you."

"I love you, too. Bye."

They hung up. Silver pulled the earbuds from her ears and closed her eyes. Too much had happened too quickly and she was going to need a minute to process everything.

Leigh's wedding was going to be its own kind of mess. Not the logistics — Pallas knew exactly how to throw the perfect event. It was more that Silver was going to have to explain her relationship to Leigh. Which meant telling people about Autumn. She was fairly confident her friends would be totally on board but she was less sure about how Drew would accept the information. Yes, he knew about their child, but nothing else.

Guilt tapped on her shoulder, but she ignored it. She hadn't done anything wrong. She wasn't the bad guy. She'd been up-front from the beginning. Her relationship with Autumn was her business. If he'd cared, he could have asked what had happened, but instead he'd gone on with his life without so much as a backward glance. Which all sounded really good, but did nothing to take away her growing sense of dread and discomfort.

A reckoning was coming — she could feel it.

"Silver, I'm really sorry. I kept hoping I would get better."

Silver told herself it would be wrong to respond with anything but sympathy. Georgiana was a steady, dependable worker and she'd never once flaked out on an event.

"It's okay. You go take care of yourself. I'll be fine."

"You won't be fine." Georgiana groaned. "I gotta throw up, and then I'll call you —"

Conversation ended with a gagging sound followed by a noise Silver didn't want to identify. It took her a second to keep from throwing up herself. She ended the call and tucked her phone into her jeans pocket, then tried to figure out what on earth she was going to do. In less than four hours, there was a wedding for three hundred and twenty people at Weddings Out of the Box. The bride and groom were expecting her to handle all their beverage needs and as of ten seconds ago, she had no staff.

She got out her tablet and double-checked the drinks menu for the night. The theme was a casual beach wedding. In order to keep costs down, the couple had chosen two signature drinks, along with beer and wine. In a pinch, Silver could get by with minimal help, but she absolutely needed at least one other person around.

All the usual suspects were unavailable for the same reason Georgiana wouldn't be in. That left friends, most of whom worked in the wedding business, so would be busy on a Saturday night with minimal notice. She tried Carol, but the call went directly to voice mail. Wynn's did the same, leaving Silver cursing under her breath. A name occurred to her, but she ignored it until there were no other options.

"Hey," Drew said when he answered. "I didn't expect to hear from you so quickly. What have you decided?"

"I haven't. I'm still considering." More things than he knew about, she thought. Not just the business proposition but how she was ever going to tell him about Autumn. Neither of which concerned her now.

"Did you mean what you said about helping me with events?" she asked. "That you'd be a real working partner?"

"I did. Why?"

"I want to give you a trial run. It will help me decide."

She knew she was assuming a lot — for one thing, that Drew would be available on a night when most single, good-looking guys had plans. Not that she'd heard of him dating anyone, but he often kept his romantic relationships private. For all she knew, he was practically engaged, something she found herself not wanting to think about.

"You want me to work a wedding?" he asked. "Tonight?"

"Yes."

"Is the last-minute thing a test or desperation?"

She sighed. "Mostly desperation. My regular hires called in sick. They worked a party at the Chapel on the Green. Someone brought in some bad shrimp and they all have food poisoning." Silver shuddered. "Based on what I heard, it's really awful."

"I don't need any details," he said quickly. "I'm happy to help. Just tell me when and where."

"Weddings Out of the Box in an hour. Wear khakis and a Hawaiian shirt. That's what all the servers are wearing."

"Should I bring anything?"

"I've got that handled." She hesitated. "Thanks, Drew. You're helping me out of a jam."

"Glad to do it. See you in an hour."

Silver hung up. She'd already changed into khaki shorts, a red bikini top with an open red Hawaiian shirt tied at the waist. Her hair was pulled back in a simple braid with a silk hibiscus clipped to the end. Her makeup was light, her earrings simple gold hoops. Her job was to provide bar service and otherwise blend in with the background. In a perfect world, she wouldn't be noticed at all.

She drove over to Weddings Out of the Box and backed the trailer into place. Once it was in position, she unhitched it and drove the truck around to the far end of the parking lot, then returned to her Airstream to start setting up. That morning she'd collected all the supplies she would need for the drinks. The decorations had been finalized and delivered at the last prep meeting on Thursday. Except for additional manpower, she was good to go.

She'd barely unlocked the trailer when she heard the sound of rapid footsteps on the walkway. She turned and saw Renee Grothen scurrying toward her.

The petite redheaded wedding coordinator had a tablet in one hand, a clipboard in the other and an air of concern pulling her eyebrows together. Looking at her, one would assume the sky was falling, but Silver had done enough weddings with Renee to know that the woman was always in full-on freak-out mode right up until the wedding started. Once the happy couple were safely married, she slowly relaxed. As the reception transitioned from appetizers to entrées to cake-cutting with nary a disaster, she relaxed a little more and the frown went away. Renee knew her stuff, but she was a little on the tightly wound side.

"I'm fine," Silver said before Renee could ask.

Renee's green eyes widened. "I heard there was food poisoning and that everyone was vomiting."

"They are, but I wasn't there and I'm fine."

Renee's hands trembled. "You can't handle the bar yourself. It's too much. Even with the limited drink menu there is simply no way —"

Silver smiled. "Renee, trust me. I have it under control. Help is on the way. This part of the wedding is totally taken care of."

Before Renee could start keening or whatever it was she did when she was really upset, Pallas, the owner of Weddings Out of the Box, joined them. Silver and Pallas had been friends for years. When Pallas had started working at Weddings Out of the Box and Silver had opened AlcoHaul, they'd begun working together on a regular basis.

The previous year Pallas had fallen madly in love with artist Nick Mitchell. They'd married and were expecting their first baby. Silver glanced at her friend's still almost-flat stomach.

"How are you feeling?"

Pallas's first trimester had been a nightmare of morning sickness.

"Better," her friend said. "I'm only occasionally queasy and it passes quickly. What a relief!" She turned to Renee. "If Silver says she has it covered, she has it covered. You can let it go." She smiled. "I mean that."

Renee's nod was reluctant. She'd only been working for Pallas for a month or so and was still in triple-checking mode. Or maybe she was always like that, Silver thought. It would be a tough way to live but she would guess it meant all the details were managed.

Pallas led Renee away and Silver finished opening up the large double doors on the side of the trailer. She connected two power cords, then turned on the lights inside. She pulled out boxes of decorations and set them aside. The folding tables and chairs came next. They were stacked together to be assembled later. The large easel and chalkboard were in the back. She got them out, along with a box of chalk.

Drew walked up, dressed as she'd requested. He looked good. Calm and capable and just a little bit sexy. When he spotted her, he frowned.

"Hey, you've already unloaded. Did you leave anything for me to do?"

"Plenty," she said, trying not to let her

relief show. Of course, she'd known he would be here, but having him actually present made her feel better about everything. Despite her promises to Renee, she was a little concerned about getting everything set up in time. Even with Drew around, she was short a body and both her helpers had known what to do. Drew was a novice.

Still, he'd always come through in a pinch. Back when she'd told him she was pregnant, the first thing he'd done was propose. Compared to that, tonight should be a snap.

She had him hook up the hose that would keep the water tanks full, then wash his hands.

"Your first job is to cut up honeydew melon," she told him. "It's messy so you'll want to wear an apron."

She half expected him to protest the coated cotton apron covered with drawings of landmarks of downtown London, but he only settled it over his head, then tied the strings behind his waist.

"Cut up how?" he asked. "Big chunks? Little chunks?"

She got out a massive cutting board, a serving spoon and large knife. "I keep it sharp, so be careful." She set two bowls in front of him. "The bigger one is for the melon. The smaller one is for the seeds. The fastest way to do this is to cut the melon in half, then seed it."

She demonstrated. She placed the flat side down on the cutting board and cut it into two-inch slices. "Cut off the rind then chop the slices into big cubes. Those go in the bowl."

"Got it," Drew said. "How much do you want me to do?"

She showed him the case of honeydews. "All of them. There are more bowls in the cupboard by your feet. When you have five full bowls, come get me."

"Will do." He winked.

The unexpected movement caught her off guard. She felt a flash of heat low in her belly. *No, no and no,* she told herself. She wasn't going down the *Drew is the sexiest man I've ever known* path. Not now, not ever. This was work only. Work and maybe an awkward conversation about the child they'd given up. There would be no funny business, regardless of how he winked at her.

Drew went right to work. He cut and chopped deliberately, being careful to keep his fingers away from the blade. After a couple of seconds, she realized she couldn't monitor him — not if everything else was going to be ready on time.

She left him in the trailer and went outside. She pulled the portable, custom-built bar from its storage hatch at the back of the trailer and carefully lowered it to the ground, then wheeled it into place. She locked the wheels, then began stacking the plastic racks that held the glasses. Beer would be served in the bottle, so no glasses needed there. She had wineglasses for the Sangria, champagne flutes for the mimosas and highball glasses for those who only wanted water. The soda/coffee/tea station was self-serve and across the way, so not her problem today.

She put out two small squat tables and set a big galvanized steel beverage tub on each. The beer was in the refrigerator and there was plenty of ice in the freezer. She would put out both right before the ceremony started. The placement — behind the bar — would keep the beer handy, but not available for guests to simply grab and run. Silver liked to know who was drinking what. Part of her job was to make sure no one got too drunk and ruined the event.

She set up the folding tables and chairs. The ones she used were slatted black faux wood. They were lightweight, durable and could fit into nearly any theme.

She only put out six tables with four chairs

each. They were there for quick conversations, not to be a gathering place away from the main party. Silver placed them on the far side of the bar so they wouldn't impede the flow of traffic, then opened the boxes of decorations.

The casual beach wedding theme was easy. She put woven mats on the grass by the trailer. There was a mason jar candle in the bride's colors for every table. She placed faux coral around the mason jars and made sure there were a couple of long gas lighters behind the bar. Once the wedding had started, she and Drew would light all the candles so they would be burning nicely by the time the guests came out for the reception.

She stacked driftwood by the bar and strung twinkle lights around the entrance to the trailer before stepping inside to check on Drew.

"How's it going?" she asked, moving beside him to inspect his work.

"Great."

He'd filled four bowls with cut-up honeydew and was working on the fifth.

"You work fast," she said.

"Speed isn't always important but today I want to impress the boss."

She ignored the speed comment, not sure

exactly how he meant it. Regardless, she had to stay focused on the job at hand. "So far, I'm impressed."

"Good to know."

She had to reach around him to pull glass pitchers from an overhead cupboard. Despite her best efforts, she brushed against him. It was worse with the stainless steel beverage dispenser. She had to shimmy and bend down, only to end up rubbing her butt against his.

"Sorry," she said, avoiding his gaze. "Small space."

"I don't mind."

She didn't mind, exactly, either; it was just so unnecessary. They were working. *Focus,* she told herself. Be strong. Businesslike. Pretend he's Georgiana. Because with Georgiana, she never noticed the tight space. They just did what had to be done without any fuss.

"Done," Drew said.

"Good. Rinse your hands, then get out the Vitamix. We'll work in small batches."

She showed him how to fill the container with ice, sugar and honeydew.

"You want to make sure the mixture is completely liquefied. No lumps. Then you'll taste each batch to make sure it's sweet enough."

"How will I know?"

"I'll taste the first couple with you so you can learn what we need."

He looked at her. "You're good at this."

"It's my job."

"No, it's more than that. You like this and it shows. The people who hire you are lucky to have your expertise and dedication."

The unexpected compliment left her flustered. What on earth was wrong with her?

"Thank you."

"Welcome. Now I'm going to master the Vitamix."

While he worked, she pulled out a three-gallon open container and poured in rosé, Burgundy, pineapple juice and fruit punch, along with the juice of both lemons and limes. She used a big, long-handled spoon to mix everything together, then tasted its result. Not her thing, but good, she thought. She'd started with chilled ingredients, so the Sangria was already cold.

The large container went into the industrial refrigerator that took up nearly a quarter of the trailer. She would fill the beverage dispenser right before the wedding started and set it outside on the bar. There was a built-in compartment for ice, which kept the drink cold without diluting it.

As she worked, Drew liquefied batch after batch of honeydew. She made random checks on the sweetness, then put the filled pitchers into the refrigerator. The mimosas were a combination of the honeydew mix and champagne. She would pour into the glass from each hand, creating a bit of entertainment along with the cocktail.

A smooth event was all about prep work, she thought as she grabbed both a champagne flute and a wineglass. She poured water into each, added a drop of purple food color from the bottle she kept tucked in a drawer and left the glasses on the counter.

"If you have to pour, that's how much," she told him, pointing to the glasses. "Sangria in the wineglass, mimosas in the champagne flute. If they ask for you to add more, tell them we'll be here all night."

Renee hurried over, clipboard and tablet in hand. "We're nearly ready. Are you ready? Is everything okay?"

Silver waved to the tables, the decorations, then opened the refrigerator to show her the pitchers filled with liquefied honeydew and the giant container of Sangria.

Renee visibly relaxed. "Thank you. I can always count on you to give me one thing to check off my list. You're the best, Silver.

69

Have a good wedding."

"You, too. Good wedding."

When she'd scurried away to check on yet another detail, Drew finished filling the last pitcher.

"She's a little tense," he said.

"Weddings are a big deal for the entire wedding party. There's rarely a chance to get a do-over so it has to be perfect the first time. Plus the whole getting married thing is always stressful. That's a lot of pressure. Renee wants each bride and groom to have exactly what they want."

"You like her."

"She's growing on me. I can respect someone who always gives their best."

He looked at her. "Was that a general comment or were you specifically aiming it at me?"

She frowned. "Why would you ask that? We weren't talking about you."

"Just checking."

"You thought I was taking a dig at you? Why? You earn a living."

"In a bank, and I suspect you have no idea if there's actual work involved."

He was right about that. What did he do to fill his day? Meetings? Reading reports? Telling others what to do?

That summer they'd dated, he'd always

been so physical — going and doing. She couldn't imagine him sitting behind a desk all day.

"Point taken," she said, then smiled. "But I wasn't talking about you at all."

"Good to know."

They looked at each other. Silver felt something grow between them. More than awareness, although that was there. Maybe it was the past, she thought, reminding herself she was over him and not interested in starting something up again. That would be stupid. Only he'd always appealed to her and —

"I think the guests are starting to arrive," he said, distracting her.

She turned and saw that people were making their way inside. She watched for wayward invitees. The bride and groom didn't want beverage service before the wedding, so when people approached, Silver guided them toward the building where the ceremony would take place.

"Do you always have to do that?" Drew asked. "Fend off those looking to get drunk early?"

"Not all the time, but it happens. As for getting drunk, we do our best to prevent that. There are things to look for."

"I know. I've been reading up on being a

bartender." He ticked off points on his fingers. "No doubles, no two drinks at a time. If you think someone's having too much, give them water and suggest they eat. At an event like this where there are likely to be parents paying or at least contributing, getting help can be useful, unless the person drinking too much *is* the parent."

Silver raised her eyebrows. "You have been doing your homework."

"I told you I would." He moved toward her. "Silver, I'm serious about being a partner in the company. I don't want to take over and I don't want to run things. I want to be a part of the business. A minority partner."

"Barely," she grumbled, trying to ignore the faint hunger that seemed to be growing inside of her. "You want a practically even split."

"What do you want?"

To have enough money that she didn't need anyone — not even Drew. But as that was unlikely to happen . . .

She thought about what he was offering her and how much she wanted to grow the business. She thought about all the weddings and parties she had to turn down and how much she really liked what she did.

"I want a sixty-forty split," she said, bracing herself for instant regret. There wasn't any. Instead she felt a sense of relief and anticipation. Drew had him some fine-looking trailers.

For a second he didn't say anything, then slowly, he started to smile. "Sixty-forty. I'm assuming you're the sixty."

"You would be correct."

Their gazes locked. For a second she felt the same flutter in her stomach that had always accompanied her Drew-time. She firmly squashed the sensation, reminding herself that had been a million years ago. They were totally different people now.

He flashed her a grin, then held out his hand. "Done. I'll have my lawyer draw up the paperwork and get it to you this week. We need to figure out what we want to do with the trailers. They're in great shape and have so much potential."

They shook hands. She ignored the tingles when they touched.

"I already have plans," she told him. "I've been working on them for a while. You can look them over and we can talk about them."

"This is going to be great," he told her. "You have a strong business plan and plenty of experience. I have a fresh eye and lots of contacts. We're going to be a good team."

"We are."

Renee hurried out of the building and waved at her. Silver waved back.

"That means the ceremony is nearly over," Silver told Drew. "Get ready for the crowd. The first rush is always the big one."

While Drew opened bottles of champagne, she filled the stainless core of the beverage dispenser with ice and put on the cap. Once it was secure, she set the beverage dispenser on the cart by the bar before carefully pouring in the Sangria mixture. She poured ice into the galvanized tubs and added bottles of beer. Drew had already brought out three pitchers of the honeydew mixture.

She set two large trays on top of the bar. "You start filling the wineglasses with Sangria," she told him. "I'll take care of the mimosas."

After filling one tray with champagne flutes, she poured in the honeydew mixture and topped it with champagne. By the time they'd filled a tray with each drink, there was a crowd of people walking toward them.

Silver smiled as the first guests approached. "Good evening. We have two signature drinks today, along with beer. The honeydew mimosa is really delicious, if you'd like to try that."

"I'll take a beer," the man said.

"I want the mimosa."

Drew pulled a beer out of the ice, wiped the bottle, then used a bottle opener to pop off the cap. Silver handed a flute to the woman and the beer to the man before turning to the next couple.

She calculated the number of people waiting and figured they would have a twenty-minute rush then a steady stream for the next two hours. Things would slow down after that.

She and Drew worked well together. When the mimosas got low, he handled the guests while she poured more. It was only when the initial crowd had dwindled that she realized she'd forgotten to tell Drew one very important thing — that she had a relationship with their daughter and that Autumn would be coming to town.

CHAPTER FOUR

Monday mornings Silver usually slept in late. Weekends were always busy with two or three bookings. This past weekend, there had been a wedding Sunday afternoon — this after the Saturday night event. The beach wedding had gone until two in the morning while the Sunday afternoon wedding hadn't ended until nearly ten at night. But despite the opportunity to stay in bed, she'd awakened at dawn.

She knew that Drew was the reason she hadn't been able to indulge in her Monday morning ritual. Between the new partnership, Leigh's upcoming wedding and the reality of Autumn, she had too much on her mind.

She got up and decided to take advantage of her extra time by cleaning her loft apartment. Then she placed her orders for the upcoming weekend and tried to figure out what to take to the girlfriend lunch.

Nearly every Monday or Tuesday she and her friends met for lunch. In a town where weddings dominated the calendar, the locals treated Monday and Tuesday as their weekend. Silver and her friends rotated hosting duties for their lunch. Whoever hosted provided the entrée while everyone else brought another dish. Silver was toying with the idea of making a salad when she realized she had a couple of leftover honeydew melons.

She cut them up, then pureed them with ice but didn't add any sugar. She put the sealed container into a cooler along with a few cans of lemon-lime soda, plastic glasses and spoons. Before she left for the lunch, she called in an order to her favorite Mexican restaurant. She picked up chips, salsa, guacamole and a dozen chicken taquitos, then drove out to the animal preserve.

In addition to being a wedding destination town, Happily Inc was the proud home of one of the most awarded recycling centers in the country. Theirs was a town that recycled and composted in earnest. There were even competitions where residents on different blocks tried to have the least amount of trash each week.

The owners of the Happily Inc Landfill and Recycling Center had also purchased hundreds of adjoining acres where they'd started an animal preserve. The nonpredatory residents — zebras, gazelles, a water buffalo and a new-to-them herd of giraffes grazed, played and added a charming element to the already-quirky town.

Carol Lund-Mitchell ran the animal preserve. Her father and uncle owned the landfill and the surrounding land, and she took care of the animals. When it was Carol's turn to host and the weather was nice, they ate outside in the preserve.

Silver followed another small pickup into the parking area by the main office, then waved as Bethany climbed out.

"Tell me you didn't bring salad," the pretty blonde called as she lifted a bakery bag off the seat next to her. "I'm very stressed these days and in desperate need of sugar and carbs."

"I brought both."

"That's why I love you." Bethany laughed. "Pallas texted to say she was bringing Renee to lunch today."

"I know. I heard from her, too."

Renee had moved to town a few months ago. Pallas had talked to Silver about adding her new employee to the girlfriend lunch. Given how tense Renee could be, Pallas hadn't been sure, but Silver had given her a thumbs-up. Renee had loosened up in recent weeks and there had been hints of a wicked sense of humor.

"I'm excited not to be the new girl," Bethany confessed.

"We can't all have been born here," Silver teased. "Some of us got lucky and some of us didn't. But even us transplants become family."

They walked onto the path leading into the preserve. After passing through a double set of gates, they made their way to the big tree where Carol usually set up lunch. She'd spread out a half dozen blankets and brought in big pillows for lounging.

Silver stared at the familiar arrangement. Carol, a sensible-looking redhead wearing khakis and work boots, looked at her.

"What? Did I forget something?"

Silver smiled. "I was just wondering how much longer we can have lunch out here. We try to get together at least three times a month and with us rotating the location through all six or seven of us, we won't be back here for at least two months." She eyed her friend's rounded belly. "I'm not sure you and Pallas will be physically capable of sprawling on the ground then."

Carol and Pallas were both pregnant. They were married to brothers, and Natalie, newly engaged to yet another Mitchell brother, had confessed to being incredibly vigilant when it came to birth control. She didn't want any surprises until after the wedding.

Carol lightly touched her stomach. "We'll move to the house when that happens. I'm not giving up my girlfriend lunches for anything."

"Labor," Bethany teased. "You might have to give up one or two when you have the baby."

"We'll see."

Wynn and Natalie arrived, followed by Pallas and Renee. Everyone settled on the blankets.

"I have chicken salad sandwiches," Carol said, pointing to a pink bakery box. "On croissants."

Pallas moaned. "Sounds delicious."

Silver explained about her wedding cocktail and how she had modified a nonalcoholic version for the lunch. Everyone helped themselves to food and Silver poured drinks. Bethany filled her plate, and then looked at Pallas.

"Thank you for still being my friend."

Pallas rolled her eyes. "You're marrying my brother. I don't really have a choice in the matter, but even if I did, I would still like you. I swear."

Bethany hung her head and sighed. "I hate my life."

"You don't," Wynn told her. "You're in love with a great guy."

"There is that, but everything else." She turned to Renee. "Do you know who I am?"

Renee put down her sandwich and cleared her throat. "Bethany Archer?"

Everyone laughed.

Pallas hugged Renee. "I think what Bethany is means is do you —" she made air quotes "— *know who she is,* as in her parents are the king and queen of El Bahar."

Renee's green eyes widened. "I didn't know that. Am I supposed to call you something like ma'am or Your Highness?"

"No. Just Bethany." She groaned and explained how her mother, an American schoolteacher, had gone to El Bahar to teach at the international school and had met and fallen in love with then–Crown Prince Malik.

"When my dad died, Malik adopted me," she continued. "So while I have El Baharian citizenship, I was born in Riverside, California."

Pallas smiled. "She brought over a stallion that my brother bought and they fell madly in love and now they're getting married."

"Maybe," Bethany grumbled.

Silver stared at her. "What? No! What happened to madly in love? Why didn't anyone say anything?" Silver might not be looking for love herself, but she very much wanted her friends to be happy.

"We're fine," Bethany said hastily. "It's not us, it's tradition." She drew in a breath. "My parents really want me to get married in El Bahar. They want to do the big royal wedding. But that means not having the wedding here, where Cade grew up. We're still working it all out."

Natalie leaned toward Renee. "Apparently marrying a princess can be complicated."

"It was never on my to-do list," Renee murmured. "But I will keep it in mind."

Everyone laughed.

"We'll figure it out," Pallas told her future sister-in-law. "I promise. You, me and your mom are still talking options."

No one knew weddings better than Pallas, Silver thought fondly, but before she could say anything, she heard an odd rustling sound in the bushes on the other side of the tree. One of the zebras stepped out into the clearing and eyed them.

"That's strange," Natalie said, pointing to the handsome boy. "I thought the zebras pretty much kept to themselves."

"They do." Carol smiled. "Don't worry — they're perfectly safe."

"Maybe they like taquitos," Pallas said, waving one. "I know I do."

Conversation shifted to Natalie's recent success at the gallery where she worked part-time and showed her art. She'd been featured in a show and had sold everything. Wynn talked about how her son, Hunter, was doing in school this year.

Silver looked around at her friends. They were an interesting mix. Only Pallas had been born in Happily Inc. Natalie, Bethany and Renee were the most recent transplants. Carol had moved here a few years before that and Wynn had arrived maybe ten years ago. Silver couldn't remember exactly. One day Wynn had arrived with a baby and enough cash to buy a print shop. There'd been no husband/father or other family. Wynn never talked about her past. She had secrets, but then who didn't. Silver had moved to Happily Inc when she'd been fifteen.

"What are you thinking?" Natalie asked her. "You have the strangest look on your face."

"Nothing specific," Silver said with a laugh. "Just enjoying time with my friends."

"Not me, though, right?" Pallas groaned. "You hate me. You have to."

"I could never hate you."

"Okay, but you hate my mother." She sighed. "I really can't blame you for that." She slapped her hand over her mouth. "Crap. I shouldn't have said that, should I? Now we have to talk about it. I'm sorry. It was private."

Silver smiled, knowing Pallas would never deliberately say anything hurtful. Plus, she was going to tell everyone everything anyway. Once she started working with Drew, the truth would come out.

She turned to her friends. "The bank turned down my loan request for the trailers."

"No!" Carol's expression turned indignant. "Why would they do that?"

"*They* didn't." Pallas's expression turned grim. "It was my mother. I know it was. Libby's horrible. I swear she's still pissed because you dated Drew all those years ago. Let me talk to Grandpa Frank. He would hate to know that she's acting like this."

"Who's Drew?" Renee asked. "And Grandpa Frank? What trailers? You're getting more trailers? They're for the business, aren't they? Because our clients love what you do."

Silver smiled at her. "Yes, I wanted to buy two Airstreams. They're gorgeous and perfect."

"There's a little one that could go up to Honeymoon Falls," Wynn said as she picked up a taquito. "A lot of people want to have small weddings there but getting any kind of food or bar up that tiny, steep road has been impossible."

"I'd worry about the competition but we're turning away business every single week," Renee said.

Pallas beamed. "This is so why I hired her."

Everyone laughed except Carol.

"But what about the trailers?" she asked, worrying her lower lip. "Can we talk to someone else or do a GoFundMe or something?"

Silver sipped her nonalcoholic mimosa. "Yes, well, I have that covered. I'm taking on a business partner. Drew bought the trailers and he's going to be a minority owner in the company."

Those who didn't know her history with Drew looked relieved. Pallas and Natalie, on the other hand, stared at her with identical looks of disbelief. Wynn's smile was a combination of smug and I-told-you-so.

Renee groaned. "I hate being the new girl.

What am I missing?"

"Drew and I have a past." Silver shrugged. "We dated some in high school."

Pallas rolled her eyes. "*Dated some?* Is that what we're calling it? You didn't date some. You two were the hot item. You nearly set the town on fire." She sighed. "It was so romantic. And then Drew went to college and was a total butthead."

"We broke up before he went," Silver said mildly. "Although I appreciate the name-calling."

"He wasn't supposed to fall for someone else, but he did. He brought that snooty bitch home and everything."

"There was a snooty bitch?" Carol asked. "Why didn't I know about that?"

"Welcome to my world," Renee murmured.

"She was awful," Pallas continued. "I can never remember her name."

"Ashley Lauren Grantham-Greene."

"She sounds very hateable," Natalie said.

Pallas nodded vigorously. "She was *so* awful. They were engaged and I can't for the life of me figure out why. When Drew broke things off, she set his house on fire."

"It was his car," Silver corrected, trying not to smile at the memory. The engagement had been hard on her, but the fire had gone a long way to easing her broken heart. "Pallas, you always say the house, but it was his car."

"Whatever. I still hate her."

"Serves him right," Natalie announced. "How could he not stay in love with you?"

"It's a mystery."

Renee looked at her. "It's nice that you've moved on and become good enough friends that you can work together. He will bring a business acumen that balances nicely with your creativity and knowledge about the industry."

Before Silver could respond, one of the gazelles walked toward them. She was slim and beautiful with huge eyes. She seemed to study them for a second before moving away.

"That was Bronwen," Carol said. "She's pretty tame, but she's never gotten this close to us before. I wonder if it's something we're eating."

"Or drinking," Wynn said, waving the mimosa. "These are delicious."

Silver watched the gazelle disappear into the bushes and wondered how to tell her friends the rest of the story. Not that it was complicated, she just wasn't sure how to begin.

She sucked in a breath and told herself

they would love her regardless. Wynn already knew and had never judged her. Just as important, her friends might have some good advice for getting through the mess she'd sort of, maybe created.

"I got pregnant," she blurted.

Everyone turned to look at her. Several gazes dropped to her stomach. Only Wynn didn't look surprised.

"When?" Pallas asked.

"Back in high school." Silver told herself to just get it out there. "I knew Drew was heading off to college and that everything would be different for him when he was gone. I didn't want him to think he owed me anything, so I broke up with him. I think I was secretly hoping he would quit school in a couple of weeks and come home to be with me."

"Which didn't happen," Wynn said gently.

"No, it didn't. About a month after he'd left, I figured out I was pregnant. I told my uncle and he asked me what I wanted to do. I decided to go see Drew and tell him face-to-face."

"Because you thought he would say he loved you and wanted to marry you," Renee said softly.

"Something like that."

Carol's eyes widened. "And?"

"And I told him and he proposed."

Pallas's mouth dropped open. "How could I not know this? You married Drew and you never told me? OMG! I can't believe it. When? Where? You have a baby?"

Silver held up her hand. "We didn't get married. I could tell he'd only proposed because he thought he should. He didn't love me anymore and he certainly didn't want to marry me."

She told herself she could say the words without feeling anything. Time had passed and she was a completely different person now, as was Drew. She'd grown up, moved on, and he wasn't on her radar as anyone but a business partner.

"What did you do?" Natalie asked, her voice soft.

"I told him I would have the baby and give it up for adoption. He signed the paperwork and that was that."

No one looked convinced by that last statement. Wynn made a circular "go on" sign with her hand.

"My uncle helped me find a nice couple in Los Angeles who wanted to adopt. I went to meet them and liked them a lot. In fact I moved in with them my last few months."

"That's where you went!" Pallas sounded triumphant. "I knew you were off doing

89

something but I always assumed you joined a biker gang."

"Really? A biker gang? Have you ever seen me on a motorcycle?"

"No, but you'd look good on one."

Silver laughed. "Thank you. Anyway I had the baby and came back here, only I couldn't seem to get my life together."

"You were still in love with Drew," Carol said.

"I was. Eventually I got over him." She smiled. "Ashley Lauren Grantham-Greene helped. Or maybe it was the car fire. Regardless, I moved on, but . . ."

She wasn't sure how to explain what had happened. "Before I figured it all out, I was pretty lost. I ended up going back to LA and living with the couple who adopted Autumn. They eventually divorced, but I stayed close to Leigh, Autumn's mom. Drew knows about the baby and that I gave her up, but nothing else. Not that I'm still in touch with her." She paused. "She's eleven."

Pallas's eyes widened. "Oh no, no, no. Your daughter being eleven isn't the big deal, is it? That's not why you're telling us this." She stared at Renee. "*The Great Gatsby* wedding."

Renee's mouth dropped open. "No way."

She spun to stare at Silver. "Seriously?"

"What are you talking about?" Carol demanded.

Pallas pressed a hand to her chest. "I can't believe it, but I'm right, aren't I?" She drew in a breath. "A couple of weeks ago, we had a couple cancel their wedding. It's too late to do much in the way of refunding them money. Too much had already been ordered. The theme is *The Great Gatsby* — not my favorite book, but the era is gorgeous and they had such cute ideas for the event."

"Did they break up?" Bethany asked.

"No. She got pregnant and they eloped. They had thought there would be fertility issues so they were thrilled to be having a baby. Not twenty-four hours later a woman called and asked if there was any chance she could have a wedding this fall. I told her about the cancellation and she was all in." Pallas returned her attention to Silver. "Her name is Leigh and she has a daughter named Autumn and they're coming here."

"I know. I'm going to be the maid of honor."

Her friends all stared at her. Natalie recovered first. "Just to recap, you and Drew had a baby together and while you gave up the baby for adoption, you stayed close with your daughter and the adoptive mother. All these years later, you're still close, so close that you're going to be in the wedding, which is being held here, in town, where you and Drew both live, with the adoptive mother and your daughter with Drew and he doesn't know a thing. Oh, and you just went into business with him. Do I have that right?"

Things sounded even worse when put like that, Silver thought, not sure if she should laugh or learn to ride a motorcycle and take off on a long road trip.

"That's pretty much it," Silver told her. "Except for the part where I'm keeping Autumn for a week or so while her mom goes off on her honeymoon."

Bethany leaned forward. "Your daughter with Drew, the one he doesn't know about, is going to be here? In Happily Inc? For a week? With you?"

"Uh-huh."

"Chances are he's going to notice," Wynn told her. "I'm just saying."

"Yes, that's what I thought, too."

"So you're going to have to tell him."

Something Silver really didn't want to think about. "That seems to be the most sensible plan."

Natalie winced. "Um, good luck with that."

"Thanks."

Renee picked up her drink. "Amazing. And here I thought life in a small town would be boring."

Despite living up in the mountains, Jasper Dembenski didn't mind New York City. For him the noise quickly faded into the background, and the constant rush of people, cars and buses made it easy to blend in. The street layout made sense to him and he enjoyed walking blocks at a time, rather than taking a cab. And if getting crammed into an elevator with too many people ever got to him, he retreated to the comical irony of his life. He'd been an average kid who had grown up in a town in Montana no one had ever heard of, yet here he was, staying at the Peninsula Hotel and being wined and dined by his publisher. Who would have thought?

He went into the building, signed in with the security guard, then made his way to the bank of elevators. His editor, Sara, a petite, dark-haired woman in her late thirties, met him when he stepped out onto the twenty-second floor.

"You made it," she said with a smile. "How was your flight?"

"Good. Easy."

From Happily Inc he could drive to Los Angeles, Phoenix or Las Vegas, and then take a plane pretty much anywhere he wanted. For his trip to New York, he'd chosen to go through Los Angeles. His publisher always booked him first class and put him up at a fancy hotel. There was little to complain about.

"Hank's already here," Sara told him. "In the conference room."

The first time he'd visited his publisher's offices, he hadn't known what to expect. He discovered that they were offices, kind of like every other business. Junior employees worked in cubicles and those higher on the food chain had nice private offices with windows. Instead of artwork, there were posters of book covers everywhere, and a gallery of author head shots. Pretty much every bit of wall space had bookshelves overflowing with books, but otherwise, there was little to distinguish this space from, say, an insurance broker.

Paper manuscripts had gone the way of the dinosaur — authors submitted digitally and were edited the same way. Copy edits were done with track changes, as were final page proofs. Cover art, from concept to finished product, was emailed. Jasper had started his writing career with a pad and pencil but had quickly learned if he was going to get serious, he had to work on a computer. Now he couldn't imagine creating any other way.

"We're all excited about the book you're working on," Sara said, leading him toward one of the conference rooms.

He chuckled. "Is that your not-so-subtle way of asking if I'm going to deliver the book on time?"

Sara smiled. "No, but now that you mention it . . ." She motioned him into a small conference room. "How is the book going?"

"I'm on track. I should be done in plenty of time."

"That's exactly what I want to hear."

He walked in and shook hands with his agent. Hank was a small, thin man pushing fifty. His unassuming appearance belied his killer instinct. They'd met at the first writer's conference Jasper had attended. He'd entered a contest where the finalists had their pages read by a New York agent. Hank was way too powerful to judge contests or bother with conferences, but when a junior agent at his firm had been too sick to attend, Hank had volunteered to go in her place. Jasper had won the contest, Hank had read the pages and signed him within a week.

"You made it," Hank said as they sat down. "Everything good on your flight and with the hotel?"

"Couldn't be better."

When Jasper had sold his first book, he'd still been fairly messed up from his time in the army. PTSD, brought on by years of fighting overseas, had a way of doing that to a person. He'd agreed to go on a book tour before realizing what that meant. The itinerary — flying all over the country to speak at bookstores and then sign books — had terrified him. Crowds were tough and airports had been impossible. They'd compromised by spreading out the events and having him drive himself from city to city.

Over the years, he'd gotten better. Flying would never be fun, but he could do it. The same with speaking to a large group. The signings were easy because he liked meeting his readers. But while he'd relaxed into the process, Sara and Hank always monitored him, as if concerned he was going to have an episode at any second. He supposed he was enough of a jerk to kind of enjoy their tension.

One of the assistants brought in coffee. Sara waited until he'd left before speaking.

"You'd mentioned this was the second to the last book in the series," she began.

96

"Next year you'll write the last book, then start something new."

Jasper nodded. "I've been playing around with an idea for a military series."

Hank and Sara glanced at each other. "We're excited about the idea," Hank told him. "Are you ready to write it?"

Jasper didn't think he would ever be ready, but he was starting to think it was time. He'd already created the main character — an amalgamation of three guys he'd known back in Afghanistan. Three good men who had been killed. He wanted to tell their stories without violating their privacy. Creating one character that took the best of each of them solved the problem.

"I've got a good handle on what I want to do," Jasper said. "I'm thinking of an open-ended series. Military crimes, some with a civilian connection."

Sara's eyes brightened. "We would love that. You're the best at what you do. Just to be clear, next year you'll write the last book in your current series, and then you'll start the new series after that."

"Yes."

Hank leaned forward. "Vidar needs a love interest."

Jasper resisted rolling his eyes. "So you've told me."

"Hank's right," Sara added. "It's time. You have female readers who adore you, but come on. You need a fully realized woman in one of your books. One who is more than a one-night stand or a victim. It will help you grow as a writer. Vidar falling in love will make readers bond with him more and bring the series to a satisfying conclusion."

A conversation they'd had before. Jasper knew the argument. Vidar, his ongoing hero, was too one-dimensional. He needed a personal life. A deeper backstory. Less grunts and more conversation.

His argument that the character borrowed heavily from the Norse mythology — the son of Odin and a giantess named Grid, Vidar was silent and known for his physical strength and therefore was unchangeable — was wearing thin.

What he didn't tell them and would barely admit to himself was his resistance wasn't about the story. He knew they were right in their assessment of his story arc. The problem was him — he wasn't sure he knew *how* to write a woman and he sure as hell couldn't figure out how anyone fell in love.

"I'll see what he can do," he told them.

"Excellent." Hank nodded. "Now Sara has some interesting ideas about next year's tour."

Sara smiled. "I hope you're going to be excited. We want to do something different."

Their idea of exciting and his had little in common, he thought, but nodded to show he was willing to listen.

Sara leaned toward him. "We want to send you to Europe. All your publishers there are clamoring to see you. England, France, Spain, Italy and of course Germany."

"You're huge in Germany," Hank reminded him.

"We're hoping for three weeks." Her tone was cautious. "If you think you could manage that."

He'd never been to Europe, he thought. Never thought he'd go. He was fairly sure his passport was out-of-date, but that was easily rectified.

"Make it four weeks so I can have a day or two off in each of the countries," he told them. "I'd like to look around and see a few things."

"Excellent." Sara jotted on her pad of paper. "Now about the US tour. We really want to push the book and have you visit as many of the accounts as possible." She smiled. "Before you glower at me, we've come up with what we think is the perfect solution."

She pulled a large, glossy brochure from under the pad and handed it to him. Jasper looked at the cover and started to laugh. "Seriously?"

The picture showed a luxury RV on a highway. He turned the page and saw a layout along with a list of amenities.

Sara's expression was hopeful. "We'd take care of renting the trailer and booking your trailer sites or camping spaces or whatever they're called. In the big cities like Chicago and St. Louis, you'd leave the trailer parked at the site and stay at a hotel for a couple of days. But most of the time you'd be on your own, driving from place to place. No escort, no airports, no rush. What do you think?"

"How long would you want me to be on tour?"

She worried her lower lip. "Three months?"

It was a long time to be gone, but it wasn't as if he had a lot waiting for him at home. He thought briefly of Wynn, but theirs was a casual relationship — no promises, no strings. He'd left Happily Inc three days ago and he hadn't heard from her. He would be gone another couple of weeks and they wouldn't be in touch until he was home. Like he'd first thought — he was free to do what he wanted.

"Let's do it," he told Sara. "I'll use the road time to get my last book in the series figured out, then go home and write it."

Hank grinned. "Fantastic. Your sales are going to go through the roof."

Jasper nodded as if that mattered to him as well, but in truth, the writing was a lot more about keeping the demons at bay and his ability to look himself in the mirror than about any royalty check. The writing had saved him when he'd thought nothing could. Without his stories, he wouldn't be here today — of that he was sure.

CHAPTER FIVE

Drew watched Silver sign the paperwork formalizing their new business relationship. He'd delivered the contract to her a couple of days ago and she'd had an attorney look everything over. This morning she'd texted to say she was ready to sign.

He'd arrived at her retail space shortly before noon. She'd been waiting, one of the display tables cleared, with two chairs on opposite sides. It wasn't until she finished with the last page that he realized he'd half expected her to change her mind. Taking on a partner was a big deal. But she hadn't and now they were partners.

He took his copy of the contract, then held out the keys for the new trailers. "Here you go."

She grinned and took them. "I have so many plans I'm not sure where to start."

"Show me."

She walked to the small alcove she used

as her office and returned with several sheets of paper and a large sketch pad. She set the latter in front of him, then moved her chair so they were sitting on the same side of the table.

"I thought we'd keep the remodel on the smaller trailer fairly simple," she began. "It's more mobile, given the size. We can take it out into the desert or up to Honeymoon Falls. It's going to be all about using the space."

She showed him the drawings she'd made of custom shelves and cabinets. A refrigerator was a must, but if they were going to be away from an electrical source, then they would be working off a portable generator.

"That means there's a noise component," she told him. "We'll have to figure out how long we can have the generator turned off. During a wedding ceremony for sure, but then it would have to be on for the party, otherwise, nothing would stay cold."

"What about solar panels?" he asked.

She blinked at him. "What?"

"Maybe we could use solar panels to power everything. We're in the desert — it's rarely cloudy. As long as the panels were fully charged, I bet we could avoid using a generator."

Her eyes widened. "That's brilliant. Yes,

let's look into that!"

Her praise made him sit up a little straighter. Stupid, but true. He'd always like impressing Silver and apparently, that hadn't changed.

They returned their attention to her drawings. She'd designed flip-up counters and plenty of storage for glasses, blenders and liquor.

"With this design, we could use the trailer for a lot more than weddings," he said. "How about graduations, birthday celebrations and office parties? Things that happen other than on the weekend."

"I was thinking about that, too. Having more trailers means having more staff. I won't be able to simply call around to find out if my preferred people are available. I'm going to have to keep at least one or two on permanently."

She didn't look happy as she spoke.

"There's money in the budget for two employees."

"I know, but it's a step further than I've ever gone." She looked at him. "We can't all be titans of industry."

"It's a small-town bank, Silver. I'm not exactly a titan."

"You're more titan-like than anyone I know."

They were sitting close enough that he could see tiny smile lines by her eyes and the pale freckles on her nose. She wore her usual nonwork uniform of jeans and a tank top. A tattoo of a dragon curled over her left shoulder, the tail trailing toward her elbow. He knew there was a small rose on the inside of her right ankle and a ladybug by her right hip bone.

The dragon was new to him. After all this time, there were probably tats he hadn't seen and he was curious about them. What other ink had she chosen to define and celebrate herself?

Silver had always been beautiful. As a teenager, she'd been in a class by herself. She still was but it was different now. Her features were a little sharper — honed by life's experiences. She still smelled like vanilla and the promise of sex, a scent he knew to be uniquely hers. Even her pheromones taunted him.

He pulled his attention back to the drawings in front of him. They went over her plans for the larger trailer, one that would be primarily for weddings. Her design was all about getting as much of a bar as possible into a trailer, and then being able to serve customers quickly and efficiently.

"We're going to have to pick a contractor," he told her. "Did you look at the names I sent you?"

"Yes. They both have great reputations. Neither of them have experience working with trailers, but that's not a surprise. It's kind of a specialized field."

"They've each worked with clients of mine and have gotten good reviews. We can go with whomever you're comfortable with." When she hesitated, he added, "I'm happy to interview them myself or set up interviews with both of us there."

"Let's do that. I'm not sure what to ask, but I want to be there. Then we'll make a decision."

He pulled out his phone and added the task to his calendar. "I'll get something out to them today so we can get going."

She nodded. "The sooner the trailers are functional, the sooner we can start booking them." She glanced around her showroom. "Now if only we could do something with this."

He followed her gaze. The retail space was big and open. One square room maybe fifty by fifty with an alcove that was her office. There were a couple of restrooms in back and a small storage area.

Silver leaned back in her chair. "I keep feeling as if I'm missing out on an opportunity to make money here, but I'm not sure what to do. Everything I've thought of seems so complicated."

"Such as?"

"Rehearsal dinners. Generally, the wedding party has the rehearsal on Friday and then the dinner after, but sometimes their wedding venue has a Friday wedding planned and so the Saturday wedding folks are out of luck. Or sometimes the wedding party is too small to meet the venue's minimum. I thought about offering this place, but there's no kitchen. Putting one in would be really expensive and take up too much space."

"Can't they use caterers? Or couldn't you contract with a caterer who would bring in everything they need."

Silver looked doubtful. "Without any kind of food prep area, it would be difficult to actually cook. All the food would have to be brought in. It makes things complicated." She paused. "Don't laugh, but I've thought about having bachelorette parties here."

"How would you make that happen?"

She pointed to the ceiling. "I'd get rods installed so I could easily hang drapes to make the setting feel more intimate. We'd have seating like at any dinner, but also a few sofas and love seats. It would all be movable so we'd be able to support what-ever theme they wanted."

"There's a theme?" All the bachelor par-ties he'd been to had focused on liquor and giving the groom a hard time.

She nodded. "Say a spa theme. So there would be a massage table and pedicure sta-tions. Those would be brought in but we certainly have the room." She looked at him, then away. "And we could put in some poles."

If she hadn't already mentioned rods for the drapes, he would have assumed she meant poles for that. "What are you talking about?"

She cleared her throat. "You know. Poles. Like stripper poles. They're actually very popular. The bride and her friends learn moves they can, ah, share later."

He kept his expression neutral and did his best not to wonder if Silver had any moves he didn't know about. "Stripper poles?"

"It's just a thought."

He reminded himself this was a business meeting and that picturing Silver doing a pole dance was wrong on many levels. "Sounds like a good one."

"Let me run some numbers. The poles have to be secured to the floor and the ceil-ing. I'd have to check my lease as well, to make sure I could do it. Or I guess I could phone Violet and just ask."

Violet was the owner of the retail space and loft above, and Silver's landlord. The previous year she'd fallen in love with an English duke and had moved across the pond, so to speak, and married him.

"If you can install stripper poles?" He laughed. "I almost want to be in on that call."

She rolled her eyes. "We're not going to talk about anything sexy."

"No, but it will still be interesting."

"You're such a guy."

"I can be, yes." He looked around. "I would say if you think renting out this space for parties is something we should try, let's spend the least amount we can. The poles shouldn't be too expensive. Better lighting and some soundproofing. But nothing that expensive, at least at first. The main business is always going to be the trailers."

"That's a really good point."

"Have you thought of starting a franchise?"

She stared at him. "Excuse me?"

"Your trailer bar idea is brilliant. What about a franchise? It would be great for a lot of people. Retirees, anyone who only wants to work a few days a week."

She made a T with her hands. "Let's take this just a little slower. You've been my business partner all of fifteen minutes. Let's put franchising on the back burner for oh, say a month."

"It wouldn't be hard. Once we got the legal stuff out of the way, we'd need to come up with a plan, then maybe do a little internet advertising."

"Is that all?"

"You have to have vision."

She folded her arms across her chest. "You weren't kidding when you said you had a lot of business experience."

"I wasn't."

"My business partner, the bank mogul."

"It's just one bank. Does that make me a mogul?"

She laughed. "It's one more bank than anyone else I know owns. I'm kind of surprised you stayed in town."

"Why would I leave?"

"You could be a bigger mogul somewhere else. Plus, you know, the parents. I've never actually met them, but I remember what you told me about them when we were going out. Your mother is very ambitious for her only child."

"Why would you remember that?" he asked.

"Because it was important to you."

It had been, and still was. He didn't normally talk about his parents, but with Silver he'd felt a connection that he hadn't experienced before or since. He'd trusted her with every part of himself, including the doubts he rarely admitted to, let alone shared.

He'd talked about his parents and their odd sense of the world — that being connected and having political and financial power mattered more than anything else, including family. His mother especially was driven to be influential. Ambition drove her to an extent that was almost frightening.

Drew had done his best to rebel against their dreams for him but it had been a losing battle. Then his father had received an ambassadorship that had sent his parents to Europe. He'd been in high school and after much discussion, they'd agreed to leave him with his Grandpa Frank.

Drew had loved the freedom, the normalcy of simply being one of the grandkids. He'd been able to relax, to learn and grow because it was what he wanted and not because of some unrealistic master plan. And he'd fallen in love with Silver.

"What is this really about?" she asked, her voice quiet. "Are you really that interested in being a business partner or are you rebelling against what your parents expect?"

"You mean run the bank for two years, then join them in their lobbying firm?"

Her eyebrows rose. "Is that the current plan?"

"Last I heard."

"What do you want?"

What he'd always wanted. He wanted to run the bank, to modernize the various processes and make every department responsive to the community.

"Remember about three years ago when there was that big push to raise the money to build a new fire station?"

One had desperately been needed, but there hadn't been the money. Business leaders had come together to raise the funds privately.

"I ran the committee," he admitted. "I wasn't the public face, but I took care of all the details, brainstormed most of the ideas. I convinced my grandfather to donate a sizable portion of our profits for the quarter. Everyone kicked in and we got the station built."

"I remember, but I didn't know that was you."

"It wasn't me. It was the whole town. That's what I want — to be more than a guy who runs the bank. I want to make the bank relevant and important. Not some heartless institution."

"Wow." She looked at him. "And here I thought you just gave orders and counted the money."

He grinned. "I let Libby do that."

He looked at Silver. She was the more mature version of the girl he'd fallen in love with. Back then she'd had attitude, but now she had life experience to back it up. He wanted to say she was fearless but didn't everyone fear something? As the question formed, he wondered what she worried about in the middle of the night.

"Do you ever think about what would have happened if we'd stayed together?"

Her eyes widened. "You and me?" She gave a strangled laugh. "Sometimes I do, but it would have been a disaster."

"Why?"

"We were too young to have a baby. You had just started college. I appreciate that you said all the right things, but we both know you would have hated to come home. Where would you have gotten a job? Where would we have lived? You would have ended up resenting me and it would have been awful."

She spoke with an authority that made

him realize she *had* thought about them staying together. She'd considered the possibilities and had rejected the premise of the question.

"We might have been okay," he said, not knowing why he wanted that to be true. It had been a long time ago — the decisions had been made and they'd both moved on.

She looked at him. "I don't think so. Besides, you'd already let me go and were ready to move on to someone else."

"I was still in love with you." Maybe a little less than he had been when he'd left for college, but there had been feelings. Not that he'd wanted a baby. Not then. She was right about them being too young for that.

"I appreciate you saying that but we both know it was long over. We'd moved on." One corner of her mouth turned up. "Besides, your mother would never have let us get married."

"We were legally adults. We could do what we wanted."

"Uh-huh." Her expression turned sympathetic. "You don't actually believe that, do you? We're talking about your mother. She would have found a way to stop us."

Silver was right about that, he admitted to himself. Not only had he been raised to respect his parents' wishes, his mother had a way of manipulating people he couldn't begin to master. Regardless, he liked to think he would have been strong.

"I would have married you," he told her. "If that was what you'd wanted."

Emotions flashed across her face. She opened her mouth, as if she were about to say something, then shook her head.

"Thank you for saying that. I, ah . . ." She drew in a breath. "I have a meeting in an hour with a lot of prep work and you have to get back to the bank. Let's talk soon."

"The sooner the better. We need to get the trailers remodeled and figure out what to do with this space."

"Absolutely."

He hesitated, unable to shake the feeling that there was more she wanted to discuss, but she only smiled.

What had she been thinking and what had she wanted to say? He was about to cross the street toward the bank when he realized what it was. He'd told her he would have married her if that was what she wanted — a long way from saying he'd wanted it, too.

Not that they were in love anymore, or even dating. But they'd been in the middle of a "what if" conversation and he hadn't played along.

He thought about going back to say something, only he couldn't think of what. What would he tell her? That he was sorry she'd given up the baby? That he wished they'd gotten married? He wasn't sure either of those statements were true. What he did know was that both he and Silver had come a long way and he was looking forward to finding out where they went after today.

Silver couldn't shake the fact that she'd been a complete and utter coward. She'd always thought of herself as reasonably brave and self-aware, but at the exact moment when she should have told Drew about Autumn and Leigh and the wedding, she'd said nothing.

Drew had given her the perfect opening. Honestly, what had she been waiting for? But instead of taking advantage of the moment, of coming clean, she'd bolted. Now, not only did she still have to tell him, she got to beat herself up. She'd been five kinds of dumb.

She walked into the conference room at Weddings Out of the Box. Renee was already there, tablet in hand, samples scattered around the table and a laptop opened to the teleconferencing program.

"Hi," she said when she saw Silver. "Thanks for coming. I know you could have just provided a drink list, but I appreciate you being here. I've never transferred a partially planned wedding from one bride and groom to another, so I can't know if I'm doing it right."

"I'm not sure there's a wrong way to do it," Silver told her with a smile. "Except for messing up all the details."

"If this is you trying to make me feel better, it's not working."

"Sorry." Silver sat across from her. "Leigh is super excited to have the wedding mostly planned. She's busy moving out of her place and working with her fiancé on the house they're having built, on top of work and getting ready for the honeymoon and raising her daughter. Leigh is very easygoing and she's going to love everything you do."

Renee smiled. "Thanks. I appreciate hearing that. I think I'll be able to relax a little after our phone call when I know she's happy with the choices already made."

Renee glanced at the clock, then tapped a few keys on the computer. The screen showed the log-on sequence. Silver had seen the program in action before. It allowed multiple viewers to see each other and the Weddings Out of the Box conference room. Slides could be displayed to everyone attending the call, so they were all on the same page, so to speak. In the past, Silver had been at the meetings as a vendor representing AlcoHaul and occasionally the caterer. Today she was also a friend of the bride.

Leigh's smiling face appeared on the screen. She waved. "Hi, Silver. Hi, Renee. Thanks for doing this. I'm so excited. Denton has patients so he's not going to join us but he said anything I love, he'll love, too."

Her happiness was so much a part of who she was that Silver felt it reach through the screen and give her a big hug. Leigh had always been an upbeat person, but since falling in love with Denton, she'd become even more joyful.

"We have a lot to get to," Renee said. "So let's dive in. There are some elements that the previous bride has chosen that can't be changed. The date for one. We can be flexible on the time of the ceremony, of course. The only thing to keep in mind is there's a wedding on Sunday afternoon, so we can't go too late."

Leigh shook her head. "A five o'clock wedding with the reception right after is perfect. We'll wrap up by ten, as the contract says. We're not really stay-up-past-midnight people."

Renee made notes on her tablet. "Okay,

on to food. You mentioned you looked over the menus. Any changes?"

"Just a couple."

Leigh and Renee worked through the various courses including the custom cookies that had been ordered.

"I love a cookie," Leigh told them. "These are super cute. We want to keep them as a party favor."

A wedding cake had already been ordered and Leigh and Denton would be taking that, as well. It was relatively simple, with pale gold frosting and a few swags on each of the three tiers.

When they were done with all things edible, Silver explained how the champagne fountain worked.

"I have enough coupe glasses so we don't have to rent any."

Leigh frowned. "Those are the round, old-fashioned champagne glasses?"

"Uh-huh. They're more sturdy. The base of the fountain will be sixteen glasses. That makes the fountain four glasses high, which looks pretty and is very manageable. Because the fountain is for display only, I've ordered crappy sparkling wine for that and we'll have it set up before the reception. But for drinking, we'll want something good."

Silver nodded at Renee. She'd already emailed her slides for the presentation. Renee hit a couple of keys and a large picture of a triangular-shaped glass appeared. There was a sugar rim and the liquid inside was pale gold.

"In keeping with the *Gatsby* theme, I've been coming up with Roaring '20s drink ideas. What if we went all champagne? Champagne by the glass, along with two or three champagne-based cocktails?"

Leigh clapped her hands together. "I love that idea. What did you have in mind?"

Silver nodded at Renee, who advanced the presentation. "This drink is called a Caribou Martini. It's coffee-flavored vodka and champagne. I know it sounds odd, but the flavors really work together. I'm also thinking a Sparkling Julep and a French 75."

"Those sound delicious. So three cocktails, plus champagne."

"Do you want an alternative for people who don't like champagne? Maybe beer or wine?"

"Denton would like a selection of Scotches, but otherwise, that's it."

Silver made some notes. She would email Denton directly and get his thoughts on the type of Scotch he wanted. Prices ranged from around ten or fifteen dollars a bottle to a couple of hundred dollars. She wanted to make sure she knew what he was expecting the final bill to be.

"I'll get with him," Silver said. "Scotch is super easy."

Renee made more notes. "Now let's talk about the decorations. We've already ordered decorative drapes trimmed in pearls. In fact, pearls are a theme here. Strands of them will decorate the table. We've ordered teardrop-shaped balloons in cream. We use fishing line so the tethers aren't visible, then hang them upside down from the ceiling. The tablecloths are pale gold, with darker gold chargers. The accents are black, including the napkins and the table numbers."

They walked through everything from flowers to the guest book. Leigh showed them a pair of shoes she'd bought that were decorated with pearls and feathers.

"Silver, I found the perfect dress for you," Leigh said. "And I ordered it, so I'm hoping you'll love it."

"If it makes you happy, it makes me happy."

Leigh laughed. "You say that now."

"I mean it. This is your day. What is Autumn wearing?"

"A little flapper-inspired dress. You're going to love it. She's going to be so cute."

Leigh glanced at Renee. "Autumn is my daughter."

Silver heard the caution in her friend's tone and knew that Leigh was erring on the side of discretion. "She knows about me and Drew and the baby," Silver assured her.

"Oh good. We're all so excited to meet Drew," Leigh said. "I've always been curious about him and Autumn can't wait to finally meet her birth father."

Words designed to make Silver feel a little nauseous. Even if she'd wanted to try to avoid Drew for the week Autumn was here, that wasn't going to be a possibility. She had to tell him, and soon.

"She understands about the adoption and everything?" Renee asked.

Leigh nodded. "I always wanted her to know the truth. When Silver came to live with us, Autumn was still a baby. I don't remember exactly when we started talking about it but by the time she was three, she was clear on the fact that she'd been adopted. I'm her mom but Silver grew her in her tummy." Leigh laughed again. "Not that we describe it that way now. She's eleven, so we can be a little more sophisticated in our conversation."

Silver's sick feeling grew.

Leigh glanced at her watch. "Oh my. I

have to run. Is that everything?"

"For now," Renee told her. "We'll schedule another call next week. Have a good rest of your day, Leigh."

"You, too." Leigh blew Silver a kiss. "Love you, Silver."

"Love you, too."

The connection went dark. Renee turned off the computer.

"Do you need to breathe into a paper bag?"

Silver frowned. "Why would you ask that?"

"You went totally white while Leigh was talking. I thought you were going to pass out."

"My stomach's a little iffy."

"Is that what we're calling it?"

Silver put her arms on the table and rested her forehead on her hands. "I'm screwed."

"You are."

"You don't have to agree with me."

"I'm an honest person." Renee put her tablet on top of her computer, then collected the napkin samples. "I take it you haven't told Drew about Autumn."

Silver straightened. "Not yet. I need to. I get that. I just don't know how to start the conversation." She sighed. "It's weird. It's not as if he doesn't know I got pregnant and therefore there was a baby born, but we've never talked about it. Not really. I'm sure he assumes I simply gave up our child and walked away. I don't know how to say it's different than that."

"You're afraid he's going to be mad, or feel betrayed?"

Silver groaned. "Yes, but that makes no sense. It's not like he asked. It's not like he ever bothered to find out what happened. I'm not the bad guy here. He's not, either. It's just . . ."

"You feel guilty."

"I do. Why is that?"

"Because you kept something from him, and while the reasons made sense at the time, you're less sure now and you're going to have to tell him and won't that be awkward."

Silver studied her friend. "You're insightful, aren't you?"

"I can be."

Why was that? Had Renee been born more intuitive than most or had life circumstances pushed her to the fringes where she was forced to observe rather than participate?

Yet another question that would be difficult to ask, Silver thought.

"I'm going to tell him," she said, as much to herself as to Renee. "Really, really soon."

"Or you could wait and let Autumn spring it on him."

"I wouldn't do that to her. When she meets her birth father, I want it to be a happy moment."

"What about for Drew?"

"I want him to understand and be sweet to his daughter."

"Are you worried he won't be?"

"Not really. I'm mostly being a coward, which isn't like me." She put both hands on the desk and looked at Renee. "I'm done being wishy-washy. I'm telling him no matter what."

Renee smiled. "You go, girl."

Chapter Six

Drew headed up to the big house. As he parked, he chuckled at the double meaning — in many ways his grandfather's estate had been the opposite of prison. When Drew had moved in, he'd felt a sense of release and freedom.

The Saturday morning air was clear with only the slightest hint of crispness. Fall in the California desert meant warm days and cool nights. It wasn't until winter that temperatures would get anywhere close to cold. He tried to get out to the house at least a couple of Saturday mornings a month. Not so much to check on his grandfather as to hang out with him. Despite his years, Grandpa Frank was healthy, active and always looking for fun. Drew hoped to be just like him when he was in his eighties.

The housekeeper let him in. She smiled. "Good morning, Mr. Drew."

"Good morning, Amelia. How are things?"

"Good. Thank you. Your grandfather is in his office."

"Thanks. I'll show myself back." He hesitated. "Is she, ah, up?"

Amelia hid a smile behind her hand. "She's gone into town already, Mr. Drew."

"Excellent."

His aunt Libby lived with her father. She'd moved back to the house where she'd grown up years ago, when Pallas and Cade had still been kids. Drew had never understood why, but he remembered his mother being livid when she'd found out. From what he could recall, his mother's fury had been more about not thinking of making the move first rather than missing out on time with her father. A few years later, his parents had left the country but the annoyance had not been forgotten.

Irene and Libby had always been competitive and not in a positive way. His other aunts were pleasant, charming women. Drew had always wondered why his mother and Libby were so, ah, different.

He found his grandfather sitting at his computer. When he spotted Drew, he smiled and stood.

"Why don't you have a life?" he teased as he walked over and hugged him. "You should be lying in bed with a beautiful young woman on a Saturday morning. Not visiting an old man."

"You're my favorite grandfather," Drew told him. "Where else would I be? Besides, I seem to be fresh out of beautiful young women at the moment."

Not counting Silver, he reminded himself, thinking about the new tattoo he'd seen and wondering about the ones he hadn't. As a teenager, Silver had ensnared him with her beauty and humor and street smarts. All these years later, she was only more enticing. Working with her was even better than he'd hoped, and he'd hoped for a lot.

They walked to the kitchen, where Grandpa Frank poured them each a cup of coffee. They sat in the sunroom. From there they could see much of the town along with the golf course and animal preserve.

"I'm thinking of buying a car," his grandfather said. "A 1968 Mustang."

"Sweet. Already restored or would you do the work yourself?"

"I'm not sure. Restored is more expensive, but at my age, I have no interest in crawling under a car. I'll have to see." He winked at Drew. "It will annoy your aunt."

"It's your money. Libby doesn't get a vote."

"She doesn't see it that way. How's your

mother?"

The question sounded casual enough but Drew still went on alert. As a rule, he and Grandpa Frank never discussed his parents.

"Last I heard, she and Dad are doing well."

His grandfather sipped his coffee. "They want you to run the bank for a few years, then join them at the lobbying firm."

"So I've heard."

"You're still not interested?"

Drew shook his head. "I like where I am. I've always been interested in how money works and that hasn't changed."

His grandfather eyed him. "You're making plans for after I retire. I know you are."

Drew grinned. "Maybe a few. I want to get more involved with the community. Be more friendly to small businesses."

"I heard about what happened with Silver's loan." His grandfather didn't sound pleased. "Libby's always had a burr up her butt about that girl. Or maybe it's how she interacts with you. Maybe she's worried that if you and Silver get back together, you'll put down roots. I suspect she's hoping your parents can lure you away and *she* can take over the bank."

Drew knew better than to be surprised by the old man's comments and insights.

Grandpa Frank had always known what was going on in his family. He listened and Drew was pretty sure he had a couple of employees acting as benevolent spies.

As for him and Silver getting back together — it wasn't the worst idea ever. Being around her, working together had been great. He'd always liked her, had always respected her. The first time around they'd been too young, but they were more mature now. Maybe they were finally ready for what they could have.

"You know I went into business with her," he said.

"I heard. Interesting thing to do. How's it going?"

"So far so good. Last weekend I worked a couple of weddings with her. I liked it a lot. The bank is such an established institution. There are so many rules and regulations. Entrepreneurs often have to make it up as they go." He picked up his coffee. "Have you ever thought of starting a venture capital firm and helping start-ups?"

"That's a young man's game."

"You're not so old."

His grandfather smiled. "Too old for that, but it's an interesting idea. You should think about it."

"I don't have the money. Besides, I'm the

bank guy, remember?"

"I do, and speaking of that, I'm going to officially retire. I'll be announcing my decision in the next week or so."

The news was a kick in the gut. Drew had always known it was going to happen. His grandfather was well into his eighties, long past when most people retired, but still.

"The bank won't be the same without you," he said honestly. "I'll miss seeing you around."

"It's time." Grandpa Frank's gaze sharpened. "I'm not naming you as my successor. I'm leaving it up to the board of directors."

Drew grinned. "You are so going to piss off Mom."

"That's not why I'm doing it. You'll have more power if the board votes you in." He softened the words with an affectionate smile. "And we both know they will."

"If they have any doubts, I'll convince them I'm the right person for the job."

"That's my boy."

Drew didn't point out he was well into his thirties. To his grandfather, he would always be the first grandchild and he was good with that. The old man had been a steady, loving force in his life.

"If I get the opportunity to run the bank,

I'll make you proud. You have my word."

His grandfather smiled at him. "You always do."

Silver told herself not to get too excited. That whatever she imagined for the Airstreams was one thing, but the meeting with the contractor was going to bring things back to reality. They didn't have unlimited funds or space.

She and Drew had interviewed several contractors before picking Walter. The barrel-chested, bowlegged powerhouse of a man had built nearly every kind of structure there was in Happily Inc. He'd been intrigued by the limitations of their project and had offered a lot of good suggestions.

As Silver walked through the fenced-in lot behind Wynn's graphics company, she couldn't help the little shiver of anticipation that tickled her belly. Both trailers were stunning, she thought, nearly giggling with happiness. Shiny and full of possibilities.

She unlocked the trailers and walked into the larger one. Instead of scuffed flooring and torn upholstery, she envisioned a gleaming new refrigerator and custom shelves the right height for the plastic racks that held clean glasses. They could have liquor storage right in the middle, where they had quick access to whatever was being poured that night and more racks in the back to hold extra bottles.

She wanted counter space that could be locked in place when they were at a job and then folded away when it wasn't needed. And more than anything, she wanted an ice machine.

She was still imagining the thrill of not having to haul ice when she spotted Drew walking toward the trailer. For a second her body went on alert and she had the most ridiculous urge to check her face in a mirror. What was up with that? She didn't care what she looked like. She and Drew weren't involved. They were business associates, nothing more.

He walked into the trailer and smiled at her. "Walter's pulling in right now." He paused. "What are you thinking about?"

"What do you mean?"

"You have an interesting expression."

She hoped she wasn't blushing and tried desperately to think of something to say. "Ah, fine. You caught me. I was fantasizing."

"About an ice maker?"

"I know it's not practical for the smaller trailer, but if we could have one here it would be so magical."

"And to think some women dream of diamonds."

"You can't make ice with a diamond."

They walked outside and shook hands with Walter. Silver had already laid out her sketches so the contractor could look them over. She'd noted dimensions as best she could. With some of the existing built-in cabinetry, she couldn't access every corner.

Walter studied the drawings, walked into the two trailers, then came out and looked at the drawings again.

Finally he rocked back on his heels and cleared his throat. "The way I see it, we have three big issues. Space, weight and practicality. We have a limited amount of space to work in. Add to that, you've got to be able to set up and break down quickly. No point in designing something amazing if it takes two hours just to set up the bar."

He pointed at the bigger trailer. "Next is weight. Airstreams are well built and can haul a lot, but you're already committed to some heavy equipment. The refrigerator alone is one big girl. Add everything else and you'll be testing the frame. We need to work with materials that are lightweight and strong. Easily cleanable, too, I'd guess. Last, practicality."

He pointed to the existing door. "That'll

134

have to be what, twice as wide? Three times would be better. You want to have access to all your raw materials, so to speak. Clean up, inside and out, needs to be fast and efficient. No deep corners for dirt to hide out. You need to have restaurant-level cleanliness with minimal weight and no space. All on a budget."

"Still interested?" Drew asked.

"I am. This is going to be a fun challenge. I'm going to make these two trailers everything they can be."

"Do you think I could have an ice maker?" Silver asked hopefully.

Walter rubbed his chin. "Let me think. It's going to be big and heavy. You won't have any control over your water source so you'll want one with a good filtration system, which means you'll need it placed such that you can change filters and hook up anything from a faucet to a hose."

He considered for a moment, then shrugged. "As long as you accept you're giving up storage space for it, I don't see why I couldn't put one in."

Silver had to consciously keep herself from dancing with excitement. "Walter, it's possible I'm falling in love with you."

He grinned. "I get that a lot. This is where I tell you that I'm happily married and the

135

missus runs a tight ship." He winked at her. "Not that I'm not flattered." He turned back to the trailer. "I've been doing a lot of kitchen remodels lately. I look forward to the change."

"And the stripper poles," Drew added.

Silver sighed. "You told him about that?"

"He did," Walter told her. "I was very impressed."

Nearly a week later, Silver drove up to Drew's house. She knew where he lived — like nearly everyone in town, she'd walked through the big houses on the golf course when they'd been under construction. But once she'd heard he'd bought one and the sold sign had gone up, she'd avoided the neighborhood.

Their conversation with Walter had gone better than they'd hoped, and the contractor had gone right to work on getting them quotes on materials along with a timetable. When Walter had sent the email with his bid, Drew had texted, suggesting they get together and talk about what they wanted to do. He'd invited her to dinner and before she could think things through, she'd accepted. A three-hour appointment with a new couple planning a wedding had kept her distracted all afternoon but as she headed up the hill toward Drew's place, she found herself fighting nerves.

Stupid man, she thought in annoyance. There was no reason he should get to her. He was just her business partner. They were going to grow AlcoHaul together. Their past made a great story but it wasn't relevant. Well, maybe a *little* relevant what with them having a daughter together. A daughter he technically knew about but didn't actually *know* about. A daughter he would be meeting in a few weeks.

Tonight, she promised herself. She would tell him tonight. She was a mature, thoughtful woman who made good decisions. She wasn't that eighteen-year-old girl too in love to think sensibly. Not anymore.

Silver's mom had always been a fool for love, going from man to man her entire life, falling madly in love, sure that this time would be forever. She'd dragged Silver all over the country until at fifteen, Silver had begged to be allowed to go live with her uncle in Happily Inc. Her mother had been about to join her latest one-true-love on his fishing boat in Alaska, so had agreed. Silver had settled in easily, loving everything about the quirky town and appreciating how she wouldn't have to worry about moving on in a few months.

Her uncle had been a kind man. Older, with absolutely no experience with children. He'd given Silver plenty of freedom and she'd paid him back by doing her best not to be any trouble. Over time, he'd become a surrogate father and she hoped she'd made his life a little brighter.

When he'd been ready to retire, he'd sold her the bar. She'd worked it for a short time, only to realize she wanted something different. She'd found a buyer and had used the money to fund AlcoHaul.

He'd died a couple of years ago. Before he'd passed, he'd made sure she'd known he was proud of what she'd accomplished and impressed with her future plans. She had no idea what he would say about her being in business with Drew and had a feeling he would warn her to guard her heart. She'd done her best to avoid being like her mother — no in and out of love for her. But she often wondered how much of her mother's wayward heart she'd inherited.

Silver pulled into the driveway of Drew's sprawling two-story house. There had to be at least four bedrooms — maybe five. She knew the back of the house opened onto the golf course with the animal preserve beyond. She thought of her small loft apartment and wondered what Drew did with all that space. Whatever it was, it didn't involve women. Since his engagement had ended, Drew hadn't been involved with anyone she knew about. Maybe he went out of town to have his fun.

Not her business, she told herself as she collected her tote bag, along with three thick folders filled with plans and preliminary budgets. In theory, this was a working dinner, or it would be right up until she dropped the Autumn-sized bombshell in the middle of things.

She'd brought along a bottle of wine, then hesitated before grabbing it. He'd invited her to dinner, she told herself. Bringing along a thank-you gift was customary and wine was always welcome. Still, with alcohol came a risk of people getting a little too comfortable. Although she supposed the wine might make it easier for her to blurt out her news. As long as it didn't cause her to notice how sexy he was and how she had occasional moments of attraction when he was around.

She picked up the bottle of Washington State Cabernet, then headed to the front door.

Drew let her in before she could knock.

"Hey," he said with a grin. "You made it."

He looked good, which she tried not to

notice, despite suddenly going breathless.

"I did. I just pointed my truck to the rich part of town and here I am." She smiled as she walked inside. "I'm very curious about what you do with all the extra space. Unless you're taking in roommates to help pay the utilities."

"Not a bad idea, but it's just me."

The entryway was large, with a two-story-high ceiling. She noted a home office on her left and a small powder room on her right before he led her into a huge open area.

The house had been built around the great room concept. One side was dominated by a huge kitchen, with a massive living space on the other. She counted two sofas, six chairs and a reading nook in the corner. The stone-clad fireplace rose nearly twenty feet. A doorway off the kitchen led to a formal dining room.

Everything she saw pointed out the gulf between them. Happily Inc didn't have a "wrong side of the tracks" literally, but Silver had always known her life was very different from his. Funny how when they'd been together, all those years ago, it hadn't been a problem. They'd just fallen in love and had wanted to be together.

"I'm cooking," he said as they walked into

the kitchen. "You should be impressed."

"That depends on what you're making. If it's grilled steaks and a salad, then no, I'm not." Although based on the delicious aromas, she would guess whatever he was serving was a lot more complicated than that.

"You always were a tough crowd." He pointed to a six-burner stove where a couple of pans were simmering away. "Roasted vegetables, pesto risotto and pan-fried chicken with a mushroom reduction."

She set down her bottle of wine. "Okay, I'm impressed. I never thought of your mother as someone who loved to cook."

"She isn't. I learned some from my grandfather's cook and I've taken a few classes here and there. I like cooking. It's relaxing, and then you get to eat."

She eyed his lean, muscular body and decided he must have converted one of the extra bedrooms into a home gym. No one who could make mushroom reduction could look as good as him without working out on a regular basis.

For a moment she wanted to reach out and touch him, to feel his warm skin against hers. She'd always liked touching Drew and what happened when he touched her in return. She took a half step toward him only to remind herself that no, sex wasn't on the menu and even if it was, she was far too smart to give in. Fool me once and all that.

"I brought wine," she said, holding out the bottle.

"Nice." He took it from her. "Want me to open it now or want to start with a margarita?"

She laughed. "You've obviously been practicing. I'll take a margarita. On the rocks."

She set her tote on a side table by one of the sofas, then sat at the runway-sized island.

He collected all the ingredients, including fresh limes and a dish of salt. He used a quarter of a lime to moisten the rim of the glass before dipping it in the salt. He poured good quality tequila, orange liqueur and lime juice into a martini shaker, then put ice in the two glasses. After shaking up everything, he poured before adding a slice of lime to the salty edge of the glass.

He passed her the drink without saying a word. She took it and studied the color, then sniffed and took a sip.

The drink was the perfect combination of sweet, salty and tart. She smiled. "It's good. Thank you."

"Those internet classes are paying off."

"Yes, they are."

He took his glass and joined her, then nodded at her stack of folders. "Business first?"

"Can dinner wait?"

"It's all at the simmering stage. Except the vegetables. They're ready to pop in the oven, so we can take our time."

She knew that last bit was about discussing business but for one heart-stopping second, she imagined he meant something else. Something that seemed to be bubbling between them — at least on her side.

Her three-month relationship with Drew had been more than falling in love — it had been about sex, as well. They'd had great chemistry, the kind that threatened good sense and made keeping their hands off each other impossible.

After they'd broken up, she'd told herself that she would find someone else just like him, or maybe someone better. She'd assumed that kind of attraction was normal but time had proved her wrong. There hadn't been a lot of guys, but the few she'd slept with had been nothing like Drew. Or maybe she was the problem. Regardless, she'd never found that all-consuming white heat she'd felt with him.

She wondered if he'd experienced the

same thing or if she was the only one forced to deal with a mild sense of disappointment.

"Then let's go ahead and look at numbers," she said, her tone light. If nothing else, she was good at hiding what she was thinking.

She took another sip of her drink, then opened the three folders. One contained the information from Walter — quotes, timetables and options on materials. The second folder had cash flow estimates based on different scenarios such as fixing up both trailers at once versus doing one and then waiting a bit to do the second one. The third folder contained cost estimates in a very professional spreadsheet. Drew had put together that one. Silver was a bit spreadsheet challenged.

He settled next to her at the island bar. He was close enough to be a distraction but not so close that she could complain he was invading her space. Dinner had not been a good idea, she thought with mild resignation. She should have suggested a coffee date at a public place. Something that wasn't so . . . intimate.

Focus, she told herself. Work and only work. Work, then dinner, then she could tell him about Autumn. The plan made sense and no matter what, she was going to stick to it.

Drew picked up Walter's quote. "We should do it. All of it. Both trailers and your retail space. I know it's a big chunk of cash all at once, but the sooner we get the trailers making money, the better. The same for the storefront. Right now it's just dead-weight."

The sudden knot in her stomach had nothing to do with how good-looking he was. "Are you insane? That's a huge risk." She reached for his spreadsheets and flipped through them until she found the one she wanted. "According to your numbers, that will take the twenty grand you're throwing in and all my savings. There won't be any reserves for emergencies. What if my truck gets totaled or we don't get any bookings or there's a tornado?"

"You have insurance for the truck." He looked at her. "Silver, you're turning down weddings every single week. We haven't even started marketing the smaller trailer for parties, but I know at least a half dozen people who would be interested in renting it."

"You say that now but interest is not the same as writing a check." She pressed a hand to her chest. "Do it all? I'm not sure I can breathe."

She wanted to expand, but to take her savings down to zero? Drew would be fine. He had a regular job and this house and God knew how much in the bank. This was just an investment for him, but for her, it was her whole world.

He flipped through the printouts. "Did you see this one? We have Walter work the trailer projects consecutively instead of concurrently." He reached for Walter's quotes and found the one that mentioned doing the work that way.

He pointed to the page. "See how it takes longer because we won't be his only job. He would get to work on the big trailer and the retail space immediately. Once the equipment is on hand, he can do the work in about two weeks. Then we'd have that trailer up and earning money. He'd start your place the second week of the big trailer work and follow up with the smaller trailer. It spreads the work out and means the second truck purchase can be put off a little and income will be coming in." He pointed to the line for the truck purchase. "Let's not pay cash for those. Get a vehicle loan. You can deduct the interest and use the money we save to pad your savings until you feel more in control. Then you can pay off the trucks early."

The bands around her chest eased a little. She went over the numbers again and studied Walter's bid. The cost of doing them all at the same time versus doing them one after the other was nearly identical but the latter bought them time and her peace of mind. With the initial shock fading, she felt her confidence return.

"I never thought about getting a loan to buy the trucks," she said. "That's a good idea and it solves a lot of problems. I wouldn't decimate my savings for one." She flashed him a grin. "Plus I'd finance through the dealer rather than at the bank."

He didn't return her smile. "Silver, you know I had nothing to do with what happened at the bank, right?"

"Of course. I don't for a second think you got in the way of me getting a business loan. You have many flaws, but dishonesty isn't one of them."

His expression relaxed. "I can't believe you said I have flaws."

"Of course you do."

"What about you?"

"Three. I have three flaws."

He laughed. The sound made her want to lean into him. Drew was her greatest weakness. He always had been. For a long time she'd told herself she was cured, but apparently that was simply because she hadn't been around him.

"I won't ask you to name them," he told her. "Why don't you think about the options and we'll talk in a couple of days?"

Silver thought about how much time they'd already waited to get all the information. The refrigerator they wanted for the larger trailer was in stock, but there was only one and once it sold, it would be at least six weeks to get another one. She looked at the drawings Walter had done of what the trailer would look like on the inside. She thought about the two weddings she'd been contacted about that conflicted with dates she already had on her calendar. But if the new trailers were ready . . .

"Let's do it," she said. "The bigger trailer and my space, then the smaller trailer. I'll finance the trucks and that will give me a cushion."

His dark gaze locked with hers. "Are you sure?"

"Yes. At some point I either have to move forward or accept what I have. Obviously I'm not willing to do the latter. I grew this business from nothing — I'm not willing to let it stagnate now. We have a good plan and I have two brides waiting to hear back from me on booking their weddings. Both of them would be using the second trailer. This is the right thing to do."

He smiled. "I think so, too."

They toasted each other with their glasses, then Drew rose. "Come on. It's still nice out. Let's go sit on the patio for a few minutes. Then I'll finish dinner."

She nodded and followed him out onto his large patio. There were several chairs set up to take advantage of the incredible view. The temperature was close to eighty, with a light breeze, and the sun was low in the sky.

He pulled two chairs close together. They sat down facing the sunset. She could see the lush grass of the golf course and the animal preserve beyond. This late in the day, the animals would have already headed back to their barns for the night, but come morning, they would be out and visible.

"You have a good life," she said. "How many people get to see giraffes over their morning coffee?"

"There is that. Just think, once we're a franchise, you can move up here and we'll be neighbors."

She chuckled. "We're not going to be a franchise."

"You say that now, but I'll convince you."

"You wish."

"I remember you being more adventurous, back in the day. Remember that party we threw up at Honeymoon Falls?"

"That wasn't adventurous, it was reckless." She smiled at the memory. "But it *was* a great party."

It had been the last weekend before Drew had left for college. They'd invited everyone they'd known and pooled their money to buy food. All their friends had brought plenty of liquor — completely illegal, considering how most of them had barely been eighteen. There'd been a live band, illegal fireworks and lots of couples sneaking off into the bushes. Silver was pretty sure that was the night she'd gotten pregnant with Autumn.

"There had to have been over a hundred people there," he said.

"At least. I'm still surprised the police didn't show up."

"It was a magical night." He glanced at her. "And a great summer."

"It was," she admitted, thinking about how amazed she'd been to find herself dating Drew. Of course she'd known who he was — everyone had known him — but she'd been surprised that he'd picked her.

She sipped her drink. "I don't remember exactly how we started dating. Do you?"

"Yes. It was the Saturday before graduation. I was driving into town and I saw you walking along the sidewalk. You had on white shorts and a pink crop top. I took one look at you and I was lost."

His words jogged her memory. "Oh yeah. You pulled over and wanted to buy me dinner."

"You told me it was nine-fifteen in the morning and dinner wasn't for hours. I said I'd wait."

"You did."

They looked at each other. She felt the heat between them, the connection, then told herself it was probably one-sided and not to read anything into it.

"You should probably add I was more than a piece of ass," she murmured, mostly to distract herself.

"You know you were."

"Because we'd gone to high school together for three years and you'd never noticed me."

"I'd noticed. I just didn't do anything." One shoulder rose and lowered. "I noticed, but I knew when you and I got together, it would be intense and high school was not the place for that."

She had no idea if he was telling the truth but she hoped he was. That what they'd been together had been as important to him as it had been to her.

"I see it with Cade," he admitted. "The intensity. The way he looks at Bethany, how he talks about her."

"They're getting married — aren't they supposed to be in love?"

"Sure, but it's a whole different level. Look at what he's giving up to be with her."

"What's he giving up? She's an actual princess."

Drew looked at her. "The royal thing isn't on any guy's wish list. In-laws can be terrifying but his father-in-law is a king. I think they still behead people in El Bahar."

She laughed. "They don't and you know it. But you might have a point about the prince thing being tough duty. There will be a lot of expectations. Still, Cade's a good guy. I want them to be happy together."

"Me, too."

The sun slipped below the horizon. The air had begun to cool, but it was still pleasant outside.

"You ever date Jasper?"

The question surprised her. She glanced at him. "No. Of course not. He's with Wynn."

"Now, but what about before?"

She resisted the urge to roll her eyes. "No, I never dated Jasper. Why would you ask?"

"I thought he might be your type."

"Because he's dangerous?" Jasper had an edge about him, a darkness. She knew he had a military background but little else about him. Wynn didn't talk about Jasper, and Silver had never had the chance to get to know him beyond saying hello.

"Because he's wounded. Chicks dig a guy who's wounded."

"Chicks? You didn't just say that. Men!" She glanced at him. "You're really not in a position to be saying anything about any guy I dated. You were engaged to Ashley Lauren Grantham-Greene."

He groaned. "No. Don't remind me. That was a hideous mistake."

"She tried to set your car on fire."

"I know."

"What were you thinking? The name alone should have been a tip-off. And she was so stuck-up and pretentious. What if you'd actually married her?"

He angled toward her. "It never would have happened."

"Oh, I think it might have. Is this where I mention the engagement again?"

"No, it's not. You think you're so smart."

"I am so smart."

He stood and pulled her to her feet. "Come on. Let's go inside. I'll serve you a dinner so delicious, you'll never mention Ashley Lauren Grantham-Greene again."

She tried not to react to the heat from where his fingers had touched hers. "That's got to be some dinner because I kind of like mentioning her."

They went into the house. He set his empty glass on the table, took hers and put it down as well before turning to face her.

They were standing close. A little too close. She had to tilt her head to stare into his eyes, and every inch of her body was aware of every inch of his.

They had been so good together. The words were whispered by a traitorous part of her body that remembered Drew far too well. Telling herself this was a different place and time didn't do much to quiet the need that flared inside of her. Telling herself she had to bring up Autumn, and soon, did a slightly better job but not enough to keep her from wishing he would . . . He would . . .

CHAPTER SEVEN

Drew's eyes locked with hers. Silver saw the exact moment he decided to make a move and told herself to get the hell out of there. To not under any circumstances give in to —

He closed the last couple of inches between them and kissed her. That was it — just one gentle, sensual brush of his lips against hers and she was completely and totally gone. Any chance of escape faded as her body surrendered to that single kiss.

What was it about lips on lips? Where did the magic live the rest of the time, and who was really to blame — her body, her head or her heart?

Involuntarily, she raised her arms and rested her hands on his shoulders. She was instantly aware that he was bigger and stronger than he had been before. At eighteen, he'd been as much a boy as a man. Now, more than a decade later, he'd filled

155

out and matured and she couldn't begin to resist that.

He pressed his mouth more firmly against hers. At the same time he settled his hands on her waist, his thumbs lightly tracing her bottom ribs.

He'd always done that, she thought hazily. Touched her like that, kissed her like that. Even as the thought formed, his tongue swept lazily across her lower lip. As if they had all the time in the world. As if there was no question about what was going to happen next.

At the first stroke of his tongue, need exploded. Heat followed, making her ache and whimper and shake. Powerful hunger took control, overwhelming common sense and self-preservation. She wanted him with a desperation that threatened her very being. This was Drew and she'd always been an eager participant in any game he wanted to play.

He eased back a little and nibbled his way along her jaw. "I've seen the dragon tat," he murmured between nipping caresses. "Any other new ones I should know about?"

"There's a heart on the right side of my back. You already know about the rose."

"The dragon and the rose." He shuddered. "You know you're killing me, right?"

He wasn't the only one dying here but she wasn't going to say that. Instead she reached for the hem of her T-shirt and pulled it off in one easy move.

His gaze skimmed over her and he shook his head, then grabbed her hand. She followed him through the house, up the stairs and into the master bedroom. She had a brief impression of lots of space and a big bed, then Drew pulled back the comforter and sheets, opened a nightstand drawer and set out a handful of condoms before tearing off his own T-shirt.

They toed out of their shoes. Jeans and underwear followed. She paused to unfasten her bra and toss it on the pile of clothes.

They were both naked, but instead of reaching for her, he simply looked. She did the same, taking in the thick muscles of his chest, the narrow waist and hips and his very large, very thick erection. He was ready, she thought with satisfaction. She could see the rapid beating of his heart in a vein in his neck.

She saw his gaze roam over her breasts before settling on her shoulder. She turned slowly, letting him see the body of the dragon and how it curved over her shoulder. She kept turning so he could see the rose. He moved close then, pressing his chest to her back and resting his hands on her belly. Her eyes sank closed.

"Remember the first time," he whispered as he shifted her hair out of the way and kissed along her neck. "I was so scared. I didn't want to hurt you or disappoint you."

She smiled and drew his hands to her breasts. His fingers immediately began to tease her tight, sensitive nipples. Heat spiraled down between her legs. She felt herself swelling in anticipation and need.

"Drew, we'd been pleasing each other for weeks," she said, struggling to keep from gasping at the pleasure as he rubbed her breasts, then rolled her nipples between his fingers. "We could practically make each other come with a joke."

"But it was different that night." He let one hand slip down her belly.

She parted her legs to give him room to work. Her eyes opened and she realized they were facing the mirror over the dresser. She could see herself . . . and him. She watched his hand slip between her thighs, saw and felt the moment his fingers found her center.

"You're wet."

"You're hard."

He raised his head and met her gaze in the mirror. One corner of his mouth turned up. "Funny how it works out that way."

"There is something to be said for elegant design."

His gaze still locked with hers, he moved his fingers around and around. "I'm going to make you come just like this. We're both going to watch it happen."

She thought about protesting that she wasn't comfortable being that vulnerable, only this was Drew and watching was the least of everything they'd ever done. They'd been young and in love, with plenty of time alone and lots of privacy. They'd tried every position, every game, everything they could think of with the goal of pleasing each other. He'd learned her body so well, he could have her wet and ready in less than thirty seconds and screaming out his name in forty-five. Wouldn't it be interesting if that hadn't changed?

She parted her legs just a touch more and raised one arm up and around the back of his neck for a little more support, then leaned into him. His erection was a hard ridge between them. He kept his right hand between her legs and used his left on her breasts.

His fingers circled her clit. "Fast or slow?"

"Fast."

"Hard enough?"

"Uh-huh."

He quickened the pace but kept the pressure steady on that one amazing spot. Tension and heat radiated out from her center to the very tips of her fingers. She wanted to close her eyes, but she forced herself to keep watching. Her naked body, his hands moving. Around and around, his fingers rubbing over and over in a rhythmic pace that took her closer and closer to the edge.

She felt her breathing coming faster and could also see the rise and fall of her rib cage. Then he pinched her nipples, sending jolts of electric pleasure through her. She watched her lips part as she moaned. Color stained her cheeks and the top of her chest. Her gaze softened.

He stopped moving. Before she could react, he gently pinched her clitoris and pressed down in a back-and-forth movement, as if trying to get to the very heart of the nerve-filled knot. Need grew exponentially, taking her to the very edge. Her strength left her and she nearly doubled over. Drew held her upright, made the movement again, then returned to the circling only going faster.

She was out of control. Silver didn't know how it had happened, but suddenly she was so close, she couldn't stop herself from crying out.

"Almost," she shouted. "Don't stop."

"Never."

He moved from breast to breast, rubbing her nipples in time with what he was doing between her legs. She was so close, so close. Just hanging there, waiting . . .

"Come for me. Silver, come for me."

She let her eyes close for a single heartbeat as she breathed in the deliciousness of his touch, then opened them and met his gaze. She saw eagerness in his eyes and felt his erection flex against her back. Without warning he pressed her clit again and she was lost.

Still watching him watch her, she came with a scream as her body convulsed in perfect release.

Just as the last ripple raced through her, but well before she'd caught her breath, he half carried, half pushed her to the bed. She'd barely fallen back on the mattress when he was parting her legs and urging her to hold herself open for him.

She wanted to tell him she needed a second to collect herself, but then again maybe not, because she knew what was next.

Her only warning was a light whisper of his breath, then he licked the very heart of her. She was so sensitive from her last release that she couldn't help shuddering. Relaxed muscles suddenly tensed. She went from satisfied to hungry in the time it took her to gasp out his name.

He was relentless. He remembered everything they'd ever done together and now used that information to his advantage. He moved his tongue just the way she liked. He sucked on her clit, drawing it in his mouth in a way that pushed her closer and closer. She dug her heels into the mattress and lifted her hips toward him, then moved her head back and forth as her body climbed higher and higher until climaxing was as inevitable as breathing.

Her orgasm lasted longer than the first one. He continued to stroke her with his tongue, getting lighter and lighter, drawing out every ounce of goodness until she was limp.

If she'd had state secrets she would have spilled them. If he'd wanted anything from her, she would have offered it times three. She'd had lovers since him, but none who were so very skilled at reading her body.

He sat up and reached for a condom, then moved between her thighs, this time his gaze locked with hers.

She reached down and guided him inside her swollen body. Nerve endings cheered as he pushed in deeper, filling her, stretching her. She felt the telltale zinging that promised yet another release — this time with him inside of her. He braced himself on his hands and began to move.

Each thrust was pure perfection. The fullness, the friction, the rhythm. He got it all right. She wanted to close her eyes and sink into the experience, only he was staring at her so intently, she just couldn't look away.

She wrapped her legs around his hips and pulled him in deeper. At the same time, she ran her hands up and down his strong arms, urging him on. She watched him get closer and felt the answering response deep in her own body.

Tiny explosions began inside of her, but she ignored them. She thought of other things and told herself to wait. That it would be better when they came together. She watched, so incredibly close that when he sped up, she nearly lost control.

He swore under his breath. "You ready?"

She nodded, barely able to keep from coming.

"Now!" He groaned.

She waited for his final, deepest push, then gave herself over to her own release. They came together, crying out, clinging to each other, as much one person as they had ever been. Time blurred and bent and for one brief second, she was eighteen and with the man she would love for the rest of her life and it was exactly how it was supposed to be.

Reality returned quickly. Drew rolled off her and sighed.

"Hell of a thing," he said, then looked at her. One corner of his mouth turned up. "I still owe you dinner."

She started to laugh. Whatever had been was long gone. The sex had probably been a mistake, but despite the potential consequences, it had been worth it.

"What was it we were having?" she asked. "Steak and something?"

He kissed her. "Pesto risotto and chicken with mushroom reduction."

"Oh right. Nice that you're more than a pretty face."

"You, too."

It was all Drew could do not to whistle. Nothing showstopping — just the happy mindless tune of a man who had been bedded well by the woman he, ah, admired very much. Because he did admire Silver. She was smart, she was ambitious, she was kind and honest and beautiful and funny and —

"Are you all right?"

The sharp tone, not to mention the question itself, pulled him out of his happy daydream and back to the present. He looked up from his desk and saw his aunt standing in the doorway of his office, staring at him.

"Good morning, Libby. I'm fine, thanks. How are you?"

Her gaze narrowed. "There's something," she muttered, half under her breath. "You're not on drugs, are you?"

He laughed. "I assure you, I'm not on drugs."

"That wasn't meant as a humorous comment. I don't do humor."

"Of that I am well aware."

She continued to stare at him for another couple of seconds before shaking her head and walking away. Drew leaned back in his chair and grinned. Oh yeah, he had it bad.

His postcoital smugness lasted the entire morning. At ten-thirty he went out into the lobby to greet clients. The Newports were a young family. Doug and Melissa were in their thirties. Doug was a plumber and Melissa a stay-at-home mom. They'd recently inherited two hundred and fifty thousand dollars from a distant relative and Drew was helping them invest the money to fund their kids' future and their retirement.

While he didn't usually handle private wealth clients, he'd gone to school with both of them and had taken them on as a favor.

He found the couple in the waiting area, then raised his eyebrows when he saw they weren't alone.

"Family day," he said happily. He crouched down in front of a little girl he knew was eight. "You must be Emily. I'm Drew. Your mom and dad told me all about you."

She had dark hair and eyes and looked like a miniature version of her mother. Her gaze was wary.

"I'm not sure I like it here. Mommy said I had to be quiet."

"It's a bank," Drew told her. "People are thinking a lot, so it helps if we keep our voices down." He glanced at Melissa and nodded at the small baby she held. "Jacob?"

"Yes. We've had him just over a week." She looked chagrined. "I'm sorry we had to bring the kids but my mom got sick and you said we were just signing some paper-work."

Drew shook hands with Doug, then smiled at Melissa. "It will be fifteen minutes, tops." He leaned toward Emily. "Are you excited about your new little brother?"

Her expression was doubtful. "I guess. He

cries and his poop smells really bad. Mommy says Jacob is too small to meet Mr. Whiskers, so I take care of him all by myself."

"Mr. Whiskers?"

"My rabbit. He's a really good pet." She eyed Jacob. "He's very quiet and his poop doesn't smell at all."

Drew knew that Doug and Melissa had been unable to conceive a second child so had turned to adoption. They'd been chosen by a pregnant teenager fairly quickly. Although they'd tried to get Emily excited about expanding their family, it seemed her heart had yet to be won.

"I think you're going to find that having a little brother can be fun," he told her, then held out his hand. "Would you like to come see my office? I'll shut the door so you don't have to worry about disturbing anyone."

Emily smiled. "Yes, please." She put her small hand in his. "Do you have cookies?"

"Emily!" Melissa stood. "Sorry. When we go see my friends, they usually give her a cookie."

Drew winked at the little girl. "You know what? I think I know where I can find cookies."

"Thank you very much. Mommy says we can trust you with our money. You're not going to steal it, are you?"

He chuckled. "I am not. I promise. Cross my heart."

Emily ate two Oreo cookies while her parents signed the paperwork to transfer the money into their account at the bank.

"I'll be in touch as soon as the money arrives," he told the couple. "We already have our investment plan ready to go. By this time next week, we should be all set."

"Thank you." Melissa smiled at him. "We really appreciate all your help. The inheritance was an unexpected windfall and we were totally unprepared."

"Happy to help."

He showed them out, winking at Emily as she turned to wave goodbye. As he walked back to his office, the urge to whistle returned. He managed to control himself but chuckled as he imagined the look of horror on Libby's face if he gave in. His good mood continued right up until he glanced at his phone and saw he had a text from his mother, then it burst like a punctured balloon.

Good morning, darling. I need to speak with you.

He groaned. His mother wanting to talk

to him was never a good thing.

I'm at work. Can it wait until tonight?

Of course. I just arrived in Happily Inc myself. I'm settling in at your grandfather's and am looking forward to speaking with you.

Arrived as in . . . "Holy crap," he muttered out loud. No wonder his aunt was in a bad mood. She was going to be sharing a house with her older sister.

Drew had two appointments after lunch. Once they were done, he shut down his computer and headed for his grandfather's house. Why was his mother back in town? Whatever the reason, it wasn't going to be good for him.

He found his mother in the largest guest suite on the second floor. He knocked on the open door and called out, "Hi, Mom."

His mother, a dark-haired, slim woman of average height, stood to greet him. Irene wore a dark pants suit, diamond stud earrings and a gold link necklace. The outfit was very elegant and probably cost as much as a car. Or five. His mother wore the best, drank the best, lived in the best. Everything in her life was about being *the best.*

"Darling, you came to see me. How lovely." She leaned in for an air kiss, then stepped back and studied him. "Let me look at you. You're keeping fit. Excellent. No one wants to deal with a fat lobbyist." Her gaze sharpened as she studied his face. "You look young but we'll try to work that to our advantage." She clapped her hands together. "Come in and sit with me. I'll order tea from one of the maids. One would think with so many running around this house the response would be faster, but alas."

Drew thought about mentioning that the slow service might have something to do with how she treated the staff, but knew there was no win in that for any of them. His mother wouldn't get the point and would take out her annoyance on everyone who worked at the house.

She picked up a house phone and dialed zero. "Yes, this is Irene. I would appreciate some tea. Quickly, if that's at all possible. Two cups."

She hung up without saying thank you, then turned to him.

"Come, darling. We have to so much to talk about."

She led the way into a small sitting room. When he took the seat across from her, she leaned forward.

"I want you to know I'm going to be with you every step of the way."

Words guaranteed to strike terror in his heart, even when he didn't know what she was talking about.

"Mom, I need a subject, first."

"The bank, of course. Your grandfather is going to be stepping down. You're the obvious choice for his successor but Libby is going to be a problem. I'm here to run interference."

"I don't need my mother helping me at work." He leaned toward her. "Mom, I mean that. Stay out of my life."

Instead of being offended, Irene smiled. "Oh, Drew, don't be dramatic. I'm not going to follow you into the office and make sure your tie is straight. I'll be working behind the scenes. This is going to happen. It's part of our plan. You run the bank for two years, then join your father and me at our firm in D.C." Her expression softened. "You're going to love it. The people we know. We're growing in our European influence and isn't that wonderful? In a few years, we'll have global reach."

"Kingmakers," he muttered, knowing she wouldn't hear the irony in his voice.

"Exactly. I'm going to ignore Libby and make nice with my father. I'll play the dutiful daughter so he sees you are the one who deserves to be chairman of the board at the bank."

"You know it's not his decision. The board makes it."

She waved her hand dismissively. "The board will do what your grandfather tells them to do. I'm not worried about him. My bitch of a sister is more concerning, but I'll take care of her, as well."

She smoothed her hair. "I will admit, when you first broke off your engagement with Ashley Lauren Grantham-Greene I was very upset. She was a lovely girl and would have made you a beautiful wife."

"Except for her temper and love of setting things on fire."

His mother ignored that. "But I've come to see it was for the best. Now you can marry someone better, someone who can really help your career."

If he got in his car right now, how far away could he be by sundown? If he drove east, he would be out of the state. Maybe all the way to New Mexico, and wouldn't that be nice?

"Mom, you've got to stop. I mean it. I don't want you interfering with my job or my future. I respect what you and Dad have done, but it's not for me. I want to stay here and run the bank. I'm not moving to D.C. and I'm not joining your firm."

"Don't be difficult."

"I'm being honest. You and Dad have big dreams, but I don't share them."

Her mouth tightened. "We'll talk about that later. For now, let's just be happy I'm here. Oh! Why didn't you tell me about your cousin?"

He had several, so wasn't sure which one she was — He held in a groan as he realized she'd heard about Cade and his engagement to Princess Bethany of El Bahar.

"Clever boy," Irene said with a sigh. "I wish you'd seen her first. I suppose it's too late for you to steal her away."

"Ignoring the facts that they're wildly in love, that he's my cousin and best friend, and that it would be wrong, tacky and ultimately unsuccessful, yes, it's too late."

"That's unfortunate." Irene pouted for a moment. "Still, there's going to be some kind of event here in town, I've heard that much. Her family is bound to attend. Your father and I would very much like to meet the king of El Bahar." Her gaze locked on his. "You can arrange a private introduction. Some kind of welcome party with just us. Royal connections in that part of the world are hard to come by and very important. El Bahar is one of the wealthiest and most forward-looking countries in the world. You need to get right on that, Drew."

He glanced at the clock and saw it wasn't yet four. Too bad, because he was ready for a drink.

He stood. "Mom, it's been great. I've got to go."

"But we have so much to talk about!"

"I'm sure we do and it's going to wait." He leaned down and lightly kissed her cheek. "Have fun with Libby."

His mother was still calling him back as he headed for the stairs. On the way to the front door, he passed Amelia carrying a tray with tea service.

"Run," he told the other woman. "Run while you still can."

Jasper got home a little after three in the morning. He'd finished his last signing at nine in Dallas, had taken an eleven o'clock flight to LAX, then had driven straight home. Despite his exhaustion, he was up by seven.

After making coffee, he walked through his house to make sure all was well. The house had started out as a two-room cabin and had been added onto over the years. The charitable description would be eclectic but the more honest descriptor was a big-ass mess.

After moving in, Jasper had added an office and gym. Last year he'd knocked out a couple of walls so the kitchen and living room made sense. The master bedroom was a decent size and had its own bathroom. He figured in a year or so, he would tear down the small extra bedrooms and maybe add a bigger bedroom. Not that he had much company. His friends had their own beds to sleep in and Wynn stayed in his. Now if things ever got serious, her son, Hunter, would be a consideration.

He carried his coffee to the back porch. The morning was cold enough that he could see his breath. He sat in a rickety chair and put his feet on the railing, then breathed in the crisp air. It was good to be home.

The tour hadn't been too bad. Next year would be better. Longer, but he was looking forward to his time in the trailer. He liked his solitude and he enjoyed a road trip. He could think — about his past, about his book, about life.

His phone buzzed. He pulled it out of his shirt pocket and glanced at the screen.

You back? Want to go hiking this weekend?

His contentment faded a little as he studied the message. The request was simple enough and he enjoyed Hunter's company. There was only one problem — Wynn.

When Jasper and Wynn had first gotten together, she'd made it clear she had boundaries he was not to cross. They weren't going to get serious, no one could know and she wasn't going to introduce Jasper to her then ten-year-old son. What she and Jasper had was between them and no one else.

At the time, he'd been fine on all counts. He'd been relatively new to town and wasn't looking to get involved with anyone. He'd kept to himself and hadn't made many friends. He and Wynn had met when he'd gone into her print shop to pick up bookmarks his publisher had insisted he take with him on a book tour. She'd been freaked out because Hunter's pet snake had escaped its enclosure and she was going to have to find it. Jasper had offered to help. She'd surprised him by accepting.

They'd gone to her house and started looking. Wynn had found the small snake but instead of grabbing it, she'd screamed and jumped on a coffee table. Jasper had rescued the snake, then her. He'd impulsively invited her to coffee. She'd declined, telling him her rules, including the fact that she didn't want anyone in town knowing she was seeing someone. It had taken him a couple of seconds to figure out there was an excellent chance she was offering to sleep with him, as long as they weren't publicly an item.

Jasper had modified his invitation to coffee, changing the location to his place. She'd accepted and within a month, they'd been lovers.

That had been nearly two years ago. People had started noticing them hanging out at tournament night at The Boardroom bar and eventually word of their relationship had gotten out. Wynn had been fine with that, but had insisted Hunter wasn't to know about them.

Last summer, Hunter had shown up on Jasper's doorstep. He'd found out about Jasper's relationship with his mom and wanted to meet him. The two of them had started talking. Talking had turned into hiking together. Jasper hadn't liked going behind Wynn's back, but Hunter had pleaded with him to keep things quiet. If Wynn found out, she would end things. Which now left Jasper lying to the woman he was sleeping with.

Or we could go fishing, Hunter texted.

Jasper exhaled. He didn't like lying to

Wynn and he wondered what it said about their relationship that he was willing to keep secrets from her about her kid. He supposed it said just as much that after all this time, she didn't want Hunter to know they were . . . What? Involved? Dating? An item?

He couldn't define what they had and he had no idea where it was going. Currently, nowhere, and while he was fine with that, a disquieting voice in his head whispered he should want more.

Not possible, he told himself. When he'd left the army, he'd had a hell of a time adjusting to civilian life. He hadn't been physically injured, but the PTSD had nearly done him in. Prescription medication, therapy and strong-willed determination had done shit to make him better. In the end, one of the therapists had admitted Jasper might never be whole. His last-ditch attempt to find his way back to something that could pass for normal had been to write about his experiences.

He'd started writing literally day and night. His incoherent ramblings had started to become a story. A different therapist had signed him up for a writing class. Jasper had figured out he might have a novel buried in his hundreds of pages and had slowly begun to put it together. He'd met his agent Hank at a conference and the rest, as they say, was history. He'd settled in Happily Inc, had bought this place and made a home of sorts. As for what he had with Wynn . . .

Hello?

Hell. Jasper texted back.

Let's go hiking. At some point we're going to have to tell your mom.

No way. She'll ruin it. She's weird about guys in my life. Something to do with my dad, but she never talks about him. Gotta run. C U Saturday.

See you.

Jasper tucked his phone back in his pocket and picked up his coffee. Only the cup was cold and the view wasn't as relaxing as it had been before he'd heard from Hunter.

CHAPTER EIGHT

Forty-eight hours later, Silver was still feeling the aftereffects of her night with Drew. She didn't want to — knowing Drew was the best sex of her life was hardly comforting — but she couldn't help it. Facts were facts. There was something about that man and her body. They got along really well.

She'd already been to the drugstore to buy a morning-after pill. Although he'd worn a condom, she wasn't taking any chances. Right after that, she'd made an appointment with her doctor to get back on birth control. Not that she was assuming there would be a second, um, event, but she would be foolish not to protect herself.

She poured the big batch of bacon jalapeño mac and cheese she'd made into a large bowl, then covered it with foil. The walk to the gallery would only take a couple of minutes, so her dish should still be plenty warm when she arrived.

She tucked her keys in her jeans pocket, then packed the bowl in an insulated tote and went downstairs.

Walter's team had already started work on her retail space. Her tables and chairs, along with the large photographs and drink setups, were in storage. The walls had been sound-proofed with some kind of siding and there were four shiny stripper poles in place. Silver had to admit they were growing on her. She'd read that stripper poles were a popular item at bachelorette parties. The ladies could get their groove on and learn something they could use later in the privacy of their bedrooms. Although she wasn't exactly sure how a stripper pole move translated to non-stripper-pole life. Hmm, she might have to check that out.

She returned her attention to her retail space. The walls would be painted this week, after the new flooring was finished. The lighting had been upgraded. While she hated to think about how much this remod-eling job was costing, she had to admit the end result was going to be fantastic. Walter and his team did good work. In a few days she would get to see the larger trailer and that would be the most exciting reveal of all.

She was still smiling at the thought as she

headed for the Willow Gallery.

The gallery was next to the river and Happily Inc's river walk. More than a tourist attraction, Willow Gallery boasted a worldwide clientele, due to the exclusive nature of its collections, including the works of brothers Ronan, Nick and Mathias Mitchell.

Natalie, Ronan's fiancée and a budding artist herself, had started at the gallery as a part-time office manager. In the past few months, her art had taken off and she was in the process of transitioning from part-time employee to full-time artist. Natalie hosted the girlfriend lunches when the gallery was closed. Silver had to admit there was something really cool about dining al fresco with zebras and giraffes one week, and surrounded by incredible art the next. It kind of made going to her place or even Weddings Out of the Box seem ho-hum.

She went around to the back entrance of the gallery and let herself in.

"It's me," she called as she walked past the offices and into the main gallery, where Natalie had set up a long table and chairs.

"Hi, you." Natalie, a pretty, curvy brunette, greeted her with a hug and peered inside the tote. "What did you bring?"

"Mac and cheese."

"You are the devil."

"I know. I can't help it." Silver carried the tote to the small table where Natalie had put out several quiches. "What happens when you don't work here anymore? Are we going to have to find somewhere else for our lunches?"

Natalie grinned. "I'm engaged to Ronan and he's Atsuko's most successful artist. I'm pretty sure even if she would say no to me, she wouldn't say no to him."

Carol walked out of the kitchenette in the back with a tray of plastic glasses and a pitcher of lemonade. "Atsuko would never say no to you, Natalie. You're like a daughter to her. Hi, Silver. I'm in the middle of a big carb craving. Please tell me you brought something decadent."

"Mac and cheese with jalapeños and bacon."

"I love you so much."

"Good. I was worried."

They all laughed.

Wynn arrived next. She brought a green salad, which had everyone groaning.

"We've got to eat at least one vegetable a week," Wynn said. "I worry about us."

"It's just plain mean," Carol complained. "I eat healthy every other meal. I look forward to hanging out with my friends and being bad. It's not like I'm drinking wine or

183

anything."

Silver put her arm around her friend. "It's okay," she murmured. "You don't have to eat the salad. I'm sure someone brought dessert." She looked over Carol's shoulder and mouthed *hormones.*

The four of them talked for several minutes before Natalie glanced at her watch. "Should I call the others? They all said they were coming, but do you think they forgot?"

"Not all three of them," Wynn said.

Just then the back door opened.

"We're here!" Pallas called. "And we're late. I'm sorry."

Bethany, Pallas and Renee walked in together.

"They're late," Renee clarified. "I tried to leave on time but they wouldn't let me."

"It's my fault," Bethany said. "I'm sorry. Two days ago we came to terms on the wedding. It's been such a chore to get everything finalized."

"I thought you were having a shower here," Wynn said. "It's not a shower?"

"No. It's a party. A really big party." Bethany sank into a chair.

"You are the princess," Silver said. "Literally. So how big is big?"

"Four hundred people," Renee said. "Including the king and queen, several other members of the royal family and a few heads of state. The president is coming."

The room went silent.

Carol cleared her throat. "Of the, ah, United States?"

"Yes. That president."

Pallas held up her hand. "We don't know that for sure. It's possible the vice president will come instead."

"Well, then." Wynn waved her hand. "That's hardly noteworthy."

They all laughed and moved toward the food.

"Wow," Natalie murmured. "A royal party. Do you get to wear glass slippers? Although it's not really a slipper, is it? It's really a classic pump."

"No glass shoes," Bethany said, scooping up mac and cheese and ignoring the salad. "I'm really, really sorry."

"Stop apologizing," Renee told her. "Planning the party will be fun."

"You say that now."

Pallas moved next to Silver. "We're going to have to talk about how we're handling all of this. Please, please tell me at least one of the new trailers will be ready?"

"It should be, but there's no way we're using trailers at a royal party. I'll set up regular bartending stations. Let's talk later.

185

Give me the date and I'll reserve my best people."

"See," Bethany said with a pout. "It's already happening. Everything is going to be different because of my parents. I don't want regular bartending stations. I want Airstreams and a fun theme and everyone having a good time. Sometimes I really don't like being a princess."

Wynn rolled her eyes. "Yeah, nobody's buying that, kid. Sorry, but there we are. You're a princess. You're going to have to deal with it."

Bethany looked at Silver. "Promise me we'll have the trailers at my party."

"You're the bride. If that's what you want, that's what we're going to do."

Pallas pressed her lips together. "This is going to be so interesting. I can't wait to see how it all turns out."

"Best party ever," Renee told her. "Or it's off with our heads."

Drew knew that Silver was at her girlfriend lunch — on his way to her place, he'd driven by the gallery and had seen several cars, including Bethany's truck — but instead of going back to the bank, he'd decided to wait. He glanced at his watch and figured they would be wrapping up

186

soon enough.

He needed to see her. Later, he would analyze what that meant but for now he was willing to go with the nagging sense of urgency that would only be satisfied when he was in Silver's presence. Too much had happened too quickly — them becoming lovers, his mother's arrival, the articulation of his parents' plan for his future. A plan he wanted no part of.

His mother was by far the more ambitious of his parents. He wasn't sure if she'd been born that way or if her personality had been formed by influences he didn't know about. Grandpa Frank wasn't at all that way and except for Libby, her other sisters were relatively normal. But his mother . . .

He spotted Silver a couple of blocks away, walking toward him. He headed toward her, consciously keeping himself from breaking into a run. As they got closer, he found himself admiring her long stride, her sleek, platinum blonde hair and her air of confidence. She was a beautiful woman and if the gods were willing, she would soon be in his bed again.

"What?" she called when they were close enough to talk. "Were you waiting for me on the sidewalk?"

"It was that or in my car."

They met in the middle of the block. She smiled at him. "Okay, this is slightly weird. I'm just saying. We're business partners. I'll get you a key to the downstairs space. Wait until you see what Walter and his team have done. It's amazing. I'm still a little unsettled by the stripper poles, but they're starting to grow on —"

She paused midstep and looked at him. "What's wrong?"

"Let's go inside and then I'll tell you."

They quickly walked the rest of the way. She unlocked the door and pushed it open, then gestured him inside.

He saw she was right — a lot of progress had been made. The soundproofing was up and the floors were in. Speakers had been mounted on the ceiling.

"I like how it's coming together," he said.

Silver raised her eyebrows. "Tell me."

"My mother's in town."

Her expression relaxed. "Is that all? I thought something bad had happened."

"My mother is here. Isn't that bad enough?"

She smiled. "Not for me. She barely knows who I am."

"This is you helping?"

"Oh, I was supposed to help. You didn't mention that. Let's go upstairs and we can talk about it." She waved her tote bag. "I have leftover mac and cheese."

"You're the perfect woman."

She laughed. "Tell me about it."

They went up to her place. Her apartment was a loft — one big room with lots of windows and light — decorated in grays and pale purples. A big sofa backed onto the compact kitchen. Screens provided privacy for what he guessed was the bedroom.

She pointed to the round table in the corner by the kitchen, then put the bowl of mac and cheese in the microwave. While it heated, she got a spare key from a drawer and handed it to him.

"You're welcome to come and go as you please, but I'd really prefer to never catch you using the stripper pole."

"That I can promise."

The microwave beeped. She set the bowl and a fork in front of him, poured them both a glass of water, then sat across from him.

"Tell me about your mother."

"Are Cade and Bethany having a big party to celebrate their engagement?" he asked instead.

Silver frowned. "How do you know about that? Pallas just told me an hour ago."

"My mother told me about it yesterday

when she arrived. I have no idea where she gets her information, but that's one of the reasons she came home. She knows I'm good friends with Cade and she wants me to arrange some kind of private audience with the royal family and anyone else who can help the business."

"Yikes, that's no fun. But Cade would help with that, wouldn't he?"

"I don't want to encourage her. I don't want her messing up Cade and Bethany's party. I don't want her here."

He ate some of the mac and cheese. "This is really good."

"Thanks. It's the jalapeños that are inspired. What else?"

He thought about his conversation with Irene and wondered how much to tell. Not that he wanted to have any secrets from Silver — he was more concerned about looking ridiculous or self-serving.

"She says she wanted to help me secure the chairmanship at the bank. She knows Libby's going to make a run for it and she doesn't want that to happen."

Silver's expression didn't change. Her gaze was steady and her mouth relaxed. "She really does have a plan, then. First the bank, then you join the family lobbying firm."

"It's not a family firm, but yes. That's her plan. She's staying with my grandfather while she's here. She wants to get on his good side and screw with Libby at the same time."

"I like that last bit," Silver admitted. "As for the rest of it, what do you want?"

He pushed away the bowl. "Not to move to D.C. I like it here. I've always seen myself as belonging with the bank."

He remembered what it had been like when he'd been a kid. His parents had been on him constantly. It wasn't about doing his best, it was about *being* the best — at everything. He was expected to be stronger, faster, smarter, funnier, meaner, nicer. He was to win every battle, conquer every foe.

When they'd left him with Grandpa Frank, he'd finally been able to relax. To be just like everyone else, and he'd liked it. Ironically, he'd continued to excel, but only because he wanted to, not because it was expected.

"I'm going to guess you've told her no and she won't listen," Silver said.

"More than once. She's going to make things difficult. You, me, the business, the party, the bank."

"Do you think she and Libby will get into a fight and pull each other's hair? Because

I'd really like to see that."

He smiled. "That would be awesome, but I doubt we'll be lucky enough to be around when it happens."

"Darn." She stretched out her arms and took his hand in hers. "So the bank, huh?"

"Are you surprised?"

"No. You have all those nice suits. Where else would you wear them?"

"I know to most people it seems boring, but not to me. I have some programs in mind that would fund small businesses. We have a lot of expertise on our board. We should be offering classes and resources to business owners to help them grow. I want to talk to the high school about sending in a few people a couple of times a year to teach the basics, like how checking accounts work and the difference between a money market fund and a Certificate of Deposit, otherwise known as a CD."

He released her hands and stood up. "Do you remember Doug and Melissa from high school? Doug Newport? They're married now, two kids. They just inherited some money and it's a big deal to them. They trust me to do the right thing. They trust me with their future. I want that."

"What you do is important," she said quietly.

"Thanks. Ironically, I'm kind of liking being half owner of a traveling bar, too. I wasn't kidding about the franchise opportunity, Silver. That could be big."

She rolled her eyes. "One crisis at a time, please." She moved close and hugged him. "We will deal with the party and your mother and the bank thing as it comes. You know what you want. Just do that and ignore the rest."

She felt good. They'd always fit together perfectly. Funny how after all this time he couldn't remember why he'd thought it was important to not be with her. Sure college had been great, but not Silver great.

She leaned back and looked into his eyes. "So, when do you have to be at work?"

"I have a little more time."

She smiled. "Oh good. I thought maybe we could take your mind off things." Her smile widened. "You know, with sex."

His body's reaction was nearly instantaneous. He kissed her.

"You have the best ideas ever."

"Tell me about it."

After Drew went back to the bank, Silver prowled around her apartment. While her body was so relaxed as to practically be liquid, her mind refused to settle. Some of the problems were relatively easy. Planning Bethany and Cade's party for one. That was just logistics. Bigger than what they usually did and probably with a lot more security, but still a party. She knew how to do that.

On the scale of least to most, her relationship with Drew probably came next. What were they doing? Sure the sex was great and they were working well together, but what did that mean and where were they going? Or weren't they going anywhere? Was this just for fun?

Questions she couldn't answer by herself and she wasn't ready to talk to him about them, either. Probably the best approach was to decide what she wanted, and then see if he wanted to follow that path, as well.

But figuring out the whole want thing was complicated. For one thing, she wasn't sure how she felt about him. She liked him but liking and *liking* were worlds apart. She knew he was a good guy. She knew he was honorable, which was great, but she wasn't sure she could see them staying together, long-term.

He said he was all in with the bank but in her gut, she couldn't help thinking he would look up one day and decide he wanted more than what Happily Inc had to offer, and then what? She was firmly settled here.

But the biggest problem facing her was the one about Autumn — namely telling Drew about his daughter. Time was ticking and she had yet to cough up the truth. It sure wasn't going to get easier as the days slipped away.

Her phone chirped, giving her a perfectly good excuse to let the guilt go. She glanced at the screen and saw she had text from Leigh. *Timing,* she thought, as she read the text.

You around for a little FaceTime?

Rather than answer, she activated the app, then called Leigh. Her friend's face filled the screen.

"Hi," Silver said with a smile. "What's up? Wedding talk?" *Please oh please don't ask me if Drew knows about Autumn yet.*

The picture became a dizzying swirl of movement, then Autumn's face filled the screen. For the millionth time, Silver saw that her daughter was all Drew, with dark hair and his eyes. The shape rather than the color, but still.

"Hi, Silver. Guess what? I have a dress for the wedding. It's so pretty. I'm super excited. I've never been in a wedding before. I've only been a guest at one in my whole life. People don't want kids at their wedding. But I get to go to this one and be in the wedding and stay up super late. Mom said she'd do my hair really special and I get to carry flowers like a real bridesmaid. We are going to have so much fun!"

"We are. I can't wait," Silver said when Autumn took a breath. "My friend Wynn says she has a bike for you to ride," she added. "You can explore the town and everything."

"Yay! I can't, can't, can't wait!"

The picture moved again, then Leigh reappeared.

"As you can tell, she's pretty excited."

"I got that."

"She's all confirmed at the Learning Center," Leigh continued. "From eight-thirty to two-thirty, Monday through Friday. I know you love her, but we're going to be gone a whole week and that's longer than you've ever had her. Autumn can be very high energy."

"We'll be fine. I'm glad she's going to stay current with her schoolwork."

Leigh's eyebrows rose. "I assume Drew is excited to meet her."

Silver winced. "He will be."

"Silver, you haven't told him?"

"Not yet. It's complicated."

"It's coming up soon. You have to let him know. I've already told Autumn and she wants to meet him. She's also asking me how many dads are too many, but I guess that's a good problem to have."

"It is. And I will tell him." She hoped she didn't sound defensive. "Soon."

"As long as he knows before we get there. I don't want to be the one who has to explain it all to him."

"You won't. I'm going to do it."

Leigh's tone gentled. "He has to be ready or he'll break Autumn's heart. I know you don't want that."

"I don't. I wouldn't hurt her for anything. I'll take care of it. I promise he'll be totally on board before you and Autumn get here."

After they'd hung up, Silver thought about her promise and hoped she wasn't lying. Telling Drew was one thing — having him okay with the information was going to be another.

CHAPTER NINE

Drew held the passenger door open for Silver.

"It's just a party," he said as he got in on his side. "Aside from food and drinks, what is there to plan?"

"Only everything. Is there a theme? What time of day? Is it lunch? Dinner? Afternoon? Will there be a band?" She glanced at him. "This isn't just a party — it's part wedding shower, part reception. For Bethany and Cade, this is the closest they're going to get to a regular wedding-type event in Happily Inc. The actual wedding and reception will be defined by protocol and El Baharian tradition."

"I stand corrected," he said as he drove to Weddings Out of the Box. There was a meeting for all the vendors as Cade and Bethany discussed what they wanted. As Silver's new business partner, Drew had been invited along to help with the brainstorming. Not that he had any idea of what they expected from him.

"What do you brainstorm?" he asked. "We're just bartenders so you do drinks and that's it?"

"I should slap you," she said with a laugh. "Technically that is the service we provide, but at this point in the process, all ideas are usually welcome. There is the occasional bride who has been planning her wedding since she was ten and doesn't want anyone else's input, but most want to know what we think. We've done a lot of weddings and can often speak to the pitfalls. Some flowers are beautiful, but if they have a scent, they can overwhelm an event. Nothing makes food taste bad faster than stinky flowers."

There was more to what Silver did than he'd first realized. As a guy, he'd known that, for the most part, weddings mattered a lot more to the bride than the groom. Ashley Lauren had been obsessed with the details and less concerned about their relationship.

They arrived at Weddings Out of the Box and parked. Silver collected her tote bag and walked next to him.

"We didn't bring any samples," he said.

"Until we know what they're looking for, there's no point. Once we pick a theme and colors, we'll get together about the specifics. From what Pallas said, we have a really tight time frame, so nothing custom unless it can be done on a rush basis."

"I suspect the king of El Bahar can pull a few strings."

"I'm sure he can."

Silver led the way to a conference room. Pallas was already there, along with Renee, Bethany and Cade.

Drew looked around. "I thought there would be more people."

"I did, too." Silver frowned. "The caterer at least and maybe a florist. Are we conferencing them in?"

"This is everyone," Pallas confirmed. "Let's take our seats and get started."

Bethany sat next to Cade. Drew took a seat on his right. Silver, Pallas and Renee were on the other side of the table.

"To answer your question about the caterer," Bethany said with a sigh, "my father wants me to use one from Los Angeles. Once we decide what the party is going to be, Cade and I will go see them and do our tasting there."

Cade took her hand and squeezed her fingers. "We're going to make this our party," he told her.

"I want to believe you but my father is

getting in the way." She made a face. "He loves to take charge. It's very annoying."

Renee sighed. "Kings. What are you going to do?"

There was a moment of silence, then everyone laughed.

Pallas activated her tablet before looking at Bethany. "Even if the caterer is coming from LA, you still get a say in what you're going to be eating. This party is for you and Cade, and we're going to make it amazing."

"There isn't much time," Bethany said, sounding doubtful. "We took so long arguing about what event was happening where and then picking a date, we aren't going to be able to do anything really fun." She looked at Cade. "I don't want this to be some big royal event. All our friends will be there — I want them to have a good time. I want the party to be about us and how we are as a couple. What we like and how we see ourselves."

"It will be," he told her. "Have a little faith."

Pallas leaned toward her. "Bethany, I know you're overwhelmed. I promise to do everything in my power to make sure you love your party. Give us a chance to make you happy, okay?"

Bethany nodded. "Sorry. I'm being whiny.

It's just if you saw what was happening back in El Bahar, you'd run screaming into the night."

Drew glanced at Silver. "Does she know it's the middle of the day?" he asked in a stage whisper.

Bethany grinned. "It's a figure of speech." She drew in a breath. "Okay, let's make this work."

Drew didn't consider himself overly intuitive when it came to women but even he could see that she was upset.

Renee picked up her pen. "Every good party needs a theme. If this were a traditional shower, it would be easier, but I'm not sure any of those ideas would work with the crowd we're expecting."

"Why not?" Cade asked.

Pallas and Renee exchanged a look. "Themes can range from spa day to lingerie. I'm not too sure we want to go there."

"No hats," Silver said with a smile. "So a Mad Hatter party is out. Let's see. You two own a ranch and work with horses. What about a backyard barbecue?" Her eyes widened. "Oh, I know. Let's do the I Do BBQ theme."

Renee began writing furiously. "Yes, that would totally work. I've seen it done with weddings and showers. There are a million ideas on Pinterest. We dress as cowboys and cowgirls, the food is a combination of picnic, barbecue and down-home cooking." She looked at Bethany. "What do you think?"

"I think I like it." She turned to Cade. "Honey, are you good with that?"

He nodded. "It's not scary. Or too pink. Men in suits will look out of place, but that was going to happen anyway."

"Dark suits?" Pallas asked.

Bethany nodded. "Security for sure. My dad, the president."

"Great, so we'll do black, white and red as the colors. The bride and groom can be in plaid shirts. Jeans for Cade and a little white leather skirt with fringe for Bethany, or a white denim skirt."

Bethany began to relax. "I like that."

"Don't forget the white cowboy hat with a veil," Silver added. "This is going to be great. All your friends can wear red Bride's Posse T-shirts."

The ideas were flowing fast and Drew wasn't sure what he was supposed to add. Telling everyone he couldn't wait to see Silver in a tight T-shirt didn't seem helpful.

"We'll make this easy," Renee said. "We can get ceramic cowboy boot vases for the centerpieces. We'll go red and white with the flowers, but have table accents in black. Burlap table runners are neutral. We can have plaid everywhere."

"Cow balloons," Silver said. "Big bouquets of them."

Bethany grinned. "I like that. This is fun."

"It gets better," Renee said. "We can put most of the tables inside because there's no ceremony. A few will be outside, but we can use a portion of the lawn for games. Croquet, horseshoes, even a beanbag toss."

"We can do spiked lemonade, margaritas and beer for the drinks." Silver made some notes. "What about food?"

"I want a cake pop stand," Bethany said. "In the shape of a tiered wedding cake."

"Done," Renee said. "How about fair food? Pulled pork, beef and chicken sandwiches. All kinds of salads, a taco bar, maybe some sliders. For dessert, in addition to the cake pops we can do s'mores." She looked at Pallas. "We can set up a grill where people can roast their own marshmallows."

Bethany leaned against Cade. "We have the best friends ever."

Drew sat back and listened to the ideas flow. In less than an hour, the party was planned. They had a preliminary menu, the list of drinks, a theme and decoration ideas.

Renee set up a time to go with Cade and Bethany to LA and do a tasting. Pallas promised to have the decorating samples in-house in less than a week and they'd agreed on three kinds of margaritas for the party. That tasting would be in a couple of days.

He hadn't offered a single idea, mostly because he'd been unable to think of any. Silver, Pallas and Renee had moved too fast. He knew they did this sort of thing all the time but he'd had no idea they were so creative. He'd figured being a part of her business was going to be easy. After all, he had a degree and worked in business. He hadn't realized how wrong he could be.

Silver's head was spinning with ideas. She had a lot of things she wanted to look up when she got home. There were some decorations she'd seen on Pinterest that she wanted to share with Renee. If they could make them work, Bethany would be thrilled.

"That was a good meeting," she said as Drew parked in front of her storefront.

"Is it always like that? So fast and creative?"

"Mostly. Sometimes the bride has an idea that we just can't make work. Those meetings can be a slog, but we always keep going until we find something she loves. Bethany is easy. She's totally open. Her big dream is to have fun party. That's a lot easier to work with than a sea horse ball."

"You've done a sea horse ball?"

She laughed. "Technically an under-the-sea wedding, but you get my idea."

They got out of his car. "You were impressive," he told her.

"I appreciate the compliment but Renee's the real creative one. She just keeps coming up with different ideas until the bride is happy. And then she goes to town on all the details. I have to admit, when Pallas first hired her, I wasn't sure I liked her, but I'm becoming a fan."

"I couldn't keep up," he admitted.

"It takes practice to get good at brainstorming. Plus, you need to have ideas."

"How can I learn about weddings and decorations and themes?"

"If you're serious, get a couple of books on wedding planning. Read some bridal magazines, and then spend quality time on Pinterest. There are a million ideas and they're all so good. I could spend hours browsing table decorations and drink ideas."

"I'll do that. I want to be a real partner."

"Not just a pretty face?" she teased.

"I don't mind being that."

He stood close enough that her body was intensely aware of him. She thought about offering him a quickie upstairs, but he had to be at the bank and she had work to do. There was also the looming issue of telling him about Autumn. She had to do it. Honestly, she was going to pick a date and time and invite him over. She knew *why* she was putting it off, but wasn't proud of herself or her actions.

"Drew? What are you doing out here? Why aren't you at the bank?"

They both turned as a middle-aged woman approached. She was beautifully dressed, with dark hair and eyes and enough of Drew's features for Silver to be able to guess who exactly this was.

Silver had never met Irene before — she and her husband had left Happily Inc shortly after Silver had moved to town. When Silver and Drew had been dating, his parents had been off somewhere in Europe — Silver could never remember exactly where.

"Hello, Mom," Drew said, his tone more dutiful than pleased. "I'm surprised to see you in town."

"I could say the same thing. You didn't answer my question. Why aren't you at work?"

"Mom, this is Silver Tesdal. Silver, my mother."

Silver smiled. "Hello, Mrs. Lovato."

"Yes, hello." Irene positioned herself so her back was to Silver. "Drew, I've heard that the royal party is going to be planned very soon. I want you to find out as much as you can for me. I want to be prepared."

Drew looked both resigned and uncomfortable. Silver lightly touched his arm, then smiled at Irene.

"You're going to love it, Mrs. Lovato. Bethany and Cade picked a cowboy theme. I Do BBQ. She's going to be in a white cowboy hat and they'll wear matching plaid shirts. The food is all down-home barbecue inspired. Oh, and there will be a s'mores station. Doesn't that sound wonderful?"

Irene turned to Silver, her expression icy. "Excuse me, but this is a private conversation."

"I'm pretty sure I was here first."

"Who *are* you?"

"Silver Tesdal. Drew already told you." She pretended confusion. "Oh, you mean *who* am I? I own a traveling bar called AlcoHaul." She gestured to the storefront bearing her company logo. "I'll be one of the vendors at the party. And a guest. Hmm, that's going to be complicated. All of Bethany's girlfriends are wearing matching T-shirts, including me."

Silver watched Irene battle with conflicting emotions. She would guess that while Drew's mother wanted to crush her like a bug, she would be too worried about offending a princess's friend.

"You know Bethany?"

"Uh-huh. I would have worked her wedding regardless, but now it's more fun."

Irene swung her attention back to her son. "And why are you here?"

Silver honestly expected Drew to deny their relationship. In that nanosecond before he spoke, she told herself she would be fine with it. Really. It was okay. Then he totally shocked her by putting his arm around her.

"Mom, Silver and I arc in business together. We're business partners. We just bought two more trailers together. AlcoHaul is expanding."

Irene went completely white. "What? What! Drew, are you telling me you own a bar?"

"Technically he only owns part of a bar," Silver clarified. "A traveling bar. We do mostly weddings, but parties, as well. A lot of theme stuff. It's fun."

Irene glared at her son. "No. You can't possibly be telling me the truth. Why would you do this? Why would you want to have anything to do with this ridiculous town? You have opportunities that most people can only dream about. Do you know who you can be?"

She turned her attention to Silver. "If you think you're going to trap him, you can forget it. He's smarter than that."

Silver shrugged free of Drew. "I already had my chance to trap him, Mrs. Lovato, and I didn't take it. There are a lot of things you can worry about but my relationship with Drew isn't one of them. Now if you'll excuse me . . ."

She gave them both a brief wave, then let herself into her retail space. As the door closed behind her, she heard Irene shrieking something about Drew ruining his future. Rather than listen, Silver hurried upstairs. She might be overthinking the situation but she had a feeling Irene wasn't going to be thrilled at the thought of being a grandmother.

Drew managed to extricate himself from the conversation with his mother, pleading an important meeting back at the bank. On the quick drive there, he tried to figure out what he was going to say to Silver. Irene had been rude, and her fixation with Cade and Bethany's party wasn't exactly normal.

He parked at the bank and walked inside. Libby was waiting for him and practically pounced when she saw him.

"You have a package," his aunt told him. "I put it in your office."

Since when did Libby do something as low-level as deliver the mail? "Thank you," he said, not sure of her point.

"It was left in the night deposit." Her smile turned sly. "It's not what you think and there's a note."

Drew was fairly confident Libby wouldn't allow anything dangerous in her precious bank, so he wasn't all that concerned until he saw the large cardboard box on his desk. A box with airholes and a big arrow showing which way was up. As he got closer, he saw the note taped to the top of the box.

Mr. Lovato, this is my rabbit, Mr. Whiskers. I can't keep him anymore and I cried a lot when Mommy told me. Mommy and Daddy trust you with our money, so I'm trusting you with Mr. Whiskers. Aaron at the pet store can tell you how to take care of him.

Your friend, Emily.

The box moved. No, what was inside of

the box moved.

"It appears to be a rabbit," Libby told him from the doorway to his office.

He lifted the top on the box and found himself eye to eye with a gray rabbit. Mr. Whiskers lunged and Drew quickly closed the box top. Rabbits weren't vicious, were they?

"He can't stay here," Libby pointed out. "You'll have to take that thing home and deal with it." She sounded positively gleeful.

"First I'm going to find out what's going on and then I'll deal with —" he glanced at the note "— Mr. Whiskers."

"Lucky you," Libby said with a smile.

Drew waited until she was gone to call Melissa. His client stunned him by bursting into tears.

"I thought we'd lost him," Melissa said. "I'm sorry to be such a mess. It's just everything is so hard right now. Jacob has a rash and the pediatrician thinks he might be allergic to the rabbit. Emily already isn't convinced she wants a baby brother and now we're going to have to get rid of her pet. She loves him so much. We're doing more testing, but until we're sure . . ." She made a choking-sob sound. "I'm sorry, Drew. This isn't your problem."

Drew glanced at the box. It was a rabbit. How hard could it be for him to take care of it for a few days?

"Tell you what. I'll deal with Mr. Whiskers until you figure out what's going on with Jacob. If it turns out he's allergic, then you can make arrangements for Mr. Whiskers to find a permanent home. If it's something else, Mr. Whiskers can come back and resume his happy bunny life. Either way, Emily will know her pet is being taken care of."

"I couldn't possibly ask you to do that."

"You didn't. I offered. It's fine. I'm good with animals."

In truth, he had no idea how he was with pets of any kind. As a kid, he'd never had one. But he was game.

"I'll swing by and pick up some supplies, then take him home." He would also visit Aaron at the pet store to get the scoop on rabbit care.

"I can't thank you enough." Melissa sniffed. "We're so happy to have a baby, but it's a much-bigger adjustment than we'd realized."

"You can take Mr. Whiskers off your worry-about list. I'll be there in a few minutes. Oh, just one other question. Do rabbits bite?"

■ ■ ■ ■

Jasper rolled onto his side and watched Wynn walk to the bathroom, his attention captured by the sway of her hips. She was naked and unselfconscious about her body. He liked that about her. She was slightly pear-shaped with an ass a man could hold on to. He liked that, too.

It was nearly noon. Wynn had arrived less than thirty minutes ago. After very little conversation, they'd taken things into the bedroom. That was their routine — she left work and came to his place. They made love. Sometimes she stayed and they had lunch, sometimes she didn't.

She returned to the bedroom, pulling her shirt over her head. She had long, dark curly hair and dark eyes. Based on her high cheekbones and her dark olive skin, he would guess she was of mixed race — but it wasn't anything he'd ever asked about. He didn't know about her family, where she was from or why, of all the places in the world, she'd chosen to move to Happily Inc. Not because he hadn't asked — he had. But with Wynn, conversation was kept superficial.

He stood and stretched. "Are you staying?"

She smiled. "I thought I'd make us an omelet before I head back to work."

"Maybe the boss would let you take off an extra hour or two." Humor, because she owned the company.

"That bitch?" Wynn laughed. "You know she's going to insist I hurry back as quick as I can. But I have time for lunch."

She left the bedroom. Jasper washed up and got dressed. He found her chopping vegetables. The eggs were already whisked together in a bowl and the pan was heating.

He walked up behind her and wrapped his arms around her waist. She snuggled in close, pressing her butt against his groin.

"This is nice," she said. "A little sugar in the middle of my day."

"Maybe we could go to dinner sometime."

She didn't look up from her chopping. "You and I go to tournament night nearly every Monday. If you want to buy me a burger along with a drink, I won't say no."

He released her and started a fresh pot of coffee, then dropped bread into the toaster. While she cooked the vegetables, he set the table.

Their routine was familiar. Comfortable. This was what it was and he liked that. So why did he feel an uncomfortable need to push for more? He thought of his recent text from Hunter and had a feeling that was a big part of it.

"How's work?" he asked as she dumped the cooked vegetables onto a plate, then wiped the pan clean before pouring in the egg mixture.

"Busy."

"You never said how you came to buy the printing business. That's all it was at first, right? You added the graphic design part?"

She kept her attention on the pan, carefully swirling the egg mixture until it was even. She collected a bag of shredded cheese from the refrigerator, then returned to the stove.

"Why all the questions?" she asked.

"It was two."

She checked the omelet. After adding the vegetables back to one side of the pan, she sprinkled everything with cheese, then carefully flipped the other half of the cooked eggs over. Using the spatula, she cut the omelet in half and slid a piece onto each plate.

They sat across from each other at his kitchen table. She sipped her coffee, then looked at him.

"Don't be curious about me, Jasper. I'm

216

not going to tell you more than I have."

"Why?"

"I don't want to talk about it. You need to respect that."

"I've known you a long time now. More than two years. Don't you trust me?"

Her dark gaze gave nothing away. "It's not about trust."

"Sure it is. Don't you want more than what we have?"

She smiled. "You mean like a commitment and a ring. Do you?"

A question he hadn't been expecting. Did he want more?

Before he could decide, she laughed. "Uh-huh. That's what I thought. This is good for both of us. I like things exactly as they are and you do, too. Every now and then you get a bug up your butt about wanting more, but it passes."

"I don't understand you."

"How many women do you understand?"

He chuckled. "You make an excellent point and an equally great breakfast."

"Thank you."

"How's Hunter?"

Her good mood faded. "Jasper, I swear, you don't give up. Maybe it's a writer thing. You know what I said about Hunter."

"I never get in touch with him, Wynn. You

know that." He didn't have to. Hunter always found him.

He supposed by not telling her that, he was being an asshole, but some part of him was willing to risk it. Partially because he liked hanging out with the kid, and partially to see what would happen when it all hit the fan. Because one day it would. Happily Inc was too small for it to end otherwise.

Was he hoping she would relent? That she would tell him what they had was worth saving? Or was the more likely scenario that she would simply turn and walk away? And if he believed that and hung out with Hunter anyway, what did that say about what he thought of their relationship?

"I do know," she told him. "Now eat your eggs before they get cold. Then you can tell me all about your trip to New York and how great your editor thinks you are."

"She does think I'm pretty great."

"Of course she does." Wynn's smile faded. "Jasper, I like you a lot. I like this, but don't be fooled. If you cross me, it's over."

"I know."

"When we started, you said this was enough. Is that still true?"

He nodded. "I'm not looking for more."

"Good."

Her smile returned and they both started eating.

Later, as he walked her to her car, he wondered if he'd been telling the truth about not wanting more. He was pushing things with Wynn; he was restless in ways he couldn't explain. What did that mean? She drove away and he retreated to the house.

Maybe it didn't have to mean anything, he thought. After all, more than one VA therapist had warned him his experiences had left him emotionally shattered. He'd been warned he might never be whole. So what he had with Wynn should be perfect. A beautiful woman, great sex and nothing more. Only he found himself in the uncomfortable position of having to admit that some days, it wasn't enough.

Chapter Ten

Silver was going to throw up. Doing the right thing was highly overrated and she was, honest to God, going to throw up. Not that she had a choice — she'd put off telling Drew about Autumn too long and now they were less than two weeks from Leigh and Denton's wedding. Autumn was due to arrive, there was a big royal party to plan for, construction was nearly finished on the first trailer and Drew's mother was back in town. Other than that, and telling Drew about their child, she was fine. Completely and totally fine.

She paced the length of the retail space, careful to avoid the stacks of new furniture still wrapped in plastic, and did her best not to bump into the stripper poles. She was still getting used to where they were and had crashed into one the previous day. An incredibly dumb thing to think about but better than her conversation with Drew.

He was going to be so angry with her, she thought grimly. No, he would be hurt and even as she told herself she hadn't done anything wrong and it wasn't as if he'd ever asked about their kid, she couldn't help feeling . . . guilty.

She heard the door opening and spun to watch him walk inside. It was barely noon. He'd come from the bank for what he thought was a business lunch.

"Hey," he said with a grin as he approached. "Tell me this isn't about my mother."

"It's not."

"Excellent. Then I have news. I have a rabbit."

The statement was just unexpected enough to momentarily distract her. "Excuse me?"

"A rabbit. Mr. Whiskers is a standard chinchilla rabbit, which means he's kind of gray and very soft. He's around seven pounds and get this — he's litter box trained. Seriously. He uses a little litter box with this wood pulp litter. He eats a special kind of hay and lots of greens. Lettuces and kale and carrot tops. He's actually not too bad to have around. He sleeps a lot. I put him in one of spare rooms, but when I'm home I let him out."

"A rabbit? As a pet?"

He pulled her close, hugged her, then chuckled. "Doug and Melissa adopted a newborn."

He explained about Emily and her new baby brother and the rash and Mr. Whiskers. "I'm keeping him for a couple of weeks, while they get everything sorted out."

She took a step back. "I really can't see you with a rabbit, but if it's working . . ."

"It is. And people say I have commitment issues." He led her to a couple of folding chairs. "What's up? Everything okay with the construction? I haven't heard from Walter except to have him say they're on schedule."

"It's not about work." She looked at him and hoped this was going to go a lot better than she'd imagined. "Drew, I want to talk about the baby we gave up for adoption."

He stared at her. "Now? It's been years."

"I know." She swallowed, then told herself to just get it over with. "We had a girl."

He looked surprised. "I figured we'd had a boy, but I guess that's because I'm a guy." He hesitated. "Did you see her after she was born?"

"I did. Her name is Autumn."

"You named her?"

"No, I didn't. I, ah, it was hard after we

222

broke up and I found out I was pregnant. My uncle helped me find a nice couple to adopt our baby. They lived in Los Angeles and I ended up staying with them until Autumn was born."

He surprised her by taking her hand in his. "Jeez, Silver, I'm sorry. I never thought about it before, but you were pregnant. I mean you had a baby growing inside of you for nine months. I signed some paperwork and I was done. I'll bet it *was* hard."

She briefly closed her eyes and wished he wasn't being so understanding. In some ways, that made it harder to tell him.

"Leigh, that's Autumn's mom, was so wonderful to me. We became like sisters. She'd known from the time she was a teenager that she couldn't have children. It was a congenital defect and she knew she wanted to adopt. We got really close and after Autumn was born, I stayed with them for a while."

He pulled back and stared at her. "You lived with our baby?"

She nodded. "Just for a few weeks. Then I came back to Happily Inc, but I couldn't settle. I started getting into trouble. My uncle gave me the tough love lecture and I ran away." She raised a shoulder. "Not my most mature moment. Anyway, I ended up

back in LA and I moved back in with Leigh." She cleared her throat. "And her husband, of course, and Autumn."

His expression tightened. "For how long?"

"Two years. I worked, went to community college and —"

"Two *years*?" He came to his feet and glared at her. "You lived with our baby for two years and never said a word?"

"What was I supposed to say?" she asked as she stood, telling herself to stay calm. This was all new to Drew and of course he would react.

"Drew, you weren't interested in our child. You said it yourself — you signed the paperwork and you were done. I'm not trying to be mean or judge you, I'm just pointing out that it was different."

"Of course it was different. You had a relationship with our child and you never told me. You kept it a secret from me all this time."

She felt her temper flaring. "It's not as if you were asking for information. You went on with your life. I'm sorry if you feel like you missed out on something, but if you do, it's only in the last five seconds. Because for the last eleven years, you haven't given her a single thought."

"You don't know that."

"Tell me I'm wrong."

He leaned toward her and lowered his voice. "You are wrong. I did think about her. I wondered. You're right — you were the one dealing with your pregnancy and I was in college. Fine. I accept that. But once you stayed in touch with her, you should have said something. You owed me that. If not then at least now." He waved his arm toward the rest of the room. "We're supposed to be business partners. We're sleeping together and starting something personal between us. How am I supposed to trust you now when you kept this from me? And where on earth do we go from here?"

Instead of waiting for an answer, he turned and walked out. The door slammed behind him.

Silver shivered slightly, then sank onto the chair. Her eyes burned, but she didn't cry. She told herself to keep breathing, that he would calm down and they would talk again later. Because there was a whole lot more he had to know.

Drew called his assistant from his car and told her he wouldn't be coming back into the bank today. He pulled off his tie, tossed his suit jacket into the backseat and drove east nearly seventy miles before turning around and driving back.

For the first hundred and ten miles, he cursed Silver and told himself he hadn't done anything wrong. For the last thirty, he thought maybe there might be more than one side to the story. He exited the freeway just before he reached town and drove for a few minutes. It was nearly two o'clock when he pulled up at a pair of big gates and pushed the intercom button to connect to the main office in the stable.

"Drew?" Cade's voice was scratchy through the speaker system. "What's up?"

"You got a second?"

"Sure. I'm in back, in my office."

"Thanks."

Drew knew the way. He drove around the large farmhouse to the parking area by the massive stables. It was a sunny day and several people were exercising the horses Cade bred. Drew got out of his car and walked toward the biggest barn and Cade's office. His friend met him just inside the open double door.

Cade took one look at him and shook his head. "How bad?"

"No one's dead."

Cade didn't say anything.

"No one is dead or injured or arrested," Drew amended. "Good enough?"

"For now."

Cade led him to his large office. There was a desk with a computer, a dry erase board mounted on the wall and a few file cabinets. In the back was a battered sofa. Drew took a seat on it and Cade pulled up his desk chair.

"It's Silver," Drew started, then paused, not sure what exactly to say. He was still processing information, still trying to figure out what he felt. Confusion, sure. Anger. Maybe a little guilt. But more than any of that, he felt a massive sense of betrayal while at the same time he wasn't sure he had the right.

"You remember when I told you Silver got pregnant that summer?"

"Sure."

"There's more. I hadn't wanted to break up when I left for college, but she insisted. She said I'd want to be free to do whatever I wanted at college. I fought her on it, but in the end I agreed. Three weeks into my freshman year, I knew she was right. I missed her but it wasn't the same."

Cade waited, his expression both concerned and patient.

"She showed up around my sixth week and told me she was pregnant," Drew admitted. "Scared the crap out of me. I was

227

angry and horrified and resentful as hell, but I didn't say any of that."

"You said before you offered to marry her."

"I did. She turned me down. She said we should give up the baby. I signed the paperwork and that was that."

Cade didn't say anything.

"I *thought* that was it," Drew continued. "Or rather I never thought about our kid again. Okay, maybe every couple of years. We had a girl, by the way." Autumn, he remembered. Her name was Autumn.

"For me, it was done, but not for Silver. She and her uncle found a nice couple and Silver went to live with them so no one knew she was pregnant."

"I wondered how that had been kept a secret."

Drew thought about the rest of it. What had seemed like such a horrendous crime a couple of hours ago suddenly didn't seem so very awful. So why was he angry?

"She stayed in touch with them. The mom and the girl. Autumn. She lived with them for a while. She knows our daughter and she never told me that. Never told me any of it."

Cade looked at him for several seconds before asking, "Did you want to be told?"

"I don't know. I never had the chance to wonder. I thought she was just gone, but she's not. Silver kept her from me." He leaned forward and rested his forearms on his thighs. "Everything is completely messed up. My mother's back and she's all about your party. She wants a private audience with the king, by the way, so you'll want to avoid that. Then Silver and I went into business together."

"How is that messed up? I thought you wanted to go into business with her."

"I do and it's great. Expanding her business is the right thing to do. She and I are getting involved and that's great. It's all coming together and now this. She dumped it on me with no warning." He looked at his friend. "She knows our kid and I don't."

"Do you want to?"

"Yes. Maybe. I think so." Drew still couldn't grasp the truth of it. "She's my daughter and I know nothing about her." Meet Autumn? Could he? Another question was why was Silver telling him this now? Why after all these years did she suddenly feel the need to share the news?

"When I moved back to Happily Inc, I knew I wanted to take over the ranch," Cade said unexpectedly. "I worked out a deal with Grandpa Frank where I would buy him out over time."

"Makes sense." All Grandpa Frank's grandchildren would be left money, but the ranch was a much-bigger prize. No way Cade could simply have it.

"I had a plan, a good one. Being able to buy an El Baharian stallion made that plan possible." He smiled. "But I didn't just get the horse — I got the girl, too."

Drew remembered how Bethany had come with Rida as a lowly stable hand. It wasn't until she and Cade had already fallen in love that she'd admitted to being a royal princess.

"Loving her was easy," Cade said. "As for the rest of it, let's just say it took me a while to figure out what was important to me. I had to give up my ideas about doing everything myself. Bethany wanted to be an equal partner. I had to be open to that, and to being a prince. But it's worth it. She's worth anything."

Drew shook his head. "I'm not in love with Silver." That he knew for sure.

"Not now, but you were. Both of you. Silver loved you and had the smarts to know what was going to happen. Loving you, she let you go. Then she turned up pregnant and when she could have trapped you into marriage, she didn't. She gave you an out and you took it." He held up a hand. "I'm not saying you were wrong, but look at it from her point of view. The guy she loved more than anyone ever had gone off to college and when she found out she was pregnant, he basically signed a couple of papers and told her to have a good life. He got off with nothing while she had to deal with finding people to adopt their baby, go through the pregnancy, recover, and then go on with her life as if nothing had happened. For you, it was out of sight, out of mind. Sorry, Drew. You're not the victim here."

His cousin's words were blunt. The emotions that had been battling for dominance suddenly retreated, leaving only shame as the winner.

He stood and looked at his friend. "I was a total shit."

"Yup."

"I should probably go hear her side of the story."

"It wouldn't be the worst decision in the world."

Silver had chosen that particular afternoon to tell Drew about his daughter for a couple of reasons — first, because time was running out and second, because she'd had a

231

feeling it might not go well and she didn't have any other appointments to worry about. Watching a vendor break down emotionally never made a bride feel good about her upcoming wedding.

After Drew walked out, Silver decided that rather than have a mini breakdown she would get busy. She cleaned her entire loft, then signed for a delivery. The large, flat box turned out to be the perfect distraction — it was her dress for Leigh's wedding.

As promised, it was perfect for *The Great Gatsby* theme. The silky, pale pink dress was sleeveless with a V neckline, but what made the dress was the beading. From the shoulder to midthigh, the dress was beaded in a swirling, elegant art deco style. She could practically hear ragtime music playing in the background.

She hurried up to her loft and got out of her clothes. She pulled on the dress and headed for the full-length mirror in her bathroom.

The fit was perfect. The material hugged her body, and then fell to the floor. It was a little too long, but she knew all the best alterations experts in town. Once she decided on her shoes, she would get the gown hemmed.

Her hair was a problem. The long, straight

style wouldn't work at all. Neither would any kind of a braid. She twisted her hair, then pulled it up. That was better, she thought and walked out in the living room area to get her phone. She was going to need a hair appointment the morning of the wedding so she could have her hair done. All she generally went in for was a trim and a little color. Her stylist would be thrilled.

She took a couple of selfies to text to Leigh and was just about to change back into her jeans when she heard someone knocking on the door to her loft. She opened it and saw Drew standing there.

In her excitement over the dress, she'd momentarily forgotten about their earlier discussion. Seeing him brought all her feelings back at once. She went from happy to defensive and unsure in less than a second. *Emotional whiplash,* she thought, feeling more than a little sick to her stomach.

She stepped back to let him in, then closed the door behind him.

"Obviously we have to talk," he said, then frowned. "What are you wearing?"

She glanced down at the dress, then back at him. "Give me a second to get changed. I'll be right back."

She hurried to her bedroom area, grateful for the screens that gave her privacy. It only took her a second to slip off the dress and hang it, then pull on jeans and her T-shirt. She returned to the living room. Drew stood by a window, facing her.

"You first," he said.

With the light behind him, she couldn't see his face and she had no idea what he was thinking. Not that it mattered, she told herself. He could be as angry as he wanted. She'd done the best she could at the time. She'd been dealing with a lot and she'd been on her own. Whatever complaints he had now were his own fault.

"I didn't tell you about Autumn for a lot of reasons," she began. "I stayed in LA with Leigh for almost two years. I helped her with the baby and went to school and worked and tried to figure out what I wanted with my life. When I came back, you were still in college, then you took that bank job back East for a couple of years and when you returned to Happily Inc, you were engaged. Why on earth would I say anything about our daughter?"

Before he could say anything, she continued. "I've continued to stay in touch with Leigh. She and her first husband got a divorce and that was hard, but he's still close to Autumn and Leigh's amazing. I talk to them on the phone or do FaceTime or

Skype regularly. I see Autumn a couple of times a year. She knows she's adopted, she knows I'm her birth mother, but it's no big deal. It's all she's ever known. She calls me Silver because Leigh is her real mom. I'm just a really good friend of the family who happened to give birth to her."

"Does she know about me?" he asked.

"She knows she has a biological father, yes."

"Why now? Why did you want to tell me now? You could have done it two years ago or in five more years. Why now?"

And there it was — the real complication in an already-difficult situation.

"Leigh's getting married. Denton is a great guy and he's going to make them both so happy." She cleared her throat. "The thing is Leigh has heard me talk about Happily Inc for years, but she's never been here. I've always gone to LA. So when she was thinking about where to have the wedding, she thought about it being here. She talked to Pallas and found out there was a cancellation."

Silver squared her shoulders. "That's, um, why I was wearing that dress before. I'm going to be a bridesmaid in Leigh's wedding. She's coming here to get married and she's bringing Autumn with her. Then, while Leigh and Denton are on their honeymoon, I'll be keeping Autumn. Here. For a week."

Drew finally moved away from the window. She could see his stunned expression. "Our daughter is going to be here for a week and you're going to babysit her?"

"Yes. That's about it. There were a lot of reasons to tell you but the biggest one is that Autumn really wants to meet you."

CHAPTER ELEVEN

Drew stepped out of his shower to find Mr. Whiskers had made his way to the master bathroom. The rabbit had no trouble going up and down stairs, which was a little startling. Drew had assumed that Mr. Whiskers would keep to the first floor, but he seemed to enjoy running amok in the entire house.

Although Drew kept the rabbit in a large cage while he was at work and when he went to bed, the rest of the time Mr. Whiskers had free run of the house. The lady at the pet store had sold him a couple more litter boxes to keep things clean.

Drew had put cord protectors on every electrical cord he could find. Mr. Whiskers loved to chew and Drew didn't think rabbit teeth and electricity were a good mix. At least having the rabbit around was a distraction of sorts — not that anything could stop him from thinking about his daughter.

In the past couple of days, he and Silver had talked a few more times. She'd shown him pictures of Autumn and he had tried to process the fact that she really was a part of him. That one sultry summer night, he and Silver had created a child. It was a lot to take in but he was going to have to figure it out.

He dressed in a suit, then went downstairs. Drew had already fed Mr. Whiskers, so he made his own breakfast before cleaning out the rabbit's hutch. He made sure there was plenty of water and fresh hay before going to look for his houseguest. After about fifteen minutes of catch-me-if-you-can, he managed to get the rabbit back in the cage and carefully locked the hutch door. Shortly after, he was on his way to the bank.

He got through his morning easily enough. Meetings kept him busy. Around noon, Libby stopped by.

"It's so lovely to have your mother up at the house," Libby said, her smile anything but happy. "It reminds me of what it was like when we were girls together."

Drew had heard plenty of stories about how the two sisters had hated each other, so he wasn't sure how to respond. Fortunately — or not — Libby kept talking.

"We've been catching up on old times.

Irene must be happy that you're finally settling down."

Drew looked at his aunt. "What do you mean?"

Libby feigned surprise. "Aren't you and Silver a couple? I've seen you together all over town." She touched her fingers to her mouth, then lowered her voice. "Is it a secret? Do you need me not to tell? Because, to be honest, Silver isn't at all who your mother had in mind for you. She owns a mobile bar, although the fact that it's on wheels may not matter to your mother. Silver's beautiful, which helps, I suppose. But she doesn't have family or connections and you know how important those are to Irene. Oh dear. What are you going to do?"

He held Libby's gaze for several seconds. "Tell her or not. It doesn't matter to me. Sorry to disappoint you, but it's the truth."

He walked away thinking that dealing with his mother about Silver was nothing when compared with actually meeting his daughter for the very first time.

"Thanks for this," Silver said as she pulled the worn bike out of the garage. "Autumn still loves riding a bike, so having this for the week is going to be great."

Wynn smiled. "No problem. Let's all be

239

grateful that I have trouble getting rid of things. Besides, Hunter is looking forward to hanging out with Autumn again." She sighed. "He's at that age where girls are stupid, interesting or scary, depending on the day. But he and Autumn had such a good time when we spent the weekend together that he seems to be more excited than anything else."

A couple of years before, while Silver had been in Los Angeles with Autumn for a long weekend, Wynn and Hunter had joined them at Disneyland. The four of them had gone to the amusement park together and the kids had gotten along great.

"Just think, in a few years Hunter will see girls as conquests," Silver teased.

Wynn shuddered. "That is not happening. I won't let it."

They put the bike in the back of Silver's truck, then went into Wynn's small house. Once they were in the kitchen, Wynn poured them each a cup of coffee.

"You doing okay?" Wynn asked.

"I'm trying. Drew's still in shock. He texts me questions when he thinks of them and says he's looking forward to meeting Autumn."

"Isn't that what you want? Them to meet?"

240

"Sure, but wanting it and having it happen are two different things. I just want the week to go well. For all of us. Leigh's getting married. That needs to be a happy day for her."

"It will be. Deep breaths. You'll get through it. Drew's a good guy. He's processing but in the end, he'll come around."

Silver hoped her friend was right. "At least I told him. That's something."

"You were very brave."

"I was running out of time. I got scared, which drove me to action. I tend to respond to emotions with energy. I want to be like you. You're always so Zen."

"On the outside. On the inside I'm as messed up as everyone else."

Silver doubted that. "How are things going with Jasper?"

Her friend raised her eyebrows. "Is this you changing the subject?"

"Yes. I'm so tired of my life. Let's focus on yours."

"There's nothing to talk about."

"But Jasper. He's yummy. Are you two talking marriage yet?"

Wynn laughed. "We're not talking marriage at all. Jasper and I have an understanding."

"Ah, so it's still just about sex." Silver

grinned. "Because we all know what the word 'understanding' means."

"Yes, it's about sex and hanging out every now and then, but nothing more. I'm not the marrying kind and neither is he. What we have is fun and easy, but that's all it is."

"Don't you want something more?"

Wynn glanced away. "Nope. This is plenty. I have my son and I have my business and that's all I need. Everything else is gravy."

Silver sensed there was a lot that Wynn wasn't telling her. Not that she was going to ask. She was in no position to deal with a big hairy secret these days. She was barely hanging on as it was. Not that anything was specifically wrong. Mostly it was anticipation that was killing her. Waiting for Leigh and Autumn to arrive. Waiting for Drew to meet his daughter. Waiting for the wedding.

Wynn surprised her by unexpectedly hugging her. "It's going to be okay. Drew is going to love his daughter and she's going to adore him. What happened, happened. You're not the bad guy."

"Sometimes I feel like the bad guy," Silver admitted. "Maybe I should have —"

"No." Wynn's voice was stern. "He didn't want your baby when you were pregnant. The fact that he's sorry now doesn't change the past. You were a kid and you made good

242

decisions. You're not responsible for Drew feeling all weepy. He had his chance and he didn't want to take it. These are his consequences, not yours."

"I had no idea you were so tough."

"I'm a single mom. I have to be. Don't let anyone convince you that you didn't do right by Drew. You told him the truth, you refused his half-assed proposal, you found a good family for your child and you became a part of her life. At no point did you not walk the walk."

"You're right," Silver said, feeling better by the second. "I did all that and I was only eighteen. I'm empowered and pretty damned amazing." She smiled at her friend. "We both are."

"You know it."

Late Thursday afternoon Drew stayed at his house, playing with Mr. Whiskers until it was time to leave. The rabbit had turned out to be a surprisingly pleasant pet. He was quiet, relatively clean and not the least bit judgmental. Something Drew could appreciate these days. His normally calm, almost-boring life had taken several unexpected turns, leaving him watching the clock as he counted down the minutes until he left to meet his daughter.

His daughter. He still couldn't believe it. After all these years, he was going to be introduced to her, spend time with her, get to know her. He was trying to figure out how he felt about everything that had happened, everything he had learned. There was anger, but he was less sure it was directed at Silver rather than himself. A case could be made that at no point had she been obligated to tell him she was in touch with their kid. He knew that in his head, but in his gut, he was dealing.

When it was time, he drove the few minutes to Silver's loft and parked. After climbing the stairs, he knocked on her front door.

"Hi," she said as she let him in. "Come on in."

She waved him inside, then motioned to the two people sitting on the sofa. There was a curvy woman in her thirties and a slim, dark-haired girl with blue eyes. He'd seen a couple of pictures, but they were nothing when compared with seeing her in person. She looked a lot like him.

"Hi." Autumn bounced to her feet. "This is strange, huh? I'm Autumn and you're Drew. Is it okay if I call you Drew? I can call you Mr. Lovato, if you'd prefer."

"Drew is fine."

"Good, because I call Silver by her first

244

name." Autumn studied him. "I think we look alike, don't you? That's kind of funny, huh?"

"You do," Silver said. "Drew, this is Autumn's mother, Leigh Frobish. Leigh, this is Drew."

Leigh stood and shook his hand. "Nice to meet you after all this time. Silver's told me a lot about you. It's great to finally meet Autumn's birth father."

Silver had set out iced tea and cookies, along with a glass of lemonade for Autumn. They all sat down, with Autumn and Leigh settling on the sofa while he and Silver took the chairs opposite. Drew did his best not to stare at Autumn but it was difficult when she was right there in front of him.

"My mom's getting married on Saturday," Autumn told him as she reached for a cookie. "I get to be in the wedding with Silver. We're super excited."

Silver grinned. "We are. I've already booked us a morning of beauty. We'll get our hair done and have manicures."

Autumn looked at her mother. "It's a very special occasion. Don't you think I should wear makeup?"

Leigh smiled. "No. Lip gloss is plenty."

"But I'm eleven."

"Yes, that would be the point."

Autumn rolled her eyes. "I have to wait until I'm thirteen to even wear mascara. Can you believe it? And no pierced ears until I'm fourteen. My life is a nightmare."

"The pain must be unbearable," Silver teased. "After the wedding, we have big plans for the week."

"I have a bike," Autumn told him. "Borrowed, but still. I love riding my bike. I'm going to hang out with Hunter and we're going to ride around the whole town."

"You know Hunter?" Drew asked.

Autumn nodded as she finished her cookie. "Uh-huh. He and his mom met Silver and me at Disneyland. We had the best time."

"You went with Wynn?"

He saw the flicker of guilt in Silver's eyes. She shrugged. "It was one of those things. She was planning a trip there and it was the same weekend I was visiting Autumn. We made plans."

He doubted it had been that simple. If he had to guess, he would say that Silver had accidentally blurted out something and Wynn had picked up on it.

He felt the slight turn of a knife in his gut — who else had known about his only child when he hadn't? Wynn had never hinted.

He turned to Autumn. "I'm glad you

already have friends here. What about school? Did your teachers send homework with you?"

"It's so much worse than that. There's a Learning Center in town for kids who are, like, homeschooled and stuff. All my teachers uploaded my assignments there. I have to go every single day. Even tomorrow!" She sounded horrified. "My mom's going on her honeymoon and I have to do my stupid schoolwork. Is that fair?"

"One day you'll go on a honeymoon and she'll have to work," Silver said mildly. "You're so dramatic."

Autumn grinned. "I know. I'm practicing for when I'm a teenager. What do you think?"

"I think your mom will have her hands full."

Leigh smiled at Drew. "I hope this isn't too awkward, but I want you to know you're welcome at the wedding. Autumn is only in town for a short period of time and I'm sure you want to spend as much time with her as possible."

He looked at Silver, who nodded slightly.

"That would be very nice," he said. "Thank you."

"You're welcome. The wedding is going to be a lot of fun." Leigh smiled at him. "I don't know if Silver told you but we're stepping into someone else's planned wedding. Denton and I couldn't make up our minds about what we wanted to do. I impulsively called one of the wedding businesses in town and they'd had a cancellation."

"*The Great Gatsby* wedding. Should be interesting."

Autumn sipped her lemonade. "There's a candy buffet and feathers and pearls as decorations. It's going to be beautiful."

"I'm having a wonderful party and I don't have to do any of the work," Leigh said.

Drew glanced at Silver. "Who's manning the bar?"

"Georgiana. You met her briefly a couple of weeks ago."

He remembered the pale, ethereal-looking blonde, who had lifted kegs as if they weighed as much as an apple.

He and Silver had yet to figure out who would be managing which trailer. She was pushing for Georgiana to take one and he wasn't sure. Not anything they would discuss today.

"I look forward to seeing her in action."

Autumn reached for another cookie. "Denton is wearing a tuxedo. What are you wearing?"

"A suit is fine," Silver told him.

"I have a lot of suits. I work in a bank."

"Do you get to play with the money?" Autumn asked.

"Not as often as I'd like."

"Denton's a pediatrician and my dad is an accountant." She sighed. "I have friends who don't have any dads and I have three." She looked at her mother. "I don't need any more."

"Good to know." Leigh laughed. "We'll stick with three."

Drew appreciated Autumn's ability to adjust to her new family members but her words were a stark reminder that he wasn't anything special in her life. She already had a father and a stepfather. What did her biological father matter? Maybe when she was older she might want to learn about his family, but now, he was just the new guy.

He remembered when Silver had shown up at his college dorm. He'd been happy to see her, but also curious as to the reason for her unexpected visit. He'd never imagined she was pregnant.

He remembered feeling trapped and scared. His future had disappeared with a handful of words. He'd wanted to deny the possibility, to tell her he didn't accept that, only that wasn't who he was. So he'd immediately offered to marry her.

She'd refused with a firmness that had re-assured him. Now, in hindsight, he wondered if she'd known him better than he'd known himself. She'd obviously guessed what he would do and was prepared to give him an out. Adoption. An out he'd jumped at.

But what if things had been different? What if he really *had* wanted to marry her? What if instead of feeling trapped, he'd been excited and happy? What if they'd gotten back together and started their life as the parents of a newborn? What if Autumn had been theirs?

He would have been her only dad. Sure, it would have been hard, but worth it. Instead he'd taken the easy way out — he'd let her go.

"You okay?" Silver asked.

He nodded. "Great." He faked a smile. "I'm really looking forward to the wedding, Leigh. Thank you for the invitation." He rose. "I should let you get settled. I'll see you Saturday."

Autumn jumped to her feet. "We're staying at the Sweet Dreams Inn. We have the princess room. I love it!" She smiled at Silver. "We could turn your room into a princess room."

"We could and yet we won't," Silver told

her. "You're going to be plenty spoiled on your visit, as it is. You don't need any more princessing."

Autumn slid onto her lap. "No one can be too spoiled."

They laughed together. Drew recognized the ease and familiarity between them — because they knew each other. Silver had been a part of her life since she'd been born. They had a connection he would never have with her.

Regret cut through him. Regret and envy and disappointment, although he couldn't say if the latter was with himself or Silver. There was too much to think about, too much to deal with. Later, he promised himself. He would figure it out later.

"Does she know about Bethany?" he asked.

Silver frowned for a second, then smiled at him. "Aren't you smart? No, she doesn't."

Autumn stood and moved in front of him. "Who is Bethany? Is she my age and can we be friends?"

"She's not your age," he said. "But she is one of Silver's friends."

"Okay." Autumn's tone was more "so?" than "wow, that's interesting!"

He grinned. "She's a princess. Her parents are the king and queen of El Bahar."

Autumn spun to Silver. "For real? Can I meet her? Do I have to bow or curtsy? A real princess? Does she have a tiara?"

"You don't have to curtsy and yes you can meet her and I don't know about the tiara." She looked at Drew. "Does Cade get a crown of some kind?"

Autumn spun to him. "Who's Cade?"

"My cousin. He's going to be marrying Bethany, which means he'll be a prince."

"Whoa! I so have to meet them both. Please, please, please?"

"We'll see what we can do," Silver told her. "Drew, I'm not sure I mentioned her energy level. You can see it's pretty high."

"It is."

They talked for a couple more minutes, then he excused himself. When he got to his car, his phone rang. He glanced at the screen and saw his mother was trying to reach him. After pushing Ignore, he leaned back in his seat and closed his eyes.

He hadn't known what to expect. Autumn was confident, charming and, as Silver had pointed out, full of energy. He wanted to get to know her better. He wanted to scream at Silver that she'd had no right to keep him from his child. Only she hadn't kept him from anything. She'd offered him whatever he wanted and he'd walked away without a second thought.

Something that was simple to do when the baby was still smaller than a marble and much more theoretical, than when that same child was a walking, breathing eleven-year-old.

He'd assumed he wouldn't ever care, wouldn't ever regret. He'd gambled and lost. So what, if anything, did he do now?

CHAPTER TWELVE

"I have guilt," Leigh admitted to Silver as they left the Learning Center after getting Autumn settled.

"She's going to be totally fine," Silver told her, unlocking her truck. "She'll have the entire staff eating out of her hand in what, ten minutes? By noon she'll be friends with everyone. Even if I'm wrong, she has her cell phone with her. She has your number and mine, so she can get in touch with either of us. You double-checked the child safety controls on her phone five times already so she can't go online unsupervised. I'm kind of missing the problem."

Leigh hugged her. "You're so rational. That's only one of the reasons I love you. Okay, let's go talk to Pallas and work through all the last-minute details, then we have Mexican food for lunch." She wrinkled her nose. "You do have Mexican food here in town, don't you?"

"Yes, and it's amazing."

Silver drove the short distance to Weddings Out of the Box. As she waited at a light, Leigh glanced at her.

"Did you talk to Drew last night?"

"No. I almost called about three times, but I didn't know if he'd want to talk to me." Not her finest hour, but she'd been very aware of the roller coaster of emotions he'd gone through during his first meeting with Autumn. He'd been in awe of his daughter and a little nervous, but there had been a lot of anger, too. She'd seen it flare, then die down.

"Do you think he's going to come to the wedding?" Leigh asked.

"He'll be there. He'll want to see Autumn and get to know her."

She hoped the crowd of people would provide a nice buffer as he found his emotional footing. She knew he was dealing with a lot and she really didn't want to fight. They only had a week with Autumn. It seemed wrong to waste even a second of that being angry.

Silver pulled into the parking lot and turned off the engine. "We're a couple of minutes early. Want to go get a coffee?"

"No, I'm good. We can just talk."

Silver rolled her eyes. "I recognize your

mom tone. You have something to say. Spit it out."

Leigh angled toward her and smiled. "Nothing dire, I promise. I'm just curious about a few things." She looked out the window. "This town is much smaller than I expected. I'm surprised you stayed."

As Silver had been braced for a question about whether or not she and Drew were sleeping together, she had to take a second to switch mental gears. "Okay. It's small but nice. When I moved back, I was ready to be a part of my uncle's business. I knew there was some opportunity there."

Leigh's gaze was steady. "I thought maybe you'd go somewhere else. When you didn't, I wondered if you were waiting for someone."

"Not Drew," she said flatly. "I wasn't waiting for him at all. We were done. Long done. Now we're just business partners. It's not anything more. It can't be. He's different and I'm not and this is just . . ."

Aware that she might be babbling just a little too much, she pressed her lips together and told herself to be quiet.

She cleared her throat. "I'm happy here. I have a great business and wonderful friends and a very fulfilling life. I don't need a man. Or want one." Love was complicated and

256

stupid and in the end, everything got messed up.

"There was never anyone else, was there?" Leigh asked, her voice soft. "I don't mean dating or sex. There was never another man for you. Just Drew."

"It's not like that. I'm careful with my emotions."

Leigh didn't say anything.

Silver groaned. "Fine. No. There wasn't anyone else. Just Drew."

"And now you're back together."

"We're not together-together. We're in business and . . ."

"Sleeping together."

"Yes, and that. But nothing else. It doesn't mean anything."

"He cares about you."

"He cares about his rabbit, too." .

"His what?"

"Long story. The point is, we're friends. We still have that and it's plenty. I don't want more. Not from him, not from any guy. I'm fine. Solid. Just happy as a clam."

Leigh patted her arm. "Good to know. I love you and I'm always going to be in your life. Even if you try to hide from me, I will hunt you down and love you forever."

Silver hugged her. "I feel the same way. Only I think I'd be a whole lot better at hunting you down."

"Probably. Now let's go inside. I want to see all the feathers and pearls and every tacky thing."

Friday afternoon Drew was surprised when Leigh walked into his office at the bank.

"I'm taking a chance that you have a few minutes for me," she said.

"Of course." He glanced at his calendar to see if he needed to cancel anything else and saw he was free for the rest of the afternoon.

"I have as much time as you would like," he told her. "Do you want to go get coffee or something?"

"I'm good." Leigh closed the door, then sat across from him. "I spent the morning going over the final details for the wedding. It's very exciting to see the setup and all the decorations. They're not anything I would have thought to pick but I really like them. We're going to have a good day tomorrow."

"When does your fiancé arrive?"

"Denton and his parents are driving in tonight. The wedding party is so small we aren't bothering with a rehearsal dinner. Autumn and I will stay together in the princess room at the hotel tonight, then tomorrow night Denton and I are driving back to LA after the wedding. We'll get there late, but we can sleep in before our flight to Hawaii." She laughed. "We promised we would take Autumn there over spring break next year. She understands the concept of a honeymoon but doesn't think it's fair when there are children involved."

"So she mentioned earlier."

Leigh was a pretty woman — a little curvy, with wavy dark hair and green eyes. She practically radiated happiness and contentment.

"I thought you might like to know about how Silver and I became friends," Leigh said, "but not know how to ask. Or what to ask. I thought you might like to know what it was like while she was pregnant and after Autumn was born."

"I would like that."

"I'd known for years that I couldn't have children. There's a whole plumbing thing I won't get into. When I married Paul, my first husband, we knew from the start we wanted to adopt, so we began the process as soon as we got engaged. We tried everything. Local, foreign, private, public. We were determined to find our baby. We met Silver through a lawyer friend who happened to know her uncle. It was just one of those things. She wanted to give up her baby and we wanted a baby. So we met."

Drew hadn't realized there was a process, but of course there had to have been. It wasn't as if she'd had the kid, then left her on a shelf somewhere. There had been meetings and decisions and paperwork. Silver would have been pregnant all nine months, knowing that in the end, she would be giving up her child. He wanted to correct that to *their* child, but he had a feeling that as soon as he'd agreed to adoption, she'd stopped thinking of the baby as anything but hers.

"I was so nervous at that first meeting," Leigh admitted. "What if she didn't like us? What if we didn't get along? It's hard when someone else has that much power over your life. I didn't know if I should bring a gift or flowers or what. But from that first meeting, we just clicked. We were talking and laughing and it just seemed right. Silver only took a couple of days to decide we were the ones."

Leigh smiled at him. "I was over the moon. You can't imagine how thrilled and delighted we were. Silver's uncle got in touch with us and brought up the possibility of Silver living with us through the pregnancy. Happily Inc is such a small town and he didn't want her to have to face everyone she knew, day after day."

Drew tried not to react to the gut punch. Something else he hadn't thought of. That if Silver had stayed in town, she would have had to deal with questions, gossip and judgments.

"We immediately said yes," Leigh continued. "We had plenty of room and we wanted to get to know Silver." Her smile turned wry. "And maybe in the back of our minds we were hoping she would like us enough not to change her mind, because that can always happen and it's heartbreaking."

"For everyone."

"Yes. So Silver moved in. We picked out baby furniture together and read prenatal books. What I didn't realize was that while Silver and I were getting closer and closer, my marriage was falling apart. Paul and I didn't have as much in common as we thought. Having Autumn allowed us to put off the inevitable, but I think because we were already drifting apart, Silver and I had more time together than we would have otherwise."

She sighed. "Autumn's birth was wonderful. Silver was so brave, and then I got to hold my daughter. It was the biggest blessing of my life. Silver went back to Happily Inc, but within a few weeks, it was obvious to all of us that she wasn't comfortable. We invited her back to stay with us. She went to community college and worked and helped me with Autumn. When Paul moved out, Silver was right there to see me through it. When I was back on my feet, she moved back home and I went on with my life." Her smile returned. "I planned on being a single parent the rest of my life."

"That obviously didn't happen."

"It didn't. Autumn spiked a fever on a Sunday morning and I rushed her to the emergency room. Denton was there, filling in for a friend. He took care of Autumn, who was just fine. Later, he followed up to see if she was all right. I was so ridiculous. I had no idea he was flirting with me. Finally I realized the man was asking me out." She laughed. "I said yes. We fell in love and here we are."

"And tomorrow you're getting married."

"Yes. So Autumn sees her dad every other weekend. She has dinner with him at least once a week and our holidays are shared. Paul married a couple of years ago. His new wife has three kids, two of whom are close to Autumn's age. She likes having stepsiblings. Her life is happy and full."

That was clear enough. "You're saying Autumn already has plenty of dads."

"No. I'm saying Autumn has lots of love and support. She's a sweet girl and we all care about her. I'm saying as far as I'm concerned, you and Silver made the exact right decision. At least for us. I'm not sure what you're thinking about yourself."

"I don't know what *to* think," he admitted. "For years she was nameless and faceless. A concept. Yes, Silver and I had a baby and we'd given that baby up for adoption. This is completely different. Autumn is real and she could have been ours."

He'd thought Leigh might get angry but instead her expression turned sympathetic. "Autumn still *is* real and she's still yours. She will always be a part of you."

"But I don't know her."

"You will after this week. And if you want to stay in touch with her, I'm fine with that. Silver talks to her online or through Face-Time. They text." She laughed. "Autumn does love to talk about herself."

"You make it sound easy."

"There's no reason in the world that it has to be hard."

When Silver's phone beeped, she read the text.

You around to talk?

Ever since the day Drew had met Autumn, she'd been waiting to hear from him. She'd thought he might call or come by last night, but there had only been radio silence. Given all he was dealing with, she'd debated contacting him herself, only to decide that the first contact should come from him.

I am. Want to bring a pizza? I have wine.

I'll call in an order and see you soon.

She set her small table, then settled on the sofa to wait. Leigh and Autumn were spending the night before the wedding together at the Sweet Dreams Inn. They were ordering room service and watching movies together. In the morning, Silver would pick them up for their few hours of beauty. They were all getting mani-pedis, then having their hair done. Leigh was getting her makeup professionally done while Silver was going to do her own. Last she'd heard, Autumn was still angling for more than just lip gloss.

They needed to be at Weddings Out of the Box by three for pictures, then the ceremony began at five. Autumn would come home with Silver to start her week.

Drew showed up forty minutes after he'd

texted, with a pizza and a bag of cookies from the bakery next door. She'd already opened the wine.

She let him in and took a second to study his face. Same old Drew, she thought with some relief. Whatever he was feeling, he wasn't angry or sad. At least not that she could see.

"You okay?" she asked as they took their seats at the table.

"I'm dealing. Leigh came by to see me today. She told me what it was like while you were pregnant and staying with them."

The information surprised her. Leigh had claimed to need the afternoon to do some last-minute errands. Silver hadn't realized one of them was to go see Drew.

He opened the pizza box and she inhaled the delicious scent of all meat and extra cheese on a hand-tossed crust.

"And?" she asked, taking a slice.

"And there was a lot I didn't know." He looked at her. "I gotta tell you, Silver, I'm confused as hell. I don't know what to think or what I feel. I'm angry, but I can't figure out at who. You? Me? The world? I know in my head that you didn't do anything wrong. I get that I wanted to give up our baby and you're right. I signed the papers and went on with my life. I never asked because I guess it never occurred to me. Or maybe I didn't want to know."

"You didn't want to be trapped," she said gently. "I'm sure that was a worry."

"You wouldn't have trapped me."

"There were times I thought I should have accepted your proposal."

"Not many." He took a bite and chewed. "You aren't that way. You would want a man on your own terms, not because he felt obligated."

Although he was right about that, she'd had plenty of weak moments. "I was scared and alone and pregnant. It wasn't easy." She held up a hand. "I'm not saying you should have been there or that I blame you, I'm just saying it was hard on me. Even being with Leigh and Paul wasn't always enough. I felt like everyone was staring at me and judging me."

"Did you ever think about not giving her up?"

"No." She sipped her wine. "That's my guilty secret. I love Autumn. I'm grateful she's in my life, but I never once wanted to raise her by myself. I was too young, too unprepared."

"And now? Do you think about having kids?"

"Not that often."

His gaze settled on her face. "Because you don't want them or because you can't see it happening right now?"

"It's more about circumstances than not wanting children. I could do it on my own, but that's a tough road. I watched Leigh go through it and she had an ex-husband who wanted to be totally involved with his kid. Not all guys are like that."

She picked up her slice of pizza. "I'm not making sense."

"Yes, you are."

They were quiet for a couple of minutes. Silver smiled suddenly. "Just think, if you'd married Ashley Lauren, you'd have a couple of kids with her by now."

"Assuming she hadn't already killed me in my sleep."

"There is that. Although it's a leap to go from trying to burn down a car to murder."

"I think if anyone is capable of traveling that distance, it's her."

She finished her slice and wiped her hands on her napkin. "Drew, I'm sorry. Now that all this has happened, I realize I should have said something to you sooner about Autumn."

He shrugged. "When was the right time? And what would you have said? What would you have expected me to do with the information? I knew our kid was out there. I could have asked if you knew anything. I could have registered with one of those agencies so she could have found me later, if she wanted. We both did what we did and now we've moved on."

She wanted to believe that. "You said you're still dealing with everything."

"I am. And I still have to tell my mother."

Silver stared at him. "No," she breathed. "No way." But he was right. Of course Irene had to know. "What do you think she's going to say?"

"Whatever it is, it won't be appropriate. I guarantee you that." He raised his glass. "To our beautiful daughter."

She smiled. "To Autumn."

"So, about this wedding. Think I could be your date?"

She smiled. "I thought you'd never ask."

Because of all the beauty prep work, about which he knew nothing, Drew agreed to meet Silver at Weddings Out of the Box on Saturday around four. While he knew the venue and had even been to a couple of weddings there, this time felt more personal.

The largest room had been divided into two spaces. In one half were rows of chairs, waiting for the guests. In the other were the

268

tables for the reception.

The place settings were layers of plates and chargers, all done in cream and gold. A champagne fountain stood in the corner, the stacked glasses ready for the champagne. The centerpieces were arrangements of flowers woven with strings of pearls and huge feathers. More pearls hung like streamers around the room. There were gilded mirrors and tables with fancy, feathered masks and flameless candles in glittering holders.

Renee greeted him at the door, a tablet in her hand. "You're with Silver? Because you're too early to be a guest. The bride's room is that way." She pointed to a hallway. "Everyone is already dressed. Just knock once and go in."

Without waiting for him to respond, she hurried off as if she still had a thousand things to do. He would guess she very well might. Weddings seemed to be a big deal and a lot of work. He didn't want to even begin to imagine what his mother would want his wedding to be.

He found the bride's room and knocked. Rather than simply entering, he waited for the door to be opened. When it was, he saw Autumn standing on the other side.

Her dress was a flapper style with rows of

pale pink fringe. She had on a headband with a feather and some kind of netting made into gloves. She grinned when she saw him.

"This is so much fun! We had mani-pedis and I got my hair done." She turned to show him the tight curls pinned up in back. When she faced him again, she rolled her eyes. "Still no makeup and I totally begged, but it was a really good morning. Mom looks beautiful."

Drew followed her gaze to where Leigh stood in a white wedding down. It was sleeveless, with a deep V, and fitted to just below her waist. From there it flared out with rows and rows of ruffly, fluffy material that cascaded to the floor. Her hair was up and she had on a triple strand of pearls. Silver was adjusting her dress as a photographer got into place.

Silver was wearing the dress he'd seen her in before. It looked different with her makeup and with her hair pinned up into fancy loops and curls. Her only jewelry was a simple pair of silver hoops.

He should have bought her jewelry. The thought surprised him. Jewelry? For Silver? When? They'd been teenagers when they'd been involved before and since then, it was hardly appropriate. Still, he couldn't shake the sense of wanting to give her diamonds and sapphires and bangles and rings.

Leigh saw him and smiled. She waved Autumn over. Her daughter rushed to her side and snuggled close for a picture. Silver joined him.

"How's it going?" she asked. "You going to be able to deal with all this?"

"I don't have anything to do. I'm just a guest."

"I meant later. When Leigh and Denton are gone and people realize you're hanging out with an eleven-year-old girl who looks a lot like you."

"I'm going to tell them I'm her biological father."

Silver looked at him. "Do you mean that?"

"Absolutely. I want to get to know her and figure out where I fit in her life. You're the one who had to give her up. How did you do that?"

"She was never mine. The second I picked Leigh and Paul, I knew that our baby belonged to them. I'm not saying it was easy, but it wasn't hard, if that makes sense."

It didn't, so he would file it away with everything else. "You look beautiful."

"Thank you. I'd say you clean up well, but you always wear a suit so this isn't that different."

He chuckled. "If there's a compliment in there, thank you. If not, I'll be quiet."

"There was a compliment." She watched the photographer. "Leigh is so happy. I'm thrilled she found Denton. They're going to be great together." She glanced at him. "Autumn is very excited about spending the week here and getting to know you."

"I look forward to getting to know her, too."

Silver's gaze was steady. "And then she goes home, Drew. We made our decision a long time ago. She's not ours."

"I know. That's not where I'm going."

"I just want to be sure. For both your sakes."

Because if he pushed on anything, Autumn would be hurt. He had no legal standing anymore — he was just the guy who gave up his kid one afternoon a million years ago. Now she belonged to someone else and he was one of three dads in her life.

They were where they were and if he didn't like it, well, he only had himself to blame.

CHAPTER THIRTEEN

Sunday morning, Silver and Autumn slept in. They'd been up late at the wedding. The cushions on the sectional sofa folded up and out of the way, making the couch wide enough to be a bed. Autumn had brought a sleeping bag and was happy to camp out there.

They got up and made breakfast. They were going over to Drew's about eleven to hang out. Silver wondered how the preteen would react to the fluffy Mr. Whiskers.

When they'd showered and the breakfast dishes were put away, Autumn pulled out her homework and Silver went through the budget on the remodels. Walter would be finishing up the larger of the trailers in a day or so. While she was excited to see the finished trailer, she knew he would be expecting payment that day. It was sad to watch her bank account dwindle, even for a good cause, she thought with a chuckle. If only there were a way to have the trailers *and* keep all the cash.

"What's so funny?" Autumn asked. "I'm doing algebra and that isn't funny at all."

"Algebra? Already?"

"It's just the intro class. I'll get more into it next year. Math isn't that hard for me. I like it. And science. I'm thinking maybe I want to be a doctor, like Denton. Or do hair."

Silver smiled. "You could do both. Doctor by day, hair stylist by night."

"Silver, you have to have life balance. I couldn't have two big jobs like that."

"An excellent point. Thank you."

"You're welcome. Now what was so funny?"

"I was thinking it would be nice to have my new trailer and not have to pay for it." She held up a hand. "I was laughing because it's a ridiculous idea."

"You have to pay for stuff. Stealing is wrong and you end up in jail. No one wants that."

"True enough."

Autumn focused on her homework for a few minutes, then said, "I'm all caught up with school. I'll bet I could just work really hard a couple of days and take the others off."

"Not happening."

"But Mom's in Hawaii."

"Lots of people are on vacation this week. Lots of people are on vacation every week, which is nice for them but has nothing to do with you."

"You're very tough on me."

"I know."

Autumn sighed. "Fine. I'll go to the Learning Center, but I won't like it."

"I'm okay with that."

The corner of Autumn's mouth twitched. She turned away as if she didn't want Silver to see her smile.

A few minutes before eleven, they headed to Silver's truck and drove to Drew's house.

"I like your loft a lot," Autumn told her. "It's more fun than an apartment. When I'm a grown-up, I want a loft, too."

"There's not a lot of privacy or storage. So you have to think about that. Although I guess some have more storage than others. Lofts are about open living plans. Some are really industrial with concrete floors and open ductwork."

"I saw some like that on *House Hunters.* They were in Chicago. They picked a different condo, but I liked the loft. The ceilings were really high."

Silver had trouble believing they were talking living spaces. Just a couple of years ago Autumn had been way more interested in Legos and her Elsa doll from *Frozen*. Time was moving so fast.

They drove into the golf course development. Autumn gazed out the window at the huge homes.

"So not an apartment."

"No. Drew's very successful."

"You're very successful, too. You created your own business from nothing. You're an entrepreneur. That takes talent and dedication."

Silver sent a silent thank-you to Leigh for teaching her daughter to be a sweetie. "I've chosen my own path. Most days it's pretty great."

They parked in front of Drew's house. The plan was to spend an hour or so here, then grab some lunch before going to the movies. She knew Drew wanted to spend as much time with Autumn as he could, getting to know her and having her get to know him.

Silver wondered if she would mind sharing, but so far she was perfectly fine with having Drew around. Maybe because he was Autumn's biological father. Maybe because she could play a little *what if.*

Drew greeted them at the door. "Come on in."

Autumn looked around as Drew ushered them into the great room.

"This is nice," she said. "You have a lot of light."

Silver grinned at Drew's look of confusion. "Autumn seems to have a flare for design. She's an HGTV fan."

"I am," Autumn admitted as she ran to the sliding glass doors. "What is that over there? Beyond the golf course." She looked more closely. "No way! Is that a giraffe?" She spun toward Silver. "You told me about the animal preserve and everything but I thought you were kidding. You have giraffes!"

"Not me personally, but yes, there are giraffes and gazelles and even a water buffalo."

"Can we go? We have to go. Please, please, please. I won't touch them or anything but can we go see them today?"

"We were going to the movies," Silver began.

Autumn shook her head. "Movies, shmovies. We can go another time. You have giraffes!"

Silver looked at Drew, who shrugged.

"I'm in," he said. "Although Mr. Whiskers

277

is going to be very disappointed not to be the most exotic pet."

Autumn spun toward him. "Who's Mr. Whiskers?"

"He's a rabbit. Some people I know are having me take care of him while they figure out if their new baby is allergic or not. He's a good guy. Kind of a deep thinker. Want to go see him?"

Autumn gave the giraffes one more yearning look before turning back to Drew. "Yes, please. I'd like to meet your rabbit."

Silver had to admit Leigh had done a heck of a job raising Autumn. "I'll text Carol while you visit Mr. Whiskers and see if we can go see the giraffes later this afternoon. Now that I know you don't care about the movie." She gave an exaggerated sigh.

"Of course I *care*. It's just not the same. We can see the movie later in the week."

"I could say the same about the giraffe," Silver teased.

Autumn rolled her eyes, then grabbed Drew's hand. "Okay, let's go see Mr. Whiskers. Does he know any tricks? Is he really soft? I bet he's soft."

"He is. He's a standard chinchilla rabbit, so he's gray and has a very soft coat. He eats hay and a lot of salad. No dressing, of course. Just the greens."

Autumn shot Silver a "he really has to get out more" look over her shoulder. Silver was still laughing as she texted Carol and asked about visiting the giraffes.

They agreed to meet later that afternoon. In the meantime, Drew barbecued burgers on his patio and Mr. Whiskers hopped around for Autumn even though it was one of his longer sleep periods.

After lunch, Drew and Autumn played checkers for a while. Leigh had set strict phone rules — Autumn had very specific periods of time when she was allowed to text with her friends. For the most part, Autumn didn't complain about it.

"Peanut butter," Drew said, continuing their conversation about what they liked as they tried to figure out what they had in common.

"It's okay, but I'm more into chocolate." She flashed him a grin. "That could be a girl thing. Green beans?"

"I like them a lot. There's a Thai place in town that does crispy fried beans that are delicious."

"Every vegetable is good when it's fried," Autumn told him, "but I like green beans, too. Morning person or night owl?"

"Morning person."

Autumn looked at Silver. "You're a night owl."

"I'm not. My job keeps me up late, but when I'm not working I go to bed at a reasonable time."

Autumn looked at Drew. "She's not really a morning person. I have to be quiet and not bouncy until she's had her coffee."

Drew winked at her. "You don't say."

Silver started to point out he already knew that about her, but realized just in time, it wasn't anything she wanted to mention in front of Autumn. While their daughter had yet to ask about their relationship, Silver was sure the question was coming.

"Ebooks or print books?" Autumn asked.

"Print, unless I'm traveling. Then ebooks."

"Me, too! Not that I travel that much, but still. Except for textbooks. Those should all be digital, especially when there's home-work. Making kids carry all those books back and forth from school is just cruel. Yet another reason I should have the week off."

"Nice try," Silver told her.

Drew hopped over two of her checkers and tapped his. "King me."

"You're way better than I thought you'd be," she grumbled as she did as he re-quested, but she was smiling as she spoke.

Silver held in a sigh of relief. Drew and

Autumn were getting along just fine. He'd reacted better than she could have hoped and Autumn was her normal friendly, upbeat self. With a little luck, they would get through the rest of the week without too much trauma.

Drew packed up the hay and greens, along with the three litter boxes he'd bought, the extra cage and the hutch. Melissa had called that morning to say the test results were back and Mr. Whiskers was not the reason for the baby's rash. Apparently it was an additive in the laundry soap. While the detergent was being donated to a neighbor, Mr. Whiskers was free to go home.

Drew had gone by Silver's to borrow her truck because there was no way the hutch would fit in his sedan. He got the dozing rabbit into a carrier, then loaded all the supplies onto the truck bed before tucking Mr. Whiskers's carrier safely in the passenger seat foot well.

The drive to the Newports' more modest neighborhood took less than ten minutes. Melissa met him at the front door.

"You've been so great, Drew. Thank you for taking in Emily's rabbit. I got the call after she'd left for school, so she doesn't know yet. I know she's going to be thrilled when she gets home."

He handed her the carrier, then brought in the rest of Mr. Whiskers's worldly possessions. Melissa showed him back to Emily's room — a bright, happy bedroom with lavender walls and a big hutch under the window. He saw the cords had been chew-proofed with special covers and that there was a litter box in the corner.

He and Melissa got fresh litter in the box and water in the bowl, then let out Mr. Whiskers. The rabbit hopped out, then looked around, as if judging his new surroundings. After a couple of seconds of sniffing and whisker twitching, he hopped into his old hutch and began burrowing in the hay.

"I think he's happy to be home," Drew said. "Please tell Emily that her rabbit missed her every day."

Melissa smiled. "I will." Her gaze turned speculative. "Why aren't you married?"

He held up both hands. "Gee, look at the time."

She laughed. "Sorry. That was too blunt, huh? I just mean, you're a really good guy and you took in our rabbit. Who does that?"

"He's not a lot of a work and he's a good listener. I didn't mind."

"Still. You helped out so much. What if

we'd given him away to someone who didn't want to give him back, and then we'd found out he wasn't the problem? Emily would have been devastated."

"She's a sweet girl. I'm glad I could help."

"You saved us. Thanks, Drew." She walked him to the front door. "And you should think about the marriage thing. You'd be a good dad."

"I'll keep that in mind."

He walked back to the truck, Melissa's comment about getting married stuck in his head.

He'd always assumed that was going to happen. That he would be a husband and a father — he'd actually expected it to have happened by now. Only it hadn't. There'd been the near-disastrous engagement to Ashley Lauren, but nothing since. No serious relationships, no falling in love. He hadn't even missed being involved until he'd noticed Silver again.

Funny how his plan to get back into her life by buying into her business had turned into something else entirely. They were together — sexually and in the business. They had a kid together. He'd gone from zero to sixty faster than he would have thought possible, and oddly enough, it all felt right. He wasn't sure it was forever or just for now, but whatever it was, she was someone he wanted to be around.

He drove back to her place and walked inside the retail space to give her back her truck keys.

"How was the reunion?" she asked.

"He seemed happy to be home. Emily doesn't know yet. She's going to find out after school. I suspect she'll be one excited girl."

Silver stared at him without speaking.

"What?" he asked, pulling her close and kissing her.

"It was really nice of you to take in her rabbit."

"It was nothing. He's an easy pet. I was happy to help."

"You're a good guy."

"Thanks."

She was so beautiful. Every now and then he was caught off guard by the perfect shape of her face or the way her long hair moved. She was smart and sexy and determined. He wanted to go back in time and beat some sense into his eighteen-year-old self. He should never have let her get away.

She took a step back. "Stop it. Whatever you're thinking, stop it."

"How do you know what I'm thinking?"

"I can guess. You have that 'I made a

mistake' look. Drew, we've been over this. We were kids. We made the right decision. There's no way we could have been half as good at parenting Autumn as Leigh and Paul were. Besides, even if we made the wrong decision, which we didn't, it's done. There's no going back. We just have to keep moving forward."

"That sounds very sensible."

"It is."

"I'd like Autumn to meet Grandpa Frank."

"I think that's a great idea. What about your mother?"

He grimaced. "Let's stick with Grandpa Frank for now. I'll tell my mom about her, but I have a feeling Autumn is not part of her master plan."

"Probably not." She moved toward him. "Do you have to rush right back to work or do you have a few minutes?"

"I can stick around for a bit. Did you have something you wanted to talk about?"

She smiled. "Not really. The new sofas are all unwrapped and in place. I thought maybe we could take one of them for a test drive."

Blood heated instantly. He went from conversational to horny in a single heart-beat. "I'm in. Let me lock the door and I'll meet you back here."

"I'll be the one who's naked."

He leaned in and kissed her. "I've always liked that about you."

"I finished all my schoolwork," Autumn said as they drove to Wynn's house. "It's not hard at all. There aren't any distractions. I could probably work a little harder and do more than a day's work at a time, and then take Friday off. We could go visit Millie and her friends. I've never hung out with giraffes before yesterday. It was the best. So, no school Friday?"

"That's one thought. Or you could do what you're supposed to do and stop bugging me."

Autumn laughed. "Okay, but I have to try."

"Apparently."

Silver had to admit, it was a really good day. The sun was out, the temperature warm, she'd had hot monkey sex with Drew and now she was going to spend the rest of the afternoon with Autumn. Well, technically Autumn would be riding bikes with Hunter, but Silver would be nearby and able to watch them, so that would be fun, too.

This was good, she thought. All of it. The business, Autumn, Drew, although she knew

she had to be careful about him. She didn't want to confuse fun with falling for him.

She pulled into Wynn's driveway. Autumn scrambled out of the truck just as Hunter flew out the front door. They met on the lawn and did some elaborate handshake they'd worked out while in line at Disneyland, then lifted Autumn's borrowed bike from the back of the truck.

Before Silver had made it to the front door, they had their helmets on and were heading down the street.

"Stay in touch," she yelled after them.

They both waved.

Wynn greeted her and invited her in. "I told Hunter he had to check with me every thirty minutes and they had to be home for good by four-thirty. You're always welcome to stay for a visit or you can come get her then."

"I'll stay for a bit, if you don't mind."

"I don't."

Silver sat at the kitchen table. Wynn pulled out cans of diet soda for them and took the chair across from her.

"How's the visiting going?" Wynn asked.

"We're having a lot of fun. Poor Carol begged her to meet us at the animal prese yesterday so Autumn could see Millie a her friends up close."

"Carol loves showing off her animals."

"She does."

"How's Drew settling into short-term fatherhood?"

"Easily. I'm surprised. Sometimes he's nervous, but he's done so well with her. They get along. They talk about stuff. It's good."

Wynn's expression was knowing.

"What?" Silver demanded. "Don't read more into the situation than there is. We're dealing with what could be a very awkward situation. Nothing more."

"You sure that's all it is? You did once love him."

"I also once thought a PB&J sandwich was the best food in the world. Tastes change."

"So Drew isn't tasty anymore?"

Silver resisted the urge to roll her eyes. Not only wasn't it mature, Wynn had the tiniest of points.

"I will admit that we've been living in the past some. After years of a Drew-less existence, it's weird to have him around all the time."

"And you're in business together."

"There's that."

"And you're sleeping together."

"Did I mention that directly?"

"You didn't have to. We all know. You've

been glowing."

"Maybe I have a new moisturizer."

Wynn ignored that. "I can respect truth avoidance as much as the next woman, I'm just saying, things are different with you two. If you're perfectly fine with all the changes, great. If you're not, you need to be careful. I say that as a friend."

"I know and I appreciate it. But I'm not that kid anymore."

"Maybe, but he's still that guy. And we're all in danger when he's around."

Not for the first time, Silver wondered about Wynn's past. There were so many unanswered questions and whenever she pried, Wynn flatly refused to discuss her life before she moved to Happily Inc.

"Do you think he loved you back then? When you were first together?"

The unexpected question surprised Silver. "Yes, I believe Drew loved me. As much as a guy his age can love anyone. I loved him, too. But there was too much against us. We made the right decision."

"*You* made the right decision."

The words were gentle, but still startling. "What do you mean?"

"You broke up with Drew before he left for college. You could see what was going to happen and you wanted to make that as easy on each of you as possible. You're the one who told him he didn't have to marry you when you got pregnant. He might not have liked giving up his future, but he would have done it."

"Drew's a big believer in doing the right thing."

"You were the adult in the room, as they say, because you had to be. But that doesn't mean you didn't feel the loss and the confusion and whatever else there was. Now he's back and all grown-up and handsome and how are you going to resist him?"

"I can't figure out if you're warning me off or enabling me?"

"A little of both, I suppose. I figure you need a voice of reason, right about now. I'm trying to be that. I think you were brave about Drew, then and now. I think you were able to see past being in love with him to know in your heart that if you had his opportunities, you would have wanted to leave, too."

A truth Silver rarely admitted to herself. "You're right. My mom was a disaster and dragged me all over hell and back. The reason was always a guy. Her next one true love, which she never found. When I figured I was old enough not to be too much trouble, I begged her to let me live with my uncle. I wasn't sure if he would agree, but he did. Once I was here, life was so much easier. I had a stable home life, friends. But I knew there were limitations on what I could do or be. That if I went to college, it was all on me. No one was going to help me pay for it. Drew's life was so different." She smiled. "Note to self. Next time be born rich."

Wynn laughed. "I know, right? Wouldn't that be nice."

Silver thought about how she'd felt after Drew left. He'd been all she had and he'd had so much. She was just one piece of his life.

"My mom always destroyed herself for the men she loved. She would become whatever they wanted. I think she did it so much, she lost who she was. I didn't want to follow in her footsteps. I wanted to be strong and be true to myself."

"Another reason you gave Drew an out."

Silver nodded. "You're right. I didn't want to be like her."

"And you're not."

Silver was less sure. Her mother had been a fool for love over and over again. Silver had been a fool over only one man — one love — but after him, she'd never let anyone else in. She'd never risked her heart.

She couldn't help wondering if not risking her heart was just the flip side of risking it too much. Had she been smart or had she simply learned the wrong lesson?

CHAPTER FOURTEEN

"We discussed this," Silver said Tuesday morning, her teeth clenched. She looked at the new sofas in her retail space and wondered if she was strong enough to throw one of them at Drew's head. "We agreed that Georgiana was going to be one of the managers."

"We agreed to talk about it," Drew said. "Hiring staff is a big deal. We owe it to ourselves to interview a wide range of people to make sure we have the best ones in place as we expand AlcoHaul."

She was going to have to kill him. That much was clear. "Why are you talking to me like this? I've been running my business successfully for years. You're the one who came to me about buying in, not the other way around. I know what I'm doing. Georgiana is honest, smart and she knows the business. I want her running one of the trailers."

"Isn't it a joint decision?"

"Why are you acting like I don't know what I'm doing? You're trying to take over, Drew. This is supposed to be a partnership. If this is how you expect things to be, you're wrong."

"I expect this to be a business and run like a business. Your opinion of Georgiana is important, but so is mine. That's why I asked her in for an interview."

"You did what?" Silver consciously lowered her voice. "You did that without talking to me first?"

"I'm talking to you now."

"No. No! This is not how we do things. We discuss our decisions together. You don't unilaterally invite someone in for an interview without talking to me first. You do not hire someone without —" She glared at him. "Dammit, Drew."

One corner of his mouth turned up. "Just making a point."

She wanted to stomp her foot, or make a run at sofa tossing. "You're saying that me wanting Georgiana as a manager without clearing it with you is the same as you inviting her in for an interview without talking to me."

"Something like that, although I didn't think you'd get so angry. My goal wasn't to upset you, although that's what I've done. I was making a point. I didn't do a very good job. I'm sorry. Next time I'll talk to you directly."

What? She stared at him. "That was so rational and thoughtful."

"Don't sound surprised. I'm a decent guy."

"I know, but you just flat-out apologized."

"I was wrong." He raised a shoulder. "I know how to date you and I know how to make love with you, but the business thing is harder. I'm not clear on my place here. That's going to take time."

"You're my business partner. Why is that confusing?"

He didn't look convinced. "Let's take your theory for a test drive. I think I should conduct the interview with Georgiana. I don't have a personal connection with her, so I'll ask different questions and we'll get a clearer picture of how she'll fit in with the organization."

She pressed her lips together, telling herself she would hear him out. "Go on."

"While we're on the subject, I think I should conduct all the interviews. I have a lot more experience with hiring people than you do. I've been doing it since I started working at the bank. I've also done performance evaluations and I've fired people. I'm the HR expert in the relationship. You should respect that and appreciate my expertise."

Her emotions told her to take him on and win. Her head said he was right. About all of it. She'd never had any employees at AlcoHaul. She'd contracted help as she'd needed it — party by party. She had a regular list of people she liked to work with and would give them a heads-up for big parties, but there were times she was scrambling because they already had booked other jobs.

She'd toyed with the idea of at least a part-time person, but the logistics had always caused her to put off the decision. It was so much responsibility. What if she didn't have work? What about all the paperwork and insurance and taxes? In the end, it was easier to simply hope for the best. Easier maybe, but not smarter, and not the best decision for her business.

Drew knew all about that sort of thing. What he didn't know, he would find out because running a business was what he did. If he didn't have the answers, he would know where to find them. In truth, she hadn't just agreed to take him on as a business partner because of the money. Some of it had been because of his experience and knowledge. Not taking advantage of that was just plain dumb.

"All right," she said slowly. "You conduct the interviews. But I want to be there, too, and if I have questions, I'll ask them."

"I hope you do have questions. You know AlcoHaul, Silver. You know what's needed far more than me."

She sighed. "Are you annoying on purpose or is it more of a gift?"

He put his arm around her and kissed her. "I think it's a gift. One of many."

"Ha, ha."

They set up a small folding table as a desk and brought in chairs. The rest of the space was finished and Silver had her first bachelorette party scheduled in a couple of days. As the bride had brought in her own catering, all Silver had to worry about was bar service and whether or not the soundproofing would hold up.

Georgiana arrived right on time. She was around forty, pale and slender, with tattoos over most of her body. She'd worn a sundress and heels, with her short hair in a spiky style that had Silver wondering if she should cut her own hair.

"This is awkward," Georgiana said with a laugh. "I'm not sure what to expect."

Drew motioned to the chair on the opposite side of the table. He and Silver sat next to each other.

"You know Silver has taken me on as a minority partner," Drew began. "We've bought two additional trailers and will be expanding the business."

Georgiana smiled. "About time. You've been turning away jobs forever."

"She has," Drew said. "We're looking to hire a full-time manager for the existing large trailer and you're our first choice."

"I was hoping you'd say that. It's a job I want. I like the work and I love the days off."

Silver glanced at Drew, hoping he wouldn't take that wrong. She knew what her friend meant. The weekends were long, but the days in between were nice and quiet.

"You from around here?" he asked.

Georgiana shook her head. "San Diego." She held up a hand. "I know, I know. What's a beach girl like me doing in the middle of the desert, but I like it here and I go home a lot. My parents are still there."

"You pissed about the Chargers?"

Georgiana sat up straighter and groaned. "What was up with that? Seriously? Because LA *needs* two football teams? Greedy bastards. And I mean the town and the owners, not the players. The Chargers were doing great in San Diego. We loved them and now they're gone. And they're going to share a stadium? How does that work? It's just plain dumb if you ask me."

Silver had no idea what Drew was doing. How did talking about football tell him anything about Georgiana?

"I'm a Giants fan," he said mildly.

"Then your life is one of pain."

They both laughed.

"Tell me about some of your most difficult customers," he said.

"I'll have to go back to my San Diego bartending days for that," Georgiana told him. "You don't get the same level of partying here, especially at weddings. Let me think."

She was quiet for a second, then said, "I have a few who were challenging. There's the guy who came in naked, the guy who hired a prostitute to blow him in front of his ex-wife. Or the time a bunch of bikers decided to move in on a cop bar." She smiled. "You pick."

Silver watched Drew, not sure what he would say. He looked at Georgiana.

"You're telling me you know what you're doing."

She shrugged. "I've been at this awhile. I

can pretty much read the crowd and I understand what's expected of me. Alco-Haul is different from a bar. It's events so the customers aren't regulars. Nobody wants a relationship with the bar staff — they want to get back to the party. My job is to keep things moving and make sure nobody gets too drunk."

She looked at Silver. "All the while dealing with the bride, her family and any number of crises."

"We have had those."

"Remember the DJ who tried to hold up the entire wedding?"

Silver groaned. "He succeeded, too. Even though he only had a flare gun."

"It looked real enough to me," Georgiana murmured.

Drew glanced between them. "Sounds like a good time."

"It was interesting, that's for sure." Silver waited to see what else he would ask.

He surprised her by shaking his head. "Okay, you were right. Georgiana's great. She has the experience and a good personality. If you want her, I'm in."

"Yes." Silver held up her hand to Georgiana for a high five. "You'd take the trailer we have now. The new one is going to be put to work this weekend, then Walter, our contractor, will have next week to work out any issues we find. I'll talk to Pallas, along with the owners of the other venues, and we'll start getting booked. We should talk about part-time staff. With three trailers, we're going to need regulars."

Georgiana nodded. "For some events we can pull from the pool of waitstaff in the area. When the drinks are simple, we don't need anyone who is a trained bartender. Not to pour wine or serve a premade cocktail."

"That's a good point. It would allow us to be flexible with our hiring."

"I agree," Drew said. "As long as we have a core group we can count on."

"I have some ideas," Georgiana told them. "Let me put a list together and I'll get it to you by tomorrow."

They set up a time to talk. Drew said he would have a formal job offer drawn up by then. Silver knew how much she was paying Georgiana now, on a per-event basis. She would have more responsibilities, which meant more pay. Plus, there would be taxes and insurance.

"She's going to be a great asset to us," he said. "You were right."

"You said that already."

"I know how you love hearing it over and

over again."

She sighed. "I do enjoy it very much. Maybe we could get a little wall hanging that says I'm always right."

"*Always* is stretching it. How about rarely right?"

"*Always*," she repeated.

"*Sometimes.*"

She thought about all the mistakes she'd made. Maybe "always" *was* pushing it. "I'll go with *sometimes.*"

"I'll go talk to Wynn about something for the wall."

As he and Silver had prearranged, Drew picked up Autumn after her day at the Learning Center. She raced out of the building right at two-thirty and headed for his car.

"You rescued me," she called. "I'm free, I'm free!" She flung her backpack into the backseat, then slid into the passenger seat and grinned at him. "What are we going to do? Go see Millie? Catch a movie? Why do people say catch a movie? Movies can't be caught."

"I have no idea," he admitted, charmed by her energy after a day of studying. "How was school?"

"Okay, I guess. You know, not as much

fun as *not* being in school. Although I like what I'm reading for English. It's *Little Women.* It's really old, like from a couple hundred years ago, but it's still good. We have to alternate between an old book and a new book."

"By an old book you mean a classic?"

She sighed heavily and fastened her seat belt. "Yes, Drew. A classic. You sound just like my mother."

"I'll take that as a compliment."

She grinned. "I guess it is, huh? Because my mom's the best. And Silver. And my dad and Denton and you. I guess I like all the adults in my life. Huh. That's nice." She turned to him. "So what are we going to do?"

He allowed himself a second of basking in the glow of being part of the adult company in her life, then let it go. "I thought we'd go visit your great-grandfather."

She frowned. "If he's my great-grandfather, then he's your grandfather?"

"That's him. I told him about you and he's really excited to meet you."

Her eyes widened. "I don't have any great-grandparents. I've always wanted them. Wow, that is so cool. He must be really, really old." Concern filled her eyes. "Is he like sick?"

"No. Grandpa Frank is healthy and strong. You're going to love him."

"A great-grandfather," she repeated as he drove toward the family home. "What about your parents? They would be my grandparents. Silver's mom is dead and she never knew her dad and she's an only child, so there isn't any family there." She grinned at him. "You're my last hope, Drew. No pressure."

"I can't produce family at will, so I'm not feeling a lot of pressure." There was the issue of his parents, but he had no idea how to handle that. He'd told Silver about taking Autumn to see Grandpa Frank and had said he would do his best to keep her away from his mom, but he'd never thought to discuss how on earth he was going to explain his parents to Autumn.

"My parents live in Washington, D.C.," he said, being factual while hedging on the truth. "I'm also an only child, but my mom is one of seven girls, so I'm guessing her sisters are your what? If they're my aunts, are they your great-aunts?"

"I don't know. We should look it up."

"We should. You could ask Grandpa Frank. He's a whiz on the computer."

She leaned back in her seat and sighed. "It's so nice when old people keep up with technology. I'm glad you know how to use a computer. We can do FaceTime and Skype and stuff when I go home. I do it with Silver all the time. Better than texting, but that's good, too, for quick stuff. But sometimes I want to show her things and a picture just isn't the same as seeing her."

He was still stalled on the assumption that he was old, although he supposed to an eleven-year-old, he was.

He drove up to the house, trying to see it through his daughter's eyes. It was large — three stories and four times as wide as it was high. There was a large flagstone porch that wrapped around the entire house and a huge circular driveway.

Autumn's mouth dropped open. "It's huge. It's way bigger than your house and I thought that was really big. Are you rich? Is your family rich?" She thought for a second. "You don't work *in* a bank, do you? You *own* a bank."

"My grandfather owns a bank. I'm just an employee. As for being rich, I'm not." He winked. "But Grandpa Frank is."

She laughed. "I wish I was seven. I could ask him for a pony."

"You still can."

"No way. What if he said yes? Mom would kill me. I'd like a kitten maybe. Or a rabbit.

I really liked Mr. Whiskers. He was so soft."

They got out of the car and walked up to the front door. Before he knocked, Drew glanced at Autumn.

"Just a heads-up. There are servants."

Her eyes widened. "No *way.*"

"Amelia runs the house. She's been with my grandfather for a long time and she's very kind and patient. She has a staff working under her. A couple of maids, two gardeners and a handyman."

Her mouth made a perfect O. "This is better than TV."

"I'm glad you think so."

He rang the doorbell. It only took a second for Amelia to answer, which had Drew wondering if she'd been hovering in the foyer.

"Mr. Drew," she said, her gaze on Autumn, her smile broad and welcoming. "How nice to see you. Come in, come in."

"Amelia, this is Autumn." He hesitated, not sure how to claim the relationship.

"Miss Autumn, it is a pleasure to meet you."

"Hi." Autumn grinned at her. "Drew said you were really nice and I can see you are. It's in your eyes." She looked at Drew. "Does she know? Am I allowed to say?"

"I'm not sure and yes."

Autumn turned back to Amelia. "I'm Drew's daughter with Silver. They gave me up for adoption when I was born. I live in Los Angeles with my mom, who was just here to get married to Denton. He's going to be my stepdad. My real dad remarried, too." She sighed. "It's a California thing."

Amelia laughed. "It sounds like it. If you'll come this way, your great-grandfather is very excited to meet you."

Autumn stepped close and lowered her voice. "He's not sick, is he?"

"No. Mr. Frank is very healthy. His new favorite sport is to go down a zip line." Amelia murmured something in Spanish and made the sign of the cross. "I worry Mr. Frank will hurt himself on his adventures, but he insists and I cannot stop him."

They went into Grandpa Frank's study. He was sitting behind his desk, but stood as they entered. Drew tried to see him as a stranger would and not as someone he'd known his entire life.

Grandpa Frank was a couple of inches shy of six feet, with tanned skin and blue eyes. He stood tall and had broad shoulders and a trim waist. He didn't look anywhere near his eighty-nine years and there was nothing the least bit feeble about his mental capacity. Drew was starting to think Grandpa

Frank was going to outlive them all.

"You must be Autumn," he said, walking around his desk and smiling at his great-granddaughter. "You're a pretty one, aren't you? I can see a lot of Drew in you, and a fair amount of Silver." He grinned at Autumn. "Drew's handsome enough but if I were a girl, I'd rather look like Silver."

Autumn laughed. "That's true. She's beautiful. I love her hair." She glared at Drew. "I did not inherit her blond hair, which I would have really liked."

He raised both hands. "I had nothing to do with that."

"You actually did. Your dark hair DNA overwhelmed hers. It's very sad." She turned back to Grandpa Frank. "Am I your only great-grandchild?"

"You are. I have one on the way, but not for a few more months. So you're the first."

"And the best," Autumn told him.

"Very much the best." He held out his hand. "Let's go to the kitchen and get something to eat. Then we'll take a tour of the house. There are some interesting things to see that I think you'll like, including a secret passage that leads to the attic."

"Really? That is so cool. A real secret passage? Our new house in LA is being built. I saw it when it was just framed and let me tell you, there are no secret passages."

Grandpa Frank chuckled. "Then you'll have to come back and use ours as often as you want."

Amelia went with them, no doubt to tempt Autumn with all kinds of treats. Drew would have to remember to warn Silver that Autumn was unlikely to be hungry for much dinner. He thought about joining them but instead decided to deal with what was likely to be an unpleasant conversation with his mother. While Grandpa Frank had been excited at the thought of an eleven-year-old great-granddaughter, he doubted his mother would be anything but annoyed to learn of her existence. She would see Autumn as standing in the way of what she thought of as his destiny.

For a second he toyed with the idea of not telling her about his daughter at all, but knew she would find out eventually. Better to learn the truth from him — in a situation where he could protect his daughter.

He went upstairs to the guest suite and knocked on the closed door. His mother opened it and stared at him.

"Drew. Did I know you were going to stop by?"

"No, and I hope that's all right."

"Of course it is," she said as she opened

the door and let him in. "I always enjoy your company."

The three-room guest suite was large and open, with lots of windows and high ceilings. There was a bedroom, a bathroom and a sitting room. Irene led him into the latter and motioned for him to take one of the chairs.

"Should I ring for coffee or tea?" she asked. "Although I should warn you, it will take hours. Honestly, I don't know why Dad keeps Amelia around. She does a terrible job."

"So you mentioned last time I was here. I've never found her anything but helpful."

"You only lived here as a teenager. I doubt your standards were much of a challenge for the staff."

Drew wanted to point out that the problem might be a lot more with his mother than with Amelia, but that wouldn't accomplish anything. More important, he needed to tell his mother about Autumn.

"I hope you appreciate what I'm doing for you," his mother continued as she took her seat. "Libby is still the biggest bitch on the planet. I can't figure out what's wrong with her. She's going to be trouble about the bank. You have to be prepared for that. Oh, and I've talked to a few friends and your father and I already have invitations to the party for the king and queen of El Bahar."

"I think the party is technically for Cade and Bethany," he said drily. "They are the ones getting married."

She waved her hand. "You know what I mean. Now we just need that private audience."

Drew told himself not to be distracted. "Mom, that's not why I wanted to talk to you. I have something important to tell you."

His mother's gaze flickered and he wondered if she already knew. Libby might have heard and she would have been delighted to spread the word.

"You remember Silver, Mom. You met her the other day."

His mother's look sharpened. "What does she have to do with anything?"

"We dated the summer before college. Silver got pregnant and we decided to give up the baby for adoption. Autumn is eleven now. Silver's stayed in touch with her and her family." He told himself that whatever his mother's issues were, she couldn't possibly turn her back on her grandchild.

"Mom, Autumn is here. In Happily Inc. In the house, actually. She's with Grandpa Frank. I know you won't want to meet her, but I thought you should know about her."

His mother's expression hardened. "Fine. And now you've told me." She pressed her lips together. "No wonder Libby's been in such a good mood the past few days. She must already know."

He waited, thinking she would want to say something else. Finally he asked, "Is that it? You don't want to know anything about her?"

"Why would I? She's not going to help you get ahead. You made a mistake when you were young. It happens." Her gaze turned speculative. "Actually it makes you seem very relatable, which we can use to our advantage. I assume you're covered legally."

"You mean did I sign all the right paperwork so Silver and our daughter can't come back and sue me or do something else to get in the way of my future?"

He'd been speaking sarcastically, but his mother didn't seem to notice that. "Exactly."

"It's taken care of."

"Excellent. Then we'll weather this storm and keep moving forward with our plan."

"She's not a storm. She's your granddaughter," he said. "Don't you have any curiosity about her?"

Irene's eyebrows drew together. "Why would I? She's nothing to me."

He and his mother had never been close, but he genuinely didn't understand her attitude.

"I couldn't disagree more," he said quietly. "She's rapidly becoming everything to me."

"It's that Silver person, isn't it? You're back together."

"We are, Mom, and it's worse than you think. You know what? I wasn't kidding before. We're working together and it's great. I like helping out with her business, improving processes and hiring people. It's different from banking. More personal. I've talked to Grandpa Frank about starting a venture capital company."

His mother went pale. "You mean him starting one. Not you. Oh, Drew, you couldn't. A venture capitalist? How does that make anything better? How does that get us where we want to go?"

"Where *you* want to go," he corrected. "Not me. Helping entrepreneurs is important work. Business drives our economy. Just think — we could fund the next Bill Gates."

"Tell me you're joking."

He *had* been messing with her, but the more he talked, the more he realized the idea appealed to him. Direct involvement was always preferable to being at a distance.

"I'm thinking about it," he said, realizing he wasn't actually lying.

"I don't want to hear about this," she told him. "I don't know why you're torturing me. Honestly, I work so hard for you."

He thought about his beautiful daughter, his mother's beautiful granddaughter, and all the time that had been lost. He thought about Silver and how she understood what was important.

He'd always known his parents were different, especially his mother. As he'd gotten older, he'd wondered if maybe he'd exaggerated their ruthlessness and their ambition, if the memories had been distorted. Now he understood the truth was the opposite — he hadn't remembered his mother as awful as she had been.

"I'm going to go," he told her. "I don't want to waste a minute of my time with Autumn. I wish . . ." He shook his head. "Never mind. You're right. She couldn't possibly help so why would you be interested in meeting her? If nothing else, Mom, you're exactly who you claim to be."

Jasper took the back way down the mountain. It was longer than the highway, which was what he wanted — time to clear his head. He'd been writing, putting in fourteen-hour days. Transitioning from his book to the real world was sometimes challenging and the drive helped.

He turned into a residential neighborhood relatively close to where Wynn lived. A quick glance at his car's clock told him it was late afternoon and Hunter would be out of school, so no quickie for him or Wynn.

He was still smiling at the thought of her when he saw Hunter riding his bike a little farther down the block. There was a girl about his age with him. Jasper didn't recognize her, but then he didn't know Hunter's friends.

He was about to drive by when he saw Hunter and the girl stop in front of a house with a For Sale sign. The kids got off their bikes and approached the sign. Without considering his actions, Jasper pulled over to watch.

Hunter pulled a small garden spade out of his back pocket and dug out the sign. Together he and the girl carried it across the street and down two houses before putting it in place there. Even from nearly a block away, Jasper could tell they were laughing. They got on the bikes and headed off.

"Damn," Jasper muttered as he picked up his phone.

Wynn answered on the first ring. "Hi, what's up?"

"There's a problem. Can you meet me?"

CHAPTER FIFTEEN

Silver still couldn't believe what Wynn and Jasper had told her. Even knowing the kids had come clean as soon as they'd been confronted wasn't much of a comfort. Autumn had been involved in something that was, if not technically illegal, really wrong. Worse, she'd admitted it had been her idea!

"You have to say something," Autumn announced from the passenger seat. "Just yell at me and you'll feel better."

Silver waited until they were at a stoplight to turn to her. "Do you think this is funny?"

"No, but it's not like it's really bad. We didn't steal anything or break anything. It was just a joke on five or six houses."

Silver drove through the intersection, then turned on her street. After pulling into her parking space in the alley, she shut off the engine and faced Autumn.

"You think it's that simple? What about

the signs, Autumn? You don't remember where they go. Right this second, Jasper and Wynn are taking Hunter door to door, trying to figure out who had their house for sale."

Silver had wanted to stay and have Autumn help, but Wynn had insisted Hunter explain to the people what he'd done by himself. Silver had been so stunned by the events that she'd agreed without thinking.

"You should be helping them," she said. "You should have to explain to these people why you thought messing with their property was a good idea."

Autumn sighed.

"You don't get it, do you?" Silver told her. "What if some family is desperate to sell because they need the money, or their mom or dad got transferred for work, but because of you they miss the one person who would have bought their house? What about the person who's going to have strangers knocking on their door and not know why? What if someone's home sick and they have to deal with all that? This isn't about you. This is about other people. I can't believe you were so thoughtless and selfish. I can't believe you came up with this idea."

Autumn's face paled and her lower lip trembled. "Some kids did it back home. I thought it was funny."

"Maybe to you, but not to anyone else. I have to tell you, I'm shocked that you're capable of acting like this. You knew it was wrong and you did it anyway. I never thought you were like that. I guess your mom doesn't tell me everything."

Autumn's eyes filled with tears. She scrambled out of the truck. "Silver, no! Don't say that. I didn't think it was a big deal. I was wrong. I'm sorry. I'm really sorry." Tears spilled down her cheeks. "Don't be mad at me. Please. I'll do anything."

"It's not being mad," Silver told her quietly. "It's being disappointed by your behavior."

Autumn started to cry harder. Silver ignored her and got the bike out of the back of her truck. She took it into the downstairs storage room, then headed upstairs. Still sobbing, Autumn followed.

When they were in the loft, Silver turned to her. "You won't be riding your bike anymore with Hunter and I'm taking your phone away for forty-eight hours. You can talk to your mom on my phone."

"That's too much! You're not being fair. You can't do that."

Autumn raced to the bathroom and

slammed the door. Silver shook her head, then opened Autumn's backpack and took out the phone. She went downstairs and put it in the small safe in her office, then called Leigh.

"Hi, you," her friend said. "I'm on a beach in Hawaii. What are you doing?"

"Questioning my parenting skills."

Leigh sighed. "Tell me what she did."

Silver explained what had happened. "I put her phone in my work safe. Is that all right? Is forty-eight hours too long?"

"No. You did the right thing. I can't believe she did that. It's horrible and thoughtless."

"I shouldn't have let her go bike riding with Hunter."

"Don't blame yourself. I love that she had the chance to do that. Our neighborhood at home is safe, but we're so close to some busy streets, I never let her go by herself. She got a taste of freedom, and then totally messed up. It happens. Now she'll deal with the consequences. Silver, you were right to do what you did. She's going to pout for a while, and then she'll be fine. Autumn is a pretty reasonable kid."

"I hope you're right."

Leigh chuckled. "I nearly always am. Now, how is everything else?"

"Good. Autumn met her great-grandfather yesterday. That was fun for her."

"Any Drew news?"

"No. It's not like that."

"Too bad, because you two make beautiful babies. Anything else?"

"That's it. Thanks for listening and have a good rest of your honeymoon."

"Will do and I'll call Autumn on your phone tonight. Bye."

Silver ended the call, then went upstairs. About five minutes later, Autumn came out of the bathroom. She'd washed her face, but was still a little weepy-looking.

"Did you call my mom?" she asked.

"I did."

"Is she mad?"

"She's sorry you were so disrespectful of your privileges here and hopes you've learned your lesson."

Autumn drew in a breath. "Okay. I finished all my homework already."

"Good. Then you can help me with dinner. We have our movies for tonight." Drew wouldn't be by. He was giving them a girls' night together, which she appreciated. He would have Autumn to himself the evening she had her first bachelorette party in the space downstairs.

Autumn surprised her by rushing toward

her and hugging her. "I really am sorry," she said as she hung on. "I'm going to work really hard to learn my lesson."

"Good." Silver hugged her back. "I love you, Autumn."

"Even when I mess up?"

"Especially then."

"I love you, too. Even when you take my phone away."

Silver laughed. "Good to know."

"Most people go grab a sandwich at lunch," Silver said as she watched Drew set up the bar. He'd told her he'd been working on his skills and wanted to show off for her on his lunch hour. She'd filled old liquor bottles with water, using food coloring to make the whiskey bottle contents brown. The mixers were real, mostly because they were inexpensive to replace.

"I'm going to dazzle you," he promised. "You'll be so impressed you'll want me at your bachelorette party tomorrow night."

"That's not happening. It's the first party in this space and I don't care how good you are, I'll be bartending." She softened her words with a smile. "Having said that, I could use a little dazzling."

She'd already told him what had happened with Autumn. After their daughter had gone to bed the previous evening, Silver had called Drew and brought him up to date on the entire afternoon.

"You still upset?" he asked.

"A little. More than a little, I guess. I don't ever have to deal with the real parenting stuff with her. I've always been the fun weekend parent and I like it that way. Leigh does a great job with her. I've always been happy on the sidelines."

"Is this the most time you've spent with her?"

Silver nodded. "I've done a couple of long weekends, but Leigh was never the kind of mom who wanted to get away from her daughter for a week. This is different — it's her honeymoon."

She thought about how the evening had gone. Autumn hadn't fussed at the loss of her phone and when she'd spoken to her mom, she'd come clean on what had happened.

"This was relatively easy," Silver said. "She didn't hurt anyone. The signs got put back in place. She's lost her bike privileges, so she won't spend much time with Hunter. I think she learned her lesson, but I'm still in shock that she was the instigator."

"We weren't perfect kids."

"That was different. It was us, not her."

Silver sank onto a chair as Drew cut up lemons, limes and oranges. "It makes me question myself. I wanted to punish her, but when it came to doing it, I felt awful."

"I think that's how it's supposed to go. I think you're supposed to feel bad. If you enjoy it, there's something wrong with you."

She smiled. "You shock me with your insights."

"Then my work here is done." He looked at her. "I told my mom about her."

Silver sat up straight. "I knew she'd met Grandpa Frank, but not . . ." She couldn't begin to imagine Irene embracing such living proof of a teenage mistake. "How did it go?"

"She didn't take the news very well."

"I'm sorry. Let me guess — she assumes everybody wants something and she reminded you to think about your future."

He hesitated just long enough for her to know the conversation had been more awful and uncomfortable than she could imagine.

"That and more," he admitted. "I don't get it. Autumn is her granddaughter. Why doesn't that mean something to her? Why is she so heartless? It's as if she and Libby are from a completely different family or something. Grandpa Frank is a sweet old man. I can't see him as some ruthless jerk when he was young, so what's up with those two?"

"I honestly have no idea why they're like that." Silver remembered being friends with Pallas in high school. Even then, Libby had been difficult, always finding fault in her daughter.

"For what it's worth, I don't think my parents would have been a whole lot more interested," she admitted. "My dad took off before I was born, so it's not like he was a kid person and my mom would only care if she could use Autumn to get a guy."

"You never talk about your parents."

"There isn't much to say. My mom lived to fall in love. She went from man to man, falling madly, wildly in love and living the dream until it all fell apart. Then she would be on a quest to find the next one and the next one. She would drag me with her from place to place. It was a nightmare."

"Is that why you never left Happily Inc?"

"What do you mean?"

"After Autumn was born you could have gone anywhere, but you stayed here. When you sold the bar, you could have taken the money and gone somewhere else. Instead you stayed here and started AlcoHaul."

"Leigh asked me the same thing." She shrugged. "I never wanted to wander the world. I didn't like it as a kid and I sure wouldn't like it now. This is my home. I like to think I belong here."

"You do."

Did she also belong with him?

That question had been whispering to her lately and she didn't know how to answer it. Saying no made the most sense. Yes, they enjoyed each other's company and the sex was great, but how could they know if any of it was real? Having Autumn around created a false sense of family. The business was all shiny and new. Once Autumn went back to Los Angeles and they got in a routine with the trailers, she wondered what would happen. Did they want to keep what they had and build on it or would they drift apart?

The thought of not having him around so much made her uncomfortable, but she wasn't sure why. As sure as she was that she would stay, she was equally confident Drew would one day leave. Happily Inc wasn't big enough for the likes of him. Even if he didn't completely follow his parents' path for his future, he had to be intrigued by the promise of money and power. World influence was heady stuff. She figured he would stay for a couple of years as the head of the bank, then head off for D.C. or maybe New York or somewhere in Europe.

When that happened, she knew he would offer to let her buy him out over time. Or maybe he would stay a silent partner in the business. Either way, he would be gone.

"You ready?" he asked, drawing her back to the present.

"Let's see what you got. We'll start easy. How about a classic old-fashioned?"

He'd set up the bar himself. He had garnishes, different kinds of glasses, mixers, a large bowl of ice, martini shakers and behind him, water-filled liquor bottles.

Drew dropped a sugar cube into a highball glass and added a couple of dashes of angostura bitters. He added a splash of club soda, then muddled everything together. He rotated the glass to coat the bottom and the first half inch or so of the sides with the mixture.

Silver was impressed. He didn't work fast, but he knew what he was doing. He added a couple of ice cubes, then poured in the bourbon.

She'd given him a couple of her pours to practice with at home. She'd been using them for years and could measure the right amount of liquor in her sleep. Each of the bottles of faux liquor had the same style of pours pushed into them. She knew the count, knew how much liquor he should be pouring and nearly came out of her seat when she realized he'd overpoured by half.

"Okay," she said slowly. "You're not using a shot glass which tells me you've been practicing your pours."

"I have." He sounded smug. "I did what you said. I filled an empty vodka bottle with water and got a shot glass with a line that marked an ounce. It took a bit, but I can pour that amount perfectly."

Or so he thought.

Just to be sure, she said, "Make me a dry martini. With a twist."

"Gin or vodka?"

"Gin."

He put ice into the shaker, poured in what she was pretty sure he thought was two and a half ounces of gin, then a half ounce of vermouth, followed by a dash of angostura bitters. He put the top on the shaker and shook it several times before pouring it into a martini glass. He added a twist of lemon peel to the edge of the glass.

"Next?"

"I'll be right back," she said, coming to her feet. "Give me five seconds."

She ran upstairs and let herself into her apartment. After rummaging through a kitchen drawer, she found a measuring spoon. When she was back in the bar, she held it out to Drew.

"You know a pour equals one ounce, right?"

"Yes. An ounce." He frowned. "Silver, I used a shot glass to make sure I had it right."

"I'm sure you did. The thing is a shot glass from a liquor store can be one ounce or it can be an ounce and a half. They don't always say and if you aren't familiar with the difference and you don't check . . ."

His shoulders fell a little. "You're saying I used the wrong one? How could you tell?"

"I watched you making drinks. I know how long it takes to pour an ounce. You did more than that. Not only will we go through too much liquor, everyone will be drunker than expected and the drinks themselves will be off." She nodded at an old-fashioned glass. "Pour me an ounce."

He did as she requested. When he was done, she handed him the spoon.

"Measure it back out."

He measured out two tablespoons. There was still liquid in the bottom of the glass.

"Damn," he muttered. "I spent hours learning that pour."

"Do you use a count?"

"Yes."

"So all you have to do is figure out what the real count is. It won't take that long for you to change it."

"I feel ridiculous."

She smiled. "You worked really hard. You know your drinks. That's impressive. You'll get this, too."

"I still can't believe you figured it out just by watching me make two drinks." He eyed her. "You knew on the old-fashioned, didn't you? You just wanted to be sure."

"It's my business, Drew. I've been doing this for a while. I have expertise."

"I can't believe I got the pour wrong. So much for dazzling you."

"I'm still dazzled. Just by other things."

Drew returned to the bank around one-thirty. He couldn't believe he'd messed up his pour, but he would fix it. Practicing the drinks had been fun and he was looking forward to being a regular member of the team. With his bank job filling his week, he would only help out a couple of times a month, but it would be an interesting change.

He sat through a meeting on banking regulations and met with a client before retreating to his office to clear his emails. Tomorrow he was spending the evening with Autumn while Silver hosted her first ever bachelorette party in the space downstairs. He'd had to figure out what he was making for dinner. Ordering in pizza seemed too predictable.

He had a great chicken enchilada recipe he could put together tonight, and then bake at her place. If he didn't make it too spicy, he was sure Autumn would like it. Maybe that with chips and salsa and a salad. He wanted something fun for dessert. He called the local bakery to see if he could pick up a dozen unfrosted cupcakes. He and Autumn could frost them together. He would grab tubes of frosting when he went to the grocery store to buy what he needed for the rest of the dinner.

"You're looking pleased about something," Libby said from the doorway to his office. "I'm glad. I was worried about you for a while."

Drew looked at his aunt. He'd always gotten along with her, even when he'd been a kid. He sensed he wasn't her favorite, but she made an effort. She'd resented him coming to work at the bank, but had recovered and from his point of view, they had a decent business relationship. Now he wondered how much of that was because he was considered the heir apparent at the bank. There was a better than even chance that she could be reporting to him in a matter of weeks.

"May I?" Libby asked as she walked in and took one of the chairs. She touched her pearl necklace. "I see you and Silver are back together. That's nice. I was afraid it was just a short-term thing, but it seems to be lasting." She gave him a smile that seemed more terrorizing than friendly. "I remember when you two were together that summer so many years ago. And to think you had a child and no one knew."

So much for playing nice, he thought as he leaned back in his chair. "My mother knows about Autumn," he said mildly. "In case you were wondering."

"Is that her name? I've seen her around town. She's a lovely girl. She seems very sweet. Your grandfather was very smitten by her."

"I'm glad. She's his first great-grandchild."

Libby's gaze was sharp. "I suppose technically that's true. Although she isn't a legitimate child, is she?"

Tension gripped him but he ignored the need to get in her face. "Are you calling my daughter a bastard?"

"Of course not. Drew, what an ugly thing to imply."

"I didn't imply it. I asked the question. Libby, let me be clear. Think what you want, do what you want, but stay far, far away from Autumn. If you try to upset her or say bad things about her, I will take you down."

Her eyes widened. "That's unnecessarily threatening."

"Maybe so, but I mean it, Libby. She's my daughter and I will stand between her and anyone who threatens her."

Color stained her cheeks. "Well, I never. You're acting like some deranged animal."

"And here I thought we were just having a conversation."

"Not anymore."

She rose and left. He watched her go, wondering if there was any way she was working with his mother to somehow screw with his life. As soon as the thought formed, he dismissed it. His mother wouldn't trust Libby with something as important as his future. Which meant his aunt had an agenda all her own. The concept was not the least bit comforting.

CHAPTER SIXTEEN

Silver couldn't remember the last time she'd been so nervous about an event. She'd handled much larger parties — Bethany and Cade's "we're getting married" shindig was going to be huge, but she was only mildly concerned about that one. The bachelorette party was only twelve women. What was the big deal?

Georgiana arrived right on time. Silver had already done most of the prep work, setting out glasses and bottles, getting the ice machine cranking and giving the space a last-minute polish. Georgiana greeted her and got right to work chopping up garnishes.

"This is going to be so fun," she said as she worked. "You and Drew did a great job with the space. I love the stripper poles. Are they bringing in an instructor tonight? I really want to see them in action."

Silver grinned. "I don't think the poles are

supposed to move."

Georgiana rolled her eyes. "You know what I mean."

"I do, and yes, bride-to-be Jessica said she was bringing in someone to teach pole dancing."

Georgiana looked over the drink list and grimaced. "Don't these girls know the more sugar in the drink, the worse the hangover?"

"The theme is forever love and the party is supposed to be all things sweet."

"Still, chocolate vodka shots and cotton candy champagne? What's wrong with a nice Cosmo or a lemon drop?"

"It's their party."

"And they can barf if they want to?" Georgiana looked around. "Oh good. The way to the bathroom is clearly marked. Because you know they're going to be throwing up later."

"I really hope not. The strawberry Jell-O shots aren't too sweet." The vodka–Jell-O mixture had been poured into actual strawberries that had been hollowed out. Silver wasn't sure if the addition of fruit was going to help or hurt.

Silver was prepared for a long night. Drew was going to stay with Autumn until Silver was done downstairs. Not only would he provide company for Autumn, he would let her know if they'd done enough sound-proofing.

The bridesmaids began arriving a little after six. They were all pretty and dressed in cute flirty dresses and heels. Silver tried to put names to faces but they were a blur of Tiffanys and Chelseas. She made sure she knew who Brittany was. As the maid of honor, Brittany was making all the decisions.

"This space turned out fabulously," the busty redhead said. "We're super excited." She pointed to the boxes the other women had carried in. "We'll just get our banners in place. Tiff is bringing the balloon bouquets."

Silver stared as several banners proclaiming One Penis Forever followed by a sad face emoji were fastened to the wall.

"Did the theme change?" she asked casually.

"Uh-huh. The forever love theme was just too cute, although we are definitely keeping the drinks and the food. We're just mixing things up. Oh, and don't worry about us getting drunk. Limos are coming at eleven. Then we're going out on the town."

At least once they left, they weren't her problem, she thought with a smile.

More decorations went up. There was a

mug shot station which Silver hoped wasn't tempting fate too much, along with posters of naked men with massive erections. White plastic first aid boxes had been relabeled as Hangover Kits.

"They're going to need those," Georgiana murmured as she walked to the bar.

Just before seven, the rest of the women arrived. Jessica, the pretty blonde bride, wore a short white sundress and nothing but a thong underneath. When Jessica bent over to drop her handbag on the floor, Silver got a view of way more than she'd bargained for. It was going to be one of those nights.

By seven-thirty, all the women were on their third drink. By eight, when the pole dance instructor arrived, they were definitely drunk.

Adam was tall and male with muscles for miles. After setting up a pair of speakers and plugging them in, he turned to the group.

"Let me be clear," he said cheerfully. "You are not the team I play for, so don't bother coming on to me. Having said that, enjoy the show."

Before Silver could figure out what he meant, he stripped down to a tiny thong that barely contained his, um, assets. He was tanned, muscled and five kinds of gorgeous, and the bridesmaids looked at him like hungry sharks at a surfing convention.

He set his phone in the docking station for the speakers. Instantly music began to pound. The girls shrieked and raced to poles.

"We're going to start with a few stretches," Adam said, winking at them as he shouted over the music. "I don't want you to be sore tomorrow morning, at least not for the wrong reasons."

Everyone laughed. Silver looked at Georgiana, who rolled her eyes. The music was incredibly loud. At least the soundproofing would get a big test.

Adam took them through basic moves. They started with the wraparound, then moved to easy climbing. More than one of the bridesmaids slipped to the ground. Two of them abandoned the lesson and started making out in a corner. Silver fought the beginnings of a headache.

While the girls continued with their lesson, she and Georgiana brought out the food. It was all appetizers.

"There's a lot of salt here," Georgiana murmured. "They're going to be hungover and puffy and hungry. Of course they'll be throwing up so they probably won't notice being hungry. This is a bad plan. What were they thinking?"

"I just want this party over," Silver told her. "Only two more hours."

Adam finished his lesson, then joined the women on the sofas. Everyone had another round, but they were eating, too. Which was something, Silver supposed.

Her sense of being slightly out of control faded a little as time went on. Adam finished his drink, dressed and left. Silver put on her own music, at a slightly lower volume. The women continued to drink, but they were chowing down on the appetizers and seemed to sober up just a little. Just as they were settling down to open presents, a guy walked in.

He looked nothing like Adam. He was of average height and attractive in an ordinary way. He wore jeans and a T-shirt. But what actually caught Silver's attention was the stricken look on his face. This was not a groom jokingly crashing his bride's bachelorette party — this was a guy with really bad news.

"Turn down the music," Silver told Georgiana. "They're going to have to be able to talk."

"Who has to talk about what?" Georgiana spotted the guy. "Oh, that's not good."

"I agree."

They both watched anxiously as the man approached Jessica. She looked up and saw him.

"Tyler! Hi! Were we expecting you?" She rose unsteadily to her feet. "Everyone, this is Tyler. He's my baby brother."

Brittany rolled her eyes. "Jess, we've known Tyler forever. Everyone here knows Tyler."

"Oh right." Jessica plopped back on a sofa and patted the seat next to her. "You're here! That's so great. You should have a drink. They're wonderful. We're having such a good time. I love you, Tyler."

Her brother sat next to her and took her hand in his. Tears filled his eyes. Actual tears. Silver braced herself for whatever was going to happen next. She knew it was ridiculous, but there was a voice in her head warning her it was going to be bad.

Tyler swallowed. "Jess, I love you so much and I'm so sorry." He brushed away more tears. "God, I don't know how to say this. Jess, Dominic slept with Mom."

The room went quiet except for the pounding beat of the music. Georgiana reached over and turned off the speakers, making the silence complete. The bridesmaids looked at each other, then at Jessica. Jessica stared at her brother.

"What?"

"Mom and Dominic. I walked in on them together at the hotel. I'm sorry, Jess. I didn't know what to do. I've been driving around, but then I came here. I had to tell you. Please, let me know I did the right thing."

His anguish was palpable. Silver's stomach twisted as she thought about the nightmare that had just been unleashed. There was no recovering from the groom sleeping with the bride's mother. The wedding hadn't just been destroyed — an entire family was ripped apart.

Jessica sprang to her feet. "My mom slept with Dominic?" Her voice was a shriek. "My *mother* and Dominic?"

Everyone started moving back. Silver had no idea what they were doing until Jessica reached down, grabbed a champagne glass and threw it against the wall. Glass and liquid went everywhere. The bridesmaids either ducked or ran for the door. Jessica bent down and overturned the coffee table, sending presents and food flying. She grabbed another drink and threw it. Tyler ducked as it sailed past his head.

"That bastard!" Jessica screamed. "I will kill him."

Silver walked up to her and got in her face. "You need to calm down. I understand you're pissed, but don't take it out on my place."

"Bitch!" Jessica screamed. "I hate that bitch. I hate them all."

She pushed Silver out of the way and began throwing packages. She ripped the banners off the wall. Silver was reaching for her phone when she saw Georgiana was already on hers. The local police were used to unruly wedding parties. They came fast and they knew how to handle a crowd.

In the five minutes it took the three police cars to arrive, Jessica chased two of her bridesmaids with a champagne bottle, destroyed all of her presents, smashed three more glasses and ran right into one of the stripper poles. She staggered around for a couple of seconds, her hand over her left eye.

"That's going to leave a mark," Georgiana said from behind the bar, where she and Silver had taken refuge.

Silver stayed put until the police arrived, then she walked out and met the officers.

It took nearly an hour to get everything sorted out. Tyler did most of the talking while Jessica held an ice pack on her eye. All the bridesmaids had taken off, leaving only maid of honor Brittany to remain by Jessica's side. Partway through the explanation, Dominic arrived. He was a big, line-backer kind of guy, who rushed toward Jessica.

"Baby, what's going on?" he asked, trying to reach for her.

"Don't you 'baby' me, you asshole," Jessica screamed. "You slept with my mother."

Dominic's look of shock and guilt only confirmed the ugly truth. Tyler shocked Silver by punching the much-bigger guy right in the nose. Blood went everywhere and Dominic screamed like a little girl.

One of the officers approached. Garrick was six years older than Silver so they hadn't been in school together, but he'd lived next door to her uncle. She'd known him for years. She'd had a bit of a crush on him the year she'd moved to Happily Inc, but at twenty-one the last thing he'd been interested in was his fifteen-year-old neighbor.

"You two okay?" Garrick asked.

Silver nodded. "Obviously Jessica will not be getting her security deposit back."

"Wasn't this your launch party?"

Silver sighed. "It was."

"You might want to rethink hosting bachelorette parties. I'm just saying."

"Thanks for the advice."

Garrick nodded toward the open door.

"Come on. Let's go take pictures and document this whole thing in case you decide to press charges."

Press charges? Why would she . . .

Silver followed Garrick inside, Georgiana trailing behind. They all came to a stop when they saw the damage.

While it had been happening, Silver hadn't had the chance to absorb the reality of the destruction. Now she saw the broken glass, the overturned and smashed tables, food everywhere. Her heart sank. She and Drew had put so much time and money into the place. They'd had such high hopes. She was sure a good cleaning would make everything look better, but still.

Georgiana hugged her. "I'm sorry," she said. "I thought the parties were a good idea, too."

"Not every party ends this way," Garrick said. "I'm sorry, Silver. This is a mess."

She honestly didn't know what to say. She stood back while Garrick took pictures. When he was done, he told her to call him if she wanted to make a statement.

He handed her his business card, then nodded at Georgiana and left. Silver stood there, not sure what to think.

"It's a big mess," Georgiana said. "But I'm not sure there's actually that much damage. Glasses, a couple of the tables. The carpet will need cleaning. What's the security deposit?"

"Five hundred dollars."

"Oh, I don't know if that will cover everything, but it should be close."

Silver hoped so. Telling herself things looked worse than they were was all fine, but she was still shaken. No, she thought as she pressed a hand to her stomach. She felt violated. She had business insurance to cover any large damages and as Garrick had suggested, she would press charges, but was that enough to make her feel better about what had happened? Who did this sort of thing? It was supposed to be a fun party.

She glanced at the card Garrick had given her and realized he'd handed her two. One was his, with his direct line. The second card was for a cleaning service that handled *unexpected emergencies,* according to the information on the card.

She had a brief vision of a gory crime scene and shuddered. At least she wasn't dealing with anything like that. But still . . .

She sent Georgiana home, then locked the doors before going upstairs. She found Drew on the sofa, reading. Autumn was sound asleep in bed. Silver went to check on her, then returned to the living area.

Drew smiled at her.

"How did it go? Was it a great party?"

She stared at him. "You didn't hear any of that?"

"Any of what?"

She motioned for him to follow her outside, onto the landing. They sat next to each other on the top of the stairs.

"You didn't hear the party?"

"No, not the music or anything." He stared at her. "What happened?"

"A bride went crazy."

Silver explained how the party had started out and how she'd totally misjudged the crowd. She told him about the pole dancing, the drinking, the arrival of the bride's brother and the revelation that followed.

"One second we were all in shock and the next, she went totally insane. Georgiana called the police. They were out in five minutes and handled everything."

Drew stood and went downstairs. Silver followed. He unlocked the door and flipped on the lights.

Seeing the damage after a little break was actually worse, she thought. It was such a kick in the gut. Their beautiful space was in ruins.

"Be careful of the glass," she said, pointing to the shards on the floor. "She shattered a dozen or so glasses. She might have broken a champagne bottle or two, as well. I'm not sure."

Drew turned and pulled her close. "I'm sorry you went through all that by yourself."

"I didn't. Georgiana was with me." She hung on to him. "I never expected anything like this to happen. With AlcoHaul, it's different. I'm pretty removed from the actual party. I know Pallas has had to deal with some rowdy revelers, but nothing like this. I know in my head not every bachelorette party ends like this, but still, it sucks."

She reached in her back pocket and pulled out the business card. "Garrick gave me the number of a cleaning service," she added. "This is going to be a big job. No dead bodies, but still a mess."

"Give me the card," Drew told her. "I'll leave a message tonight and get with them in the morning. I'll arrange to have this place cleaned, then we'll assess."

"Assess what?"

"What we want to do. If we're going to rent out the space, we need better ground rules and larger deposits. If this is going to happen, we have to figure out if it's worth it or if we should rent out the space to someone else. That's still an income stream."

His words surprised her for a second, then

she sighed. "You're right. We have to talk about it but not tonight."

"You going to be okay?" he asked. "Want me to stay? I can sleep on the floor."

"I'll be fine," she told him. "I was shaken up, but I'm all right now. Thanks for looking after Autumn. Did you have a good time?"

"We did. We've graduated to chess. She's just learning but she's going to be really good. Dinner was fun and we didn't hear anything from downstairs." He kissed her. "Come on. I'll walk you to your door."

She smiled. "That's so romantic."

"I know. Face it, Silver. I'm irresistible."

As promised, he walked her upstairs, kissed her again and left. She went inside and collapsed on the sofa. She told herself she had to get up and wash her face and brush her teeth. *In a minute,* she thought, her eyes closing. For right now, she wanted to think about Drew because he was a much-nicer topic than remembering her horrible night. As for him being irresistible, she happened to know he was right.

Drew sat with Autumn on the back patio of his house. They watched as Millie and her friends walked around the animal preserve.

"You have the best view ever," his daughter told him. "I know everyone always wants to look at the ocean or a lake, but this is way cooler. Don't you dare move. I want to come back and sit right here next time I visit."

"I want that, too," he told her.

Autumn's time in Happily Inc was over. In a couple of hours, Leigh and Denton would arrive to take her back to Los Angeles. He couldn't believe how quickly the week had sped by.

Less than two weeks ago, Autumn had been little more than a theory. Now he knew her laugh, her smile, how she rolled her eyes when she thought an adult was being stupid. He knew she was smart and irreverent and caring and funny. He knew *her* and he was going to miss her more than he'd ever thought possible.

"Are you and Silver going to get married?" Autumn asked, glancing at him. "And don't tell me you aren't dating because you totally are. I've seen how you look at her."

"When did you grow up?"

"That's not an answer."

He was mentally scrambling for what to say. He and Silver were together, but neither of them had defined their relationship, probably because neither of them wanted to. A definition would box them in. They were in business together and sleeping together and he liked her a lot. For now that was enough.

"She's great," he began.

She sighed. "Boys are so lame."

"What's wrong with thinking she's great?"

Autumn looked at him. "I'm only eleven and even I get it. If you're not going to marry her, you need to find someone. Men don't do well alone. You need a life partner. I had to read a bunch of articles for my health class and one of the ones talked about that."

She was a constant surprise, he thought with a smile. As for getting married, while he was perfectly fine single, he'd always assumed he would find someone and settle down. Ashley Lauren had put him off commitments for a while, but he'd recovered and now . . . And now . . .

He realized he honestly had no idea why he wasn't involved with someone and falling in love. He enjoyed women. He liked being in a relationship. Look how well he and Silver got along. It had been great when they'd been kids, but in some ways, it was even better now. They were older and they could appreciate what they had.

"You could start with a dog," Autumn told him. "You took care of Mr. Whiskers, so a dog would be good. Once you can manage that, you can look for a wife."

"I'm not feeble," he grumbled.

Autumn smiled. "Mom and Denton said we could get a dog when we get settled in the new house. Not a puppy, though. I want a rescue dog. One that's older. I want to make a difference, which is really hard when you're eleven." She sighed. "I'm sorry about the real estate signs. The more I think about it, the worse I feel. I need to be more mature."

"You're pretty mature now."

"I'm trying."

"I'm going to miss you."

"I'll miss you, too, but we can text and talk on FaceTime and stuff. Plus, you can come visit me whenever you want."

"I'd like that." He was hoping that Leigh and Denton would want to leave her here more often and go off on vacation. Or maybe he and Silver could have her for a couple of weeks in the summer.

He wasn't sure how that was going to work, but he wanted to give it a try. He'd just found Autumn — he didn't want to let her go now. He would, of course, but he didn't want to.

CHAPTER SEVENTEEN

Silver did her best to rally. Walter had texted to say the smaller trailer remodel was going more quickly than he'd anticipated, which meant their labor costs would be reduced. The cleaning company had been able to come out the morning after the party and had worked a miracle. The damage was less than Silver had first thought. The bride had blown through the security deposit, but not by much. The weddings over the weekend had been low-key events with no drama at all, so why was she feeling so incredibly sad?

The answer was simple — she missed Autumn. Three days after Leigh had picked her up and taken her home, Silver's apartment was empty and her days seemed long. She usually felt unsettled when she returned home from visiting Autumn, but this time was worse. Probably because getting back into her routine didn't help. Autumn had been here, in her life, and that made it harder to stop missing her.

On the bright side, she and Drew had done well together with their daughter. Autumn had had a good time, they'd all gotten along. The only problem had been with the real estate signs, but even that had turned out okay. Autumn had admitted that she felt awful several days later and promised to think the next time she wanted to pull a prank.

As Silver stocked the trailer for the upcoming weekend, she told herself to be grateful for the week and move on. That playing the "what if" game didn't help anyone, especially not her. She couldn't go back in time and even if she could, she knew she wouldn't change anything.

She had a feeling Drew would disagree with that. He'd taken Autumn's leaving much harder than she would have thought. Of course, hanging out with Autumn was new for him, and so was the pain of letting her go.

He'd been restless the past couple of days. Almost on edge. She wondered if he was thinking about the past or wondering about the future. She'd found herself doing a lot of the latter since Autumn had left. The future with and without Drew.

The problem was she couldn't figure out

what was going to happen. Was he really going to take over the bank and stay here in Happily Inc?

She finished loading mixers and liquor. She wanted to get the trailer ready before she had to leave for a meeting about Bethany and Cade's big event. That was coming up fast. The cute Bride's Posse T-shirts had been delivered. They'd all decided to wear them with blue denim skirts that were similar to Bethany's white denim skirt. Pallas had been nervous that she was too pregnant to buy one that fit, but had found the cutest skirt with a tiny stretch panel for her growing tummy. Carol was several weeks less pregnant, so her shopping hadn't been so challenging. Silver had dug a denim skirt out of her closet.

She was looking forward to the party. It wasn't every day a regular person like her got to hang out with royalty. She had no idea what Bethany's parents were like, but based on Bethany herself, she would guess they were pretty cool.

Silver had just finished the second trailer when an unfamiliar car pulled up by the open gate to the parking area where she stored the trailers. The car door opened and Silver's stomach sank as Drew's mother stepped out. Silver looked around desperately for an escape route. Before she could find one, Irene was approaching and there was nothing to do but smile as graciously as she could.

"Mrs. Lovato. This is a surprise."

Irene, well dressed and well preserved, looked her over. "Yes, I would imagine it is. I want to talk to you about my son."

Silver instantly flashed on the scene from the A&E version of *Pride and Prejudice* — the one where Lady Catherine de Bourgh told off Lizzie for being involved with Mr. Darcy. She hoped this conversation went just a little better.

"All right," she said slowly, telling herself that regardless of the assault, she could more than handle herself.

"Drew is going to be taking over the bank from his grandfather," Irene began. "Do you know this?"

"Of course. He loves working at the bank." She smiled. "I suppose they're well suited for each other."

Irene waved her hand as if dismissing the humor. "It's all but done. I'm sure Libby will make a run at it but no one wants to work for her. No, it will be Drew." Her expression softened. "He's such a wonderful man. Warm and caring, intelligent. He understands people."

Silver sensed a trap, but she couldn't see it. "Okay," she said slowly.

"He has a wonderful future ahead of him. He could go anywhere, do anything. Opportunities are just waiting for him. His father and I have connections all over the world. We know people. People in power. People with money. Drew was meant for more than this ridiculous little town."

"Then he should take advantage of what you're offering," she said, not sure of the other woman's point.

"Unfortunately, Drew has an oversize sense of responsibility. His default position is to take care of someone else, rather than himself."

Silver wanted to say that was a good thing, but she suddenly realized where Irene was going.

"You think I'm standing in the way." Silver shook her head. "It's not like that between us." She didn't know what it was, exactly, but she knew that there was no permanent commitment. If Drew wanted to leave, he would.

Irene's expression turned calculating. "I would believe you except you have a child together and doesn't that change everything?"

"Autumn is eleven. She has parents.

Whatever Drew and I are to her, they come first. They always have. It's how we wanted it."

As she spoke, she felt something odd in her chest — something she couldn't define. It wasn't a pain, exactly. More of a certainty about . . . She pushed the feeling away.

"I've never used Autumn to trap Drew," she said firmly. "Not back when I was pregnant and not now. I don't know what hold you think I have over Drew, but you're wrong. Any problems you have with him are of your own making."

Irene motioned to the trailers. "Really? This isn't you trapping him? This isn't you trying to seduce him into thinking this tiny world is enough for him? Doesn't it strike you as odd that he chose to go into business with you? Why this? Why not a tech company start-up?"

"I have no idea. You should ask your son."

"You think you're so smart, but you're wrong." Irene leaned toward Silver, her gaze intense. "You can keep him in the short term, but one day he's going to wake up and realize he doesn't belong here, and then he's going to leave you. And you'll have nothing."

Shades of Lady Catherine de Bourgh, Silver thought, trying to find the humor in the situation. She half expected Irene to say she did not send regards to Silver's mother.

"Whatever you think I want from Drew, you're wrong. You don't know me or anything about me."

Irene smiled. "You're mistaken. I know far more than you think. I know you're in love with him and that, my dear, will be your downfall."

Irene walked away without saying anything else, which was probably for the best as it was all Silver could do to stay upright. She felt as if she'd been hit in the stomach and all her air had rushed out.

Love him? Love him! No. She didn't. She couldn't. It was a ridiculous idea and only a crazy person would ever imagine she and Drew were anything but business associates who, ah, slept together and had a kid. But that didn't mean anything — it couldn't. She knew better. She'd worked so hard not to be like her mother, falling in love at the drop of a hat. She'd been determined to be strong, to define her own life on her own terms. She'd never done anything simply because of man.

Only she had. Not in a volume way, like her mother, but she'd done plenty in the name of Drew. Even doing things so she didn't have to deal with him was sort of the same thing as doing things because of him, wasn't it? She hadn't gone from man to man, but maybe that wasn't about being strong. Maybe it was about . . . about . . .

She sucked in a breath and hung on to the side of the trailer to keep from collapsing to the ground. The truth bitch-slapped her a couple of times while her brain slowly, oh so slowly started to believe.

The reason there hadn't been a string of men in her life wasn't because she was some badass who had her act together. No, the truth was far more humbling. She'd never fallen in and out of love like her mother because she couldn't. She'd given her heart to Drew when she'd been all of eighteen years old and she'd never taken it back. She'd been in love with Drew this entire time.

While the feelings had been dormant, they'd never gone away. They'd been there, lurking like some recurring virus. Being around him had brought everything to the surface.

She was a fool and she'd always been a fool. In some ways she was worse than her mother. At least her mom had always had the dream of finding *the one.* At least she had hope. All Silver had was the realization that she would love Drew for the rest of her life, and the knowledge that, as Irene had pointed out, one day he would wake up and realize this town wasn't for him, and then he would be gone, taking her shattered heart with him.

Silver arrived at the party-planning meeting still reeling from her emotional realization. She didn't know what to do with the information, let alone what it meant. The only thing she was sure of was that she had to try to act as normal as possible — a goal that proved impossible the second she walked into the conference room.

Drew was already there. Not only did her heart start thudding the second she spotted him, she was instantly overcome by indecision. Did she sit next to him? As far away from him as she could? What was she supposed to say? How should she act? What if he guessed? What if he felt sorry for her?

The last thought had her wanting to bolt for the door, but she forced herself to square her shoulders and move into the room. At all the meetings, she'd sat next to Drew. She would do the same today, and then she would be fine. Perfectly fine.

"You okay?" Drew asked as she sat next to him. "You seem upset."

"I'm fine," she told him.

Fortunately, Renee and Pallas arrived before he could ask anything else. Bethany and Cade followed. Pallas fiddled with her computer.

"We have the head of the office of protocol joining us today," Pallas said with a tight smile. "Just so you're all braced."

Bethany hung her head. "I'm sorry. Did I say I'm sorry? Because I'm sorry."

Cade put his arm around her. "It's not your fault. Look at me."

She did as he requested.

"I love you," he said firmly. "I love you and this is going to be a great party."

Bethany nodded. "I know. I love you, too. I'll stop apologizing." She looked at Pallas. "Let's do this."

Silver tried to focus on the meeting, but the happy couple's sweet words were like a knife in her chest. She wanted that, she thought desperately. She wanted Drew telling the world he loved her. She wanted to know she was safe and had family she could hang on to. She wanted to belong and all those other stupid things she'd never had in her life.

Pallas connected with the El Baharian protocol expert via video. When he appeared on the screen, Silver managed to pretend to listen, taking notes so later she could figure

361

out what everyone was talking about.

"The vice president is confirmed," Pallas said. "Between the El Baharian security forces and our own Secret Service, we'll have really tight security. I don't know how we're going to manage that. Everyone will be screened, then I guess the security team stays in the background."

"They won't interfere with the party," the protocol expert said. "His Royal Highness will have security, as will the queen and the vice president, of course."

"They're all good at this," Bethany added. "Basically you have hot guys in suits who nod politely. I'm sure there's more going on, but to the layperson, that's what it looks like."

"We can handle that," Renee said, as she entered information on her tablet. "Now, on to the menu."

The meeting went on for a couple of hours. When they were done, Silver tried to make her escape before Drew could catch her, but she was too slow. Before she'd even made it to the hallway, he fell into step with her. Because of their partnership, she couldn't even claim a work emergency. He knew all the events already on the books.

"You sure you're all right?" he asked.

"Of course. How are you doing? Still missing Mr. Whiskers? Maybe you should get a rabbit."

"Autumn thinks I should get a dog."

They walked outside. She'd parked at the far end of the lot, but instead of going to his car, he kept pace with her until they got to her truck.

"There's something," he said, watching her. "Is it Autumn? I miss her, too. I don't know how you do it, seeing her, then having her leave. It's hard."

"It is." She did her best not to feel guilty as she steered the conversation to a safer topic away from what was actually upsetting her. "Usually I visit her at her place, so when I get home, I have my routine. But this time was different. I'm missing her in my day-to-day life. That's more difficult."

"Yeah, it would be. I'm glad I got to spend time with her. She's a great kid. I see a lot of you in her."

"Not as much as you're projecting. I see a lot of Leigh in her."

"Nature versus nurture," he teased. "The age-old argument."

"I'm a nurture girl," she lied, trying not to think about how, despite everything, she'd turned out to be just as pitiful as her mother.

"I wish," he began, then shook his head. "No point in that, right? No point in thinking about what would have happened if we'd —"

The cracks in her heart widened. "Don't," she snapped. "Just don't. Neither of us needs to spend any time dwelling on the past. It's done. We did the right thing and however much fun it is to pretend otherwise, it doesn't accomplish anything. There is no second chance and even if there was, I wouldn't change anything."

"I would," he said, his voice and gaze steady. "I would change it all."

"Oh please. For how long? How long would you have wanted to play at being a dad? It wouldn't have worked. You would have resented giving up all your opportunities. You would have wanted more. That life is too small for you, just like this town."

She realized she might have said too much, so she pressed her lips together and did her best to look defiant.

"What are you talking about? What does Happily Inc have to do with —" He swore under his breath. "When did my mother come to see you?"

"This morning."

"Dammit, Silver, you know better than to listen to her. Whatever she told you is a complete lie."

"Is it? You're in the running to be in

charge of the bank and you're probably going to get it. Then what? How long will you be happy with that? Face it, Drew, you're not a run-the-bank kind of guy. You want more and you're not going to find it here. One way or another, you're leaving. You were always leaving."

She thought he'd get mad. Instead he simply raised and lowered his shoulders. "An interesting premise, but don't you think that kind of wanderlust would have kicked in by now? I've been back in Happily Inc nearly a decade. My need to take off sure has a slow burn."

She opened her mouth, then closed it. He had a point. A really good one. One she was having trouble arguing with.

He moved close enough that she had to tilt her head to meet his gaze. "I'll admit I do want more," he told her. "Funny how working with you has started to change my perspective. I like being involved in your business. I've been thinking a lot about what it takes to grow a company. I haven't figured it all out yet, but maybe there should be more to my future than the bank." He smiled at her. "But whatever that is, it's happening here. I like it here. I'm not interested in being a power broker with my parents. This is my home and I'm staying. You have

365

to trust me on that, Silver."

Trusting him was relatively easy, she thought. It was loving him that was hard. Not that she'd had a choice. Her destiny had been set the second she'd handed over her heart.

She wanted to say she wished she'd known that at the time, but she knew it wouldn't have made a difference. Loving Drew had always been unavoidable. She needed him as much as she needed air.

"What I need is to stop listening to your mother," she said with a sigh.

"Yes, you do. Are we okay?"

She nodded and raised herself up on her toes, then she kissed him. "We're fine."

"Good. I need to get back to work, but I will see you soon. We have a big weekend planned."

She thought of the events they were committed to. The smallest trailer was finished and would celebrate its debut on Saturday.

"Don't remind me," she told him. "I'm not emotionally ready to be an empire."

He chuckled. "You're going to do just great. After all you have the best business partner ever."

"You wish."

He kissed her. "You have no idea."

■ ■ ■ ■

Jasper paced the length of his office. Sometimes the writing was easy and sometimes it was hard. Today it was being just plain mean.

He thought about throwing his computer out the window, but that would only create more problems. He'd have to replace the damn thing, download his work in progress from the cloud and he'd still have pages to write.

He swore under his breath, stalked back to his desk and sat down, determined to write at least two more pages. That should get him to the end of the scene, then he'd eat lunch and maybe go for a walk. With his head clear, he would come back and finish out the day's quota.

Twenty agonizing minutes later, he saved his work and practically sprinted out of the room. He'd barely made it into the kitchen when he heard a car pull up. He looked out the front window and saw Wynn walking up the path. As far as he knew, they didn't have any plans to get together, but he wasn't about to say no to whatever she was offering.

He was smiling when he opened the front

door, but that smile faded when he caught sight of the anger in her eyes.

"What's going on?" he asked.

She stepped into his foyer and pointed her finger at him. "You broke the rules. We were clear and you broke them. You've been lying to me for months, Jasper. How could you?"

Before he could tell her he had no idea what she was talking about, she shook her head and continued.

"Don't you dare look like you're confused. You know what you've done. You made friends with Hunter. And don't bother denying it. He told me. He said you two hang out together a lot. You play video games and you've taught him some fighting techniques with your stupid sticks. You're friends."

He thought about suggesting they go into the living room to talk, but he didn't think Wynn was in the mood to do anything but blame him for everything wrong.

"You're right," he told her calmly. "I'm friends with Hunter. For what it's worth, he approached me. We do hang out. We talk about guy stuff. I helped him with his throw in baseball. Sometimes I've helped him with his English homework. You sure do have every right to be pissed. I'm such an asshole."

"You may think because of what you do for a living that you're more verbal than the rest of us, but you're wrong. And sarcasm isn't going to help you out of this. We had a deal."

The last four words came out in a scream.

"We had a deal," she repeated, just as loud. "You weren't to go near him."

"Your son needs a man in his life, Wynn. I'm sorry you don't like that, but it's true. If you don't want it to be me, then fine, but it needs to be someone."

"He is doing just fine without a man in his life. He's a good boy."

"He needs to learn how to be a good man. You're a terrific mother, but your skill set is only going to get you so far."

"You don't get to say," she told him, her voice thick with rage.

Her fury was so out of proportion with what had happened that he just couldn't wrap his mind around the problem. "Is it me or all men?"

"I don't want him knowing about my personal life. I told you that."

"Yes, you did. So I have a question. How is he supposed to know how relationships work if he never sees one up close? How is he supposed to learn how couples navigate things if that never happens in his house?

He's never seen a fight or an apology or watched as someone other than you figured out a budget or a Christmas list. What are you so afraid of?"

"You will not distract me from my point. I told you the rules and you violated them. We're finished."

He'd had a feeling that if she found out about him and Hunter, she would do as she'd always said she would. Wynn was a woman of her word. Now, as what she'd said sank in, he waited to feel crushed by the news. Or at least experience a strong sense of loss. But there seemed to be only some sadness and the knowledge that this moment had been inevitable from their very first night together.

"Just like that?" he asked.

"The rules exist for a reason."

"Which is?"

"That's not your business."

"You're breaking up with me, which makes it my business, but that's okay. Here's the thing. What I want to know is who hurt you so badly that you have to be this scared? There's something in your past that makes you act like this. I know you could do a lot better than me, but let's ignore that. On the surface, I'm a pretty decent guy. I've always treated you well. I don't cheat, I don't lie and I'm sure not after your money. As for Hunter, you're right. I broke the rules, but you know what? I'm not sorry. Because however much you love him, it's not enough. Hunter can't grow up in your little bubble. He needs more, and when you keep him from that, you're only hurting him."

For a second he thought he'd gotten through to her. Her mouth twisted and she looked like she was going to cry. But before he could say anything, her anger returned. Her whole body stiffened and she glared at him again.

"Stay away from me and stay away from Hunter," she said loudly. "We are done. I don't want to hear from you ever again. Is that clear?"

"I'm sorry, Wynn. Not about the breakup. We'll both get over it quicker than we should, but about whatever you went through. I wish I could have convinced you not to be scared. I hope you find whatever it is you need to be whole."

One tear slipped down her cheek. She brushed it away angrily. "Go to hell."

"You're upset. Be careful driving back to town."

She stalked off without saying anything. Jasper watched until she disappeared down the driveway, then he closed the door and leaned against it.

His gut churned, but not because he missed her. He would, and then he would get over it. What got him was the realization that there were so many times he thought he was the only one in pain, the only one with ghosts. He had to keep reminding himself that everyone out there had a story. Some were great, with love and laughter and all things good. And some sucked.

He walked toward his office, the end of his scene suddenly clear. He hoped Wynn could figure out what was wrong and how to fix it because hiding never worked. He knew that for sure.

CHAPTER EIGHTEEN

The boxing workouts were always challenging, but Drew had a feeling there was something else driving Jasper. His friend went after the bag like it was the enemy and only he could defeat it. The punch combinations were lightning fast, and hard enough to break bone.

Cade watched him, a worried frown drawing his brows together. "I'm not sparring with him," he muttered. "Bethany would kill me if I came home with a black eye or split lip this close to the party."

Drew had no reason to worry about his face, but he wasn't eager to spar with Jasper, either.

Jasper stayed on the bag another five minutes, his blows sounding like machine gunfire. He finally stepped back and dropped his arms to his sides.

He was dripping sweat and barely able to catch his breath. There was a look in his eyes Drew had never seen before — something bleak and lost. No, not lost — gone forever.

"Want to talk about it?" Cade asked.

Jasper unfastened his gloves and pulled them off, then he walked to the refrigerator and pulled out three bottles of water. After tossing them each one, he said, "Wynn found out I was friends with Hunter and she ended things."

Jasper didn't talk much about his personal life but he'd mentioned Wynn's strict rules when it came to her son. Hunter wasn't to know that Wynn and Jasper were involved. Drew knew that shortly after Wynn and Jasper had started seeing each other, Hunter had approached Jasper. The two had become friends.

Cade sank onto the floor mat and opened his water. "Let me get this straight. You're friends with her son and that's bad?"

Drew and Jasper sat down. Jasper shrugged. "She didn't want me involved with Hunter at all. She'd made that clear from the start. I guess I always knew this was going to happen."

"You okay?" Drew asked. He knew how bad he felt now that Autumn was gone. For Jasper, it had to be worse. He'd lost Hunter *and* Wynn.

"I will be. I knew the relationship wasn't going to last. It couldn't. Not with Wynn's ideas about Hunter. She didn't want more than we had."

"Did you?" Cade asked.

Jasper thought for a moment. "No. Sometimes I think about being in a real relationship, but that's not going to happen. It can't. I saw too much in Afghanistan. Things got broken and they can't be fixed."

Drew didn't know enough about Jasper's background to agree or disagree with what he'd said, but he couldn't help thinking that the human spirit was amazingly resilient. Jasper had changed since he'd first moved to Happily Inc. He was less reclusive, he had friends, he'd been seeing Wynn.

"I'm sorry," Cade said.

"Me, too," Drew told him.

"Thanks, but I'm okay."

Drew looked at the battered boxing bag and wondered if that was true. He had a feeling even if it wasn't, it would be, with time.

Cade looked at Drew. "My mom's being weirder than usual. I think she has something planned at the bank. About the chairmanship. Consider this a heads-up."

"Thanks, but I can handle whatever Libby has going on."

He was more concerned about Silver. Specifically his mother approaching Silver. Things were good right now — he didn't want anyone messing with what he and Silver had. He wanted . . .

He realized he wasn't sure what he wanted — not completely — but he did know he'd already lost so much with her. No way he was going to lose any more.

The smaller of the trailers had been delivered and it was perfection on wheels. Silver went over every inch of it, loving how Walter had executed all their ideas. If she could have wrapped her arms around the remodeled trailer and hugged it, she would have. She settled on hugging Walter.

"You're the best," she said. "Thank you. The craftsmanship is amazing. I couldn't be happier."

"I'm going to have my wife call you the next time I make her mad," he told her with a chuckle. "You can explain to her that she's lucky to have me so I don't have to sleep on the sofa."

"Give her my number."

She handed him the check for the final payment and was honestly too happy to even mind the decrease in the company's bank account.

When Walter left, she practically danced around the trailers. There were three. Three! She had an empire and right this second, it felt magnificent.

It took her about two hours to load the smaller of the trailers. When she was done, she ran her hands up and down the outside of the trailer, then sighed happily and locked it up. Wynn would secure the gate to the parking area before she left so the trailers would be perfectly safe. That evening, Silver would probably drive by to double-check on everything, but only because she was excited and not because it was necessary.

She returned to her retail space and sat on one of the sofas. After the disastrous bachelorette party, she honestly wasn't sure what to do next. She hadn't booked anything — she just couldn't face the prospect of another hideous party. Not that she didn't like the local police force, but she would much rather go months and months without having to call them to shut things down.

She got out her laptop and opened her spreadsheet program. She entered in the cost of the remodel, how much she paid in rent each month and the average profit she and Drew had come up with, based on the assumption there was no physical damage to the space. The numbers were exactly what they had been before. It only took a handful of parties a month to make a tidy profit. Using her retail space for the parties made financial sense.

She and Drew had already talked about the three trailers. Georgiana would take one, they'd promoted another bartender to take the small one and she would handle the third. Drew would be available to help deal with any issues.

But that was a short-term solution and she knew it. With three trailers, she needed three full-time employees — one for each trailer. The rest of the staff could be part-time. She should be managing things, not pouring drinks. Drew couldn't be expected to keep every weekend night open in case he was needed. She should be booking events, handling ordering and prepping the trailers for each reception or party. And if she was doing all that, did she really want to also be throwing bachelorette parties?

Her lease with Violet allowed her to sublet the space. She already had the trailers and her supplies stored at Wynn's business. When her friend had expanded to the current location, she'd had more room than she needed. Silver's rent check had made the move possible. Silver knew there were several small offices in the back that weren't used. Why not rent one of those for a nominal sum and lease out this space to someone who would use it? Financially she would come out the same and she could focus on the part of the business she really liked.

While the idea made sense, she had to face the uncomfortable reality of having a business partner. The decision wasn't hers to make alone. Not that she was worried about what Drew would say, but there was someone else involved. Still, she had her three trailers and that was definitely worth having to talk things over with Drew.

Silver's confident mood lasted until one-thirty on Saturday afternoon.

"We can't do this," she said, trying not to sound as panicked as she felt. "Don't take this wrong, but you're not ready. Worse, I'm not ready."

Drew and Georgiana exchanged a look. Georgiana spoke first.

"It's going to be fine. I'm handling the big *Alice in Wonderland* wedding at Weddings Out of the Box. You know if I get into trouble there, I can ask Renee for help. She probably has three extra people stored in a closet somewhere that she'll whip out to deal with the crisis."

Silver nodded slowly. "She is frighteningly organized. You're right. It will be fine." She looked at Drew. "But you don't know what you're doing. You're a novice. Who's going to make sure everything goes all right?" She pressed a hand to her writhing stomach. "We shouldn't have booked three weddings right away. What if the small trailer hadn't been ready on time? What if this is a disaster?"

She thought she might be stressing a little too much and that Drew might be offended by her obvious lack of faith in him, but instead of getting upset, he chuckled.

"I think I like you this way."

"What way?"

"Off balance. You're always so confident."

Was that how he saw her because honestly, she didn't feel confident about anything.

He opened the tablet he was holding. "My wedding is small. Only fifty guests. The cocktails are premade and chilling in the two-gallon containers. The only other choices are beer and wine. Even I can open a wine or beer bottle. I have two people helping me because I'm new. I'm to get there at five and leave at eight, although I suspect the party will go on without me.

The bride and groom are bringing their own water and soda. It's all good. You need to breathe."

"I'm breathing." Maybe a little too fast and shallow, but she was breathing.

"Okay," she said, glancing at her watch. "I have to go set up." Her wedding was early. A three o'clock ceremony with a reception going from three-thirty until whenever, although her services had only been requested until seven. The bride and groom had a limited budget and wanted a big blowout party. They were having both the ceremony and the reception outside in the park. The families had gotten together to make the food themselves. The bar was easy. Beer and margaritas. Silver had all the blenders in her trailer, along with two hundred margarita glasses, a couple of dozen cases of beer and two crates of limes.

"Then we're good," she said, trying to sound more confident than she felt. "Okay, I'm heading out to set up." She looked at Georgiana and Drew. "Call me if you need anything."

They exchanged a look, then both nodded.

"We'll be fine," Georgiana promised her. "Go have fun."

Fun when there was so much to worry

about? Not that she was going to tell them that.

Silver drove to the edge of the park. Vehicles weren't allowed past a certain point. She and the bride and groom had discussed the best place to position the trailer. She carefully backed the trailer into its spot, then rotated the solar panels to catch the sun's energy. Once that was done, she began her setup.

At two, the rest of her staff showed up. By the time the wedding started, they were ready for three hundred guests to descend. As the groom kissed his bride and everyone applauded, Silver began popping the tops off bottles of beer. The margaritas — both frozen and on the rocks — were in glasses and on trays ready to be offered to guests. Water and soda bottles sat in galvanized tubs filled with ice.

There was the usual twenty-minute crush while everyone got their first drink. Silver was pleased that her guess on how many would go for margaritas versus beer had been dead-on. By four they were down to a steady stream of customers. That would continue until they were ready to shut things down.

The reception was a boisterous, happy affair with lots of dancing and laughter. No one threw anything or started screaming. Even the kids were well behaved.

Right on time, Silver and her crew started cleaning up. They loaded empty bottles into crates and put them in the back of the truck. Silver would drive them and all the others over to the recycling center Monday morning. The tables were wiped down and stored, along with the trays, blenders and dirty glasses. At seven-thirty, she pulled out of the park and headed back to Wynn's place to stow her trailer.

She hadn't heard from Drew, which wasn't surprising. There wasn't great cell reception up at Honeymoon Falls. She debated waiting for him, then decided to go check on Georgiana. Her wedding was about the same size as the one Silver had staffed, but it was more fancy.

She walked in to find the party in full swing. Everyone looked more happy than stressed, which was good. The *Alice in Wonderland* theme played out in red, black and white. All the food was labeled Eat Me. There were decorative rabbits everywhere, along with huge playing cards. The tableware was all oversize or undersized, which must have made dinner interesting.

Silver walked over to the trailer.

"How's it going?" she asked Georgiana.

"It's been good. We're doing fine — people are drinking the usual amount. No one's thrown up."

"Always a plus."

Georgiana smiled. "The bride's father refused to walk her down the aisle. Apparently he hates the groom. He and the bride's mother had a massive fight in front of everyone, but it's fine now. One of the groom's cousins has irritable bowel syndrome and insisted one of the bathrooms be hers alone. That didn't make Renee happy. They settled the problem by giving her the bathroom in the bride's room." Georgiana shrugged. "You know, the usual. I have it handled."

"I can see that."

Silver excused herself and walked around. As Georgiana had said, the wedding was going well. Before she got back to the trailer, Drew joined her.

"Checking things out?" he asked.

She stared at him. "You're back. How did it go? Everything okay? Is the trailer okay? What did you think?"

He grinned. "This worry thing is so interesting. The wedding was fine. Forty people who hiked up to the falls rather than drive. It was very outdoorsy and nice and we left when they decided to go skinny-dipping. The trailer is back in its happy home."

Silver took a deep breath, her first in hours. "Thank you. So we did it."

"We did." He put his arm around her. "Now what do you say we leave these people to their very odd reception and let Georgiana do her job? I have a bottle of red wine waiting at my place, along with a very nice cheese and meat plate I ordered. We'll eat, we'll drink, we'll talk and later there will be sex."

She laughed. "You do know how to entice a girl."

"Not just any girl," he told her.

If only that were true, she thought wistfully.

They told Georgiana they were leaving. Drew said he'd gotten a ride with one of his helpers so they went to Silver's truck and headed for his place.

It only took a few minutes to open the wine and set out the cheese plate. Silver grabbed plates and crackers and they carried everything to the table in the corner. It was only after they sat down that she realized she was exhausted.

"That was a long day," she said. "Good, but long."

He poured them each a glass of wine. "I

agree. But it was way too much. We're going to have to hire someone for each of the trailers. You can't manage everything going on and run an event. Not every weekend."

She'd been thinking the same thing herself. "I know. I hate to give up control, but you're right. I can be a backup person in an emergency, but otherwise, I need to be handling the logistics and booking events."

She tried to sound upbeat as she spoke, but it was difficult.

"What?" Drew asked.

"Everything is changing so fast," she admitted. "I'm happy about the expansion and this is what I want, but now suddenly I'm stepping away from the day-to-day operations to be in management. It's going to be an adjustment."

"We could hire a general manager and you could still handle one of the trailers."

"That doesn't make sense. I know the business better than anyone. If I have any big management questions, you can answer them."

He touched his chest. "You're saying you trust me and my expertise?"

He was joking — she heard that in the tone of his voice and saw it in the smile lurking at the corners of his mouth. But she didn't see the humor in the question, probably because her faith in him was a whole lot less about his career and a whole lot more about who he was — and the fact that she loved him.

She'd been doing her best to avoid that truth, but it wouldn't stay hidden forever. She loved Drew. She didn't know what that meant or if it changed anything, but it was now a part of her.

She sighed. No, it had always been a part of her. The difference was now she was willing to acknowledge it.

"You have some very small amount of expertise," she told him. "I plan to exploit that for my own gain."

"That's my girl."

"Let me know when you have time to do interviews," she said. "We'll get in some candidates. In the meantime, I'll work up the budget with us bringing on two more employees." She sliced some cheese and put it on her plate.

"We have to talk about the retail space," she told him. "I ran numbers again and they're exactly what we expected. We can make a nice profit from the parties, only . . ."

"Not your thing?" he asked.

"How did you know?"

"The first party would have been off-putting to anyone. You never expressed any interest in expanding the services offered, only in offering the same services to more people. There's a difference. You like what you do and you want to do that. Hosting bachelorette parties and rehearsal dinners isn't a natural expansion."

She appreciated that she didn't have to explain herself. "But we spent all that money. The whole space is refurbished. We bought stripper poles."

"Hey, it's okay. Not every expansion works out exactly as expected. Better to cut our losses and move on. Can you sublet the space?"

She nodded. "I checked my lease already and it's perfectly fine. With rents going up in town, we should about break even."

"Sounds like you have your answer."

"You sure you're okay with the decision?"

"Absolutely." He held out his wineglass. "All right, partner. Problems solved?"

"They are."

He was so easy to be with. So easy to love. Funny how long it had taken her to see that.

"Admit it," she teased. "Buying into my business was the best decision ever. The hardware store isn't going to be nearly as exciting."

Something flashed in his eyes, but before

she could figure out what he was thinking, the emotion was gone. He smiled.

"You're right about the hardware store, but I'm starting to think I could really get into the dry cleaning business. There's just something about all those clean clothes."

"Now you're scaring me."

"Really?"

She laughed. "No. Not really."

Although knowing he had possession of her heart was its own kind of terrifying.

"Fancy," Natalie said as she walked into Silver's retail space Tuesday at noon. "I like the stripper poles. I'm not sure I could dance around one, but I like them."

Silver was hosting the girlfriend lunch at her place. She'd pulled the sofas into a loose circle. She'd set up a taco bar along one wall and had flavored herbal iced tea in one of her drink dispensers.

The rest of her friends arrived. Bethany handed out the Bride's Posse T-shirts, then everyone went to fill their plates for lunch. When they were seated on the sofas, Pallas leaned back in her seat and sighed.

"No offense, Bethany, but this is the last royal party I'm throwing for you. Do you know your father texts me every single day? He does. I get royal texts. The man adores you and wants everything to be perfect. It's sweet but so annoying."

Bethany wrinkled her nose. "That's my dad."

"Pallas is exaggerating," Renee told her. "I think it's wonderfully challenging. As for the next party, don't worry about it. By then Pallas will be busy with her new baby and I'll handle it all."

Silver looked at Bethany. "What next party?"

"I have no idea."

Carol smiled. "She means a baby shower."

Bethany held up both hands. "No and no. I mean, sure, I want kids, but not for a couple of years. I want to enjoy being married to Cade first."

"Me, too," Natalie said. "Only Ronan, not Cade. I'm not like you two." She pointed at Carol and Pallas. "No babies for *moi* until at least our second anniversary. Now that I've found Ronan, I want a little just-us-two time before we start our family."

"The Mitchell men appear to be very fertile," Silver murmured. "Make sure you're on really good birth control."

Everyone laughed. Well, everyone but Wynn, who only smiled. Silver glanced at her.

"You okay?"

"I'm fine. I agree. Birth control is important. You want to control when you get pregnant."

Pallas's eyes widened. "OMG, are you telling us you're pregnant? Does Jasper know?"

Wynn practically choked. "No. No! I'm not pregnant. Trust me, I'm not pregnant. In fact . . ." She looked at them, then back at her plate. "You're going to find out anyway, so I might as well tell you. Jasper and I broke up."

"What? No."

"What happened?"

"Are you okay?"

"Was he stupid? Sometimes men are stupid."

Wynn held up her hand to stop the barrage of questions. "It's no big deal. Our relationship was always casual. I only had one rule and that was for him not to get involved with Hunter. I found out he and Hunter were hanging out behind my back. He lied to me about the thing I told him was most important, so now I can't trust him and it's over."

"Just like that?" Natalie asked.

"It was my only stipulation. He couldn't respect my opinion, so yes, it's done."

Silver knew Wynn had her reasons, but breaking up with Jasper like that sounded a little arbitrary. "Was he mean to Hunter?"

"No, nothing like that. I'm sure if you ask him, he'll tell you he was just stepping in to be a substitute father." Something flickered in her eyes. "It doesn't matter. I wouldn't have said anything except you all knew we were seeing each other. I figured I'd just tell you and be done with it."

Carol looked at her. "I can't figure out if you're upset or not."

"I'm not. I knew it wasn't going to last. I never wanted anything permanent. I don't miss him. He was just a short-term fling."

"He can short-term fling me anytime he wants," Renee said. As soon as the words were out, she flushed. "I'm sorry. I only meant to think that."

After a second of silence, everyone laughed. Wynn reached over and patted her hand.

"You go for it. I won't mind at all."

Renee shook her head. "I'm not exactly the go-for-it type, but he is handsome and sexy." She flushed again. "Not that I've really noticed."

"Of course not," Pallas said. "I have to say, Renee, the more I get to know you, the more I like you."

"Thanks. I feel the same way about all of you."

Bethany grinned. "I'm liking this lunch. We're getting some really juicy bombshells. Wynn dumped Jasper. Renee has a crush on Jasper."

"It's not a crush," Renee protested. "It's whatever is less than that. A mild interest."

"He's free now," Natalie teased.

"We've already discussed my inability to quote unquote 'go for it.' Can we please change the subject?"

"I think Millie and Dave had sex," Carol said.

It took Silver a second to piece together the couple. "You mean giraffe Millie and giraffe Dave?"

"Who else? I really hope they're doing it because I would love a giraffe baby. Of course we won't know if she's pregnant for months."

Pallas looked at Carol. "We could all be pregnant together. That's so sweet."

"Giraffes gestate about fourteen or fifteen months," Carol said. "We don't want to share that with her."

Pallas shuddered and touched her stomach. "No, we don't."

"Pregnant giraffes," Natalie said. "That's so nice."

"She's weakening," Silver murmured. "Just wait. She'll be pregnant by the end of the year."

"Not happening," Natalie said firmly.

Conversation moved on to other topics. Silver joined in even as she kept an eye on Wynn. Since making her confession, there was no sign that anything was wrong. Was Wynn really over Jasper that quickly? Had their relationship really been that casual for both of them?

What must it be like to be able to move on that easily? Something she would never know. If Drew left or walked away from her, she would be devastated. She'd spent the last decade unable to get over him. There was no reason to think she would ever be able to recover and move on. When it came to Drew, she was well and truly stuck — for life.

CHAPTER NINETEEN

Drew's perfectly ordinary day hit the fan when he got a text from his father. It wasn't hearing from his old man that bothered him so much as the message itself.

Thanks for letting us stay at your place while we're in town. Looking forward to seeing you.

Last he'd heard, his mother was still at Grandpa Frank's place. Drew had assumed his father would join her there, but obviously he'd been wrong. He wasn't worried about how they'd gotten into his house so much as why they were there.

He finished out his day, then headed home. As he pulled up, he saw an unfamiliar rental car in the driveway. So his dad hadn't been kidding. His parents had moved in.

He told himself he could deal with whatever they had going on. They would stay through the royal party, and then they would be gone. As a rule, his mother was the more intense parent — his dad erred on the side of normal.

He braced himself for whatever was to come, vowed to be pleasant and understanding, then walked into the house.

"I'm home," he called.

"We're in the kitchen," his mother called.

He went into the back of the house and sure enough found his parents at the island.

"Darling, you're home," his mother said, hugging him. "Your father is here."

"I can see that." Obviously the fight was well behind them, never to be mentioned.

Howard, his father, was tall and fit. Drew had inherited his height from his father, along with his sense of humor.

The two men shook hands, then his father hugged him.

"You're looking good," his father said. "Very exciting about the party. That's going to be good for us. I have to head back home after that but your mother will stay for the board meeting next Monday."

"Good to know." Drew turned to his mother. "Mom, when did you decide to move in, and why didn't you tell me?"

Howard frowned. "What do you mean, move in?"

"Mom's been staying up at the big house."

Irene waved away the information. "I didn't want to impose for too long, so I decided to stay with my father until you arrived, Howard. I borrowed the key from the rack in the pantry and here we are." She smiled. "We're going to have a lovely visit."

He thought of the spare key he kept at his grandfather's house and thought perhaps he needed a different place for it, although that was a concern for later. His more pressing problem was the fact that he had no idea what his mother was up to, although knowing her, it was something.

His father offered him a Scotch. The three of them settled at the kitchen island.

"As I said, I'm going to have to head back to D.C. right after the party," his father said. "I have meetings I couldn't get out of. I'm very much looking forward to when you join us. You mother says you're thinking two years. Is that right?"

Drew stared at his mother, who carefully avoided his gaze.

"Mom," he said tightly. "What is he talking about?"

"Drew, we've been over this and over this." She touched her husband's hand. "This is why I came back to Happily Inc early. So I could speak to Drew and spend time with my father. We have to make sure he runs the bank and not Libby."

"Of course. That's always been the plan." Howard looked between them. "What am I missing?"

"Nothing, dear," Irene said. "Drew, you have to be more cooperative. We've gone to a lot of trouble to make things right for you. Now we'll talk about this later. Right now you have to meet Julie."

"Who's Julie?"

His father smiled. "You're going to like her. She's one in a million. When she came in for her first interview, I sensed something special about her. The more we've worked together, the more certain I've been." He patted Drew's arm. "Son, I think she's the one."

As Drew was reasonably confident his father didn't mean that Julie was the one for him, it stood to reason that he meant she was the one for Drew. His mother, it seemed, had told his father nothing.

"Okay, that's enough." He stood and walked around the island so he was facing both his parents.

"Dad, there are some things you should know."

"Drew, don't," his mother said. "You're being ridiculous."

"Am I? Okay, then I'm going to keep on being ridiculous." He looked at his father. "Dad, while I'm sure Julie is lovely, I'm not interested. I'm already in a relationship."

"You're not," his mother protested. "You're sleeping with some woman. There's a difference."

Drew felt his temper flare. "Don't push me, Mom. Silver is important me. You may not like her but you will respect her. Is that clear?"

His mother sighed heavily. "Fine. You're sleeping with Silver and it's magical, but in time you will come to see that you need and want more."

Howard looked at his wife. "You knew he was with someone and you let Julie come with us anyway?"

"Once he meets Julie, he'll forget all about that other woman. Silver's not all that."

"Mom," he said slowly. "Stop it." Silver was the mother of their child and someone he cared about. Some great truth lurked just out of mental reach but before he could get to it, he was forced back into the conversation.

"Drew, you've always had a problem knowing what is best for you," his mother continued. "We're just trying to help."

"You're trying to make me do what I don't

want to do. You've always seen me as a way to further what you want. That stops now. Whatever happens with the bank, I'm not joining you in D.C."

His father stared at him. "Drew, is that true? You're not interested in our firm?"

"I'm not. I'm sorry, Dad. I've been telling you both for a long time now, but you won't listen. I belong here."

"Lizards and ordinary people belong here," Irene snapped. "Everyone with half a brain gets out while they can. Drew, you don't belong here. You never have."

Before anyone else could speak, they heard the sound of footsteps on the tile floor. A tall, stunningly beautiful brunette walked into the kitchen. She was in her late twenties, with violet eyes and an easy smile. When she spotted Drew, the smile widened.

"Finally we meet. I've been hearing about you forever. I'm Julie Leighty."

She crossed to him, her arm outstretched. Drew shook hands with her.

"Nice to meet you, Julie."

She looked at the three of them. "Am I interrupting?"

"Not at all," Irene told her. "Drew, darling, why don't you get Julie a drink and take her out on the patio? While I'm not one for rural vistas, the view is quite lovely.

Tell her about the animal preserve."

There was more to be said, but Drew knew that now that Julie had joined them, this wasn't the time. He poured a second Scotch and they made their way out onto the patio.

Once they were seated he asked, "How much of that did you hear?"

She laughed. "That only lizards and ordinary people belong here. Oh, and that you don't belong here. Is that true?"

"No. This is exactly where I belong." Here, with Silver. Because she was a significant part of his life. *Hell of a time to have that revelation,* he thought. This was perhaps the definition of awkward.

"Tell me about yourself," he said by way of distraction.

"I grew up in Ohio. I'm from a big family." She smiled. "I'm one of six and a middle child, so I can get along with anyone."

"One of six? That's a lot of kids."

"It is. My house was loud all the time." She laughed. "One of the great things about having my own apartment is that it's very, very quiet. Oh, and no one eats my leftovers."

"Nirvana," he teased.

"You have no idea. Anyway, I went to

Georgetown, where I majored in Political Economics and I minored in Chinese and German."

"You're kidding."

"I have a great sense of humor, but no. I'm not kidding. I wanted to get involved internationally. I toyed with the idea of law school but honestly politics is so much more interesting. I love to travel and I'm a huge cat person. One day I will turn into a scary cat lady with sixteen cats." She smiled impishly. "Just so you're warned."

She was perfect, he thought. Smart, beautiful, funny, charming. Under other circumstances he would have been interested. But sitting with her now wasn't anything more than time spent with a friend of his parents. No matter what she said or did, he would rather be with Silver.

"Why did you join a lobbying firm?"

"I had a lot of job offers out of college, but this one was the most intriguing." She took a sip of her drink. "Not just because of the money, although that was very tempting. My parents had six kids to put through college so I had to pay for some of it myself. It's nice to clear out those student loans. And my darling little apartment is lovely. But it's more than that. I've helped change laws so charities can do good work. I'm focusing on international women's issues, coordinating with multinational corporations so when they go into a developing country, they make decisions that are good for the people there, along with themselves."

She shrugged. "I'm interested in financial security and I'm altruistic. I suppose that makes me human." She looked at him from under her lashes. "You do know this is a setup."

"I got the message. Why did you agree?"

One corner of her mouth turned up. "I kept hearing about you. Your parents talk about you all the time and I thought even if only half of it were true, I would be foolish not to come to Happily Inc and check things out." She sipped her drink. "While I'll admit I'm intrigued, I sense little or no interest on your part."

"I'm with someone."

Her eyes widened with shock. "Your mother swore you were single."

"My mother doesn't listen."

"Ah, so she doesn't approve of your lady love."

Despite everything, he smiled. "My lady love? That seems a little old-fashioned."

"But accurate."

"Very." He looked at her. "I'm sorry she misled you."

"Me, too. That makes this all uncomfortable." She sighed. "You'd think being as smart and successful as I am, I would be able to find a guy on my own. Obviously it's time to get started on those cats."

"I'm sorry."

"Me, too." She leaned back in her chair. "The same words with totally different meanings. You're being polite while I am genuinely sorry. Oh well." She pointed to the animal preserve. "Your mother promised me giraffes and gazelles. Is that true or also misrepresented?"

"There are giraffes and gazelles, I promise. They've gone in for the night, but you will see them first thing in the morning. I swear."

"I'm holding you to that."

Drew's text asking her to stop by was oddly brief. Silver debated calling him to find out what was going on but his place was only a few minutes away. She got in her truck and drove over, only to find more than just his car in the driveway. What on earth?

She walked up to the front door and knocked. When the door opened, she found herself face-to-face with a stunningly beautiful woman.

Silver considered herself on the high side of average when it came to looks. She wasn't beautiful, but she could hold her own. Next to this woman, she was cat gack.

"Hi," the brunette said, stepping back to let Silver in. "I'm Julie. You're either looking for Drew or his parents, right? Drew's in the shower, but Irene is . . . right here."

Irene pulled the door open wider. "Oh good. You came. Come in, Silver."

She stepped into the foyer and instantly knew she'd made a mistake. This was not a safe place. She had no idea what was going on but whatever it was, it was very, very bad.

"Julie and I are fixing dinner," Irene said, her tone far too friendly. "Julie works with us in D.C. Oh, be a dear and check on the chicken. We don't want it to overcook."

Julie looked a little confused, but agreed. "It was nice to meet you, Silver."

"Same here."

Once Julie was gone, Irene's friendly tone hardened. "She's here for Drew. I thought you should know. They have so much in common and as you can see, she's beautiful. Also accomplished and someone we would welcome into the family. Unlike you. You would never be welcome. You understand that, don't you? That if you try to trap him, you will be forcing him to choose. It's a difficult way to start a marriage — estranged from everyone you love. Drew has always been a man who loves his family."

Her smile was cold and brittle. "Did I mention Julie is one of six children? She's fluent in German and Chinese. She belongs with him and you don't. You never have. You might be just a small town girl, Silver, but you're not stupid. You can see what Drew could be. Are you going to be the reason he's always unhappy? Always looking? It's not a very nice way to show him you care, now is it?"

The words were like body blows. They came from every direction and left her struggling to stay upright. Her head kept screaming that Drew had no part of this. No matter what, he would never play her. He might not love her, but he was a good guy. Honorable. Which meant all this was on his mother. Silver would bet just about anything Irene had been the one to send the text. So this wasn't Drew's fault.

But that didn't mean it didn't hurt. Silver stared at Irene, not sure what to say. Vowing that she would win in the end seemed presumptuous and tempting fate just a little too much. Because the truth was, Silver didn't know if she could win. Not with Drew. She might have loved him her entire adult life, but she'd never been able to keep him. Wanting was not having.

"I need to go," she said, and backed out of the house. Once she was in her truck, she found she was shaking too hard to put the key in the ignition. It took her three tries before she was finally able to start the engine.

When she got back to her apartment, she carefully closed and locked the front door, then sank onto the floor and pulled her knees to her chest. She closed her eyes and told herself she would be fine. That whatever happened, she was strong and capable and she would get through this. But as the tears fell and the sobs ripped through her body, she had a very bad feeling that she wasn't strong enough by half.

Silver spent a long night tortured by thoughts of Drew with Julie. Not only did she have a horrible sobfest hangover, she'd never heard from him. She told herself it was because he was busy with his parents, but couldn't help picturing him having dinner with the beautiful Julie — laughing and drinking wine, as the other woman told him stories about her perfect life.

This was everything that was wrong with their relationship, she thought as she drove over to check on inventory for the upcoming royal party. The lack of clear definition.

She had no idea what he was thinking about them, where — if anywhere — he saw their relationship going. Was it casual sex? Was it more than that? What did he want?

She knew the more self-actualized question was what did *she* want, only she didn't have to ask that. She already knew. She wanted it all. With Drew. Forever.

While there was a slight chance he wanted the same from her, she wouldn't know without asking, although that meant putting herself out there. That might be the smart, mature thing to do, but she would need to be a whole lot stronger than she was this morning.

By noon, she'd confirmed she had everything they needed for Bethany and Cade's big party. She'd already reserved all the staff she would need. Georgiana would be in charge and she'd made it clear she expected Silver to enjoy herself at the party and be a guest rather than a manager. Silver wasn't sure she could do that, but she was going to try.

She'd just finished locking up the trailers when Drew drove into the parking lot. He got out of his car, his face tight with concern.

"There you are," he said as he walked up to her. "I've been calling and texting you all morning. Why didn't you answer?"

She didn't want to look at him, didn't want to stare into his dark eyes and see guilt or regret or any other emotion that would send her over the edge. Honestly, she'd never felt more like her mother's daughter than she did at that moment. She was a fool for love — she probably always had been. She was trapped, loving a man who had never truly committed to her.

"I turned my phone off," she told him. "I needed to focus on work. We're good for the parties. Everything is in place. I'll get the fresh ingredients on Friday and we'll be ready."

"What's wrong? You're upset. What happened? Are you feeling all right?"

"I didn't hear from you last night," she said, avoiding the questions.

He groaned. "I know and I'm sorry. My father arrived in town, which wouldn't be a problem except he and my mother moved into the house with no warning. I was with them." He shook his head. "It's a mess. They brought some woman who works for them. Julie. My mother led her to believe we would be perfect together. I had to explain that I was in a relationship, which my mother still refuses to believe and now Julie feels like an idiot."

He'd told her about Julie, she thought with relief. He hadn't hidden it or lied or anything. He was being who he had always been.

"I have to tell you," he continued, "I genuinely don't understand how someone as nice as Grandpa Frank had two horrible daughters. Some sociologist should make a case study of my family."

I love you. That was what she'd been about to say. That she loved him and wanted him to know. That she hoped they could be together always because everything was better with him around. She was going to tell him that they should get married and have more babies because they sure made good ones and . . .

But what came out instead was, "Julie seems really nice."

His eyes widened. "You met her?"

"I got a text asking me to stop by."

He swore under his breath. "That was my mother."

"I figured it out after I got there and you were nowhere to be found."

"I was there the whole night." He swore. "I took a shower. I must have left my phone downstairs and she took advantage of that. I'm sorry, Silver. This has been a mess." He moved toward her. "I promise, once the party's over, they'll be gone. I will make sure we don't have to deal with them again."

Would he really do that? She thought about what Irene had said — that he would have to choose between her and his family. That he'd always been a family guy and what would it mean if he had to give that up. Grandpa Frank would be fine with her, but what about everyone else?

She couldn't do this, she thought. Couldn't trap him. She hadn't before and it had been the right decision. Maybe it was the right decision again.

"Drew, you belong with them," she said slowly, taking a step back. "With Julie or someone like her. Out in the world. This town is too small. Go be what you were meant to be. You should have stayed away after college. You shouldn't have come back."

She ignored the pain in her chest, the way it hurt to breathe. She had to get it out now.

"Leigh won't keep you from Autumn," she told him, fighting tears. "She'll always be your daughter."

"What about us?"

His face was blank. She had no idea what he was thinking, which was probably for the best.

"We knew this was going to be temporary,

just like it was before. I'm not the one for you."

"You can't know that."

She managed what she hoped was a decent smile. "You've never fought for me, Drew. Yours are not exactly the actions of a man desperately in love. I appreciate the help with the business. I'll figure out a way to buy you out."

"Just like that?" he asked. "You're done?"

"I'm done."

"You can't mean that."

"I let you go before. This time isn't any different."

Finally the truth, she thought as the pain ripped through her. It had hurt then and it hurt now. She'd been in love with him then and she was in love with him now. But what mattered most was she'd been right to let go before and she was still right. Trapping Drew would destroy both of them. By letting him go, she was giving him a chance to be happy. Slightly twisted logic, but truth nonetheless.

"You're wrong," he told her. "You can't —" He turned on his heel. "Fine. If this is what you want, I'm out of here."

He got in his car and drove away. Silver double-checked that the trailers were locked, then went to her own place. Once she was inside, she sat on the sofa and told herself to just breathe. For the next few days, that was all she had to do. She would figure out how to fill the hole in her heart later.

CHAPTER TWENTY

Drew couldn't settle on an emotion. Rage, sure. Hurt, blinding hurt, yes. But as to the rest of it, he was clueless. Feeling swirled through him, building and retreating, kicking him in the gut before moving on.

He got to his house only to realize he didn't want to go inside. He was afraid of what he would say if he saw his mother. Not knowing what else to do, he retreated to his garage, where he stood at the small workbench on one side and tried to figure out what the hell had gone so wrong.

He'd assumed that if anything broke them up it would be Autumn. But when it came to their daughter, they'd pulled together, working through their issues. But this . . .

He laughed without humor. This? He didn't even know what this was.

"Son, you all right?" His dad walked in from the house. "You've been out here awhile."

Drew looked at his father. "I can't do this, Dad. I know what the plan is, but I won't be a part of it. You're screwing with my life."

"I have no idea what you're talking about."

"Silver and Autumn."

His father frowned. "Silver? That girl you knew in high school?"

"Yes, we're back together. It's serious." Or it had been.

"I didn't know. I thought —" He shook his head. "Wait. Who's Autumn?"

Drew couldn't believe it. "Mom didn't tell you?"

"Tell me what? Drew, what's going on? Start at the beginning, please."

Had his mother really not said anything about Autumn? Even as he thought the question, Drew realized he already had the answer. Of course, she'd kept the information to herself. It was inconvenient.

"Silver got pregnant over that summer," he began. "We agreed she would give up the baby for adoption. What I recently found out was that Silver stayed in touch with the woman who adopted our child.

"She was here, Dad," he said, unable not to smile when he talked about her. "She's great. Smart and funny and still a kid but on the verge of growing up. I got to know her and I can't wait to see her again."

His father looked stunned. "I don't understand. You told your mother about this?"

"Every word. I told her when Autumn was in town. It didn't go well."

His father leaned heavily against the workbench. "I can't believe it. We have a granddaughter?"

Drew got out his phone and showed his father several pictures.

"She's beautiful," his dad breathed. "I want to meet her. Please tell me I can."

"I'm sure Leigh would be open to it. Autumn would be thrilled. She's very into having a lot of family. She met Grandpa Frank."

His father stared at him. "She was in the big house? And your mother didn't meet her?"

"She didn't want to, Dad." There was a lot to be said about that, but he had more pressing issues. "I gave her up without a second thought. I was all about college and my future. I signed the paperwork and that was it. Silver had to deal with being pregnant but not me. I went on with my life."

He walked the length of the garage, then returned to his father. "Dad, I don't want to join your lobbying firm. That's not me. I want to help people one-on-one. I want to enjoy my friends and I want to fall in love and settle down."

"With Silver?"

"I'd hoped so. Now I'm less sure." She'd cut him loose — for the second time. She'd been the one to insist they break up before he went off to college. She'd been right that first time, but now? He didn't think so.

"We were so young and I made so many mistakes. I don't know what she's thinking these days. She won't tell me."

"Did you ask?" His father studied him. "Did you fight for her? Does she know you're in love with her?"

And there it was, he thought, almost not surprised. Sometimes the truth just walked out in front of a man and smiled up at him. He was in love with Silver. That was it — that was why everything else seemed out of kilter in his life. He was looking at it all without realizing he was totally and completely in love with Silver.

Before he could respond, the door to the house opened. Julie stepped out, then came to a stop.

"Wow," she said with a sigh. "I have incredibly bad timing." She turned to go back in the house.

"Wait," Drew called. "What's going on?"

"I, ah, booked a flight back to D.C. for tonight." She gave Howard an apologetic smile. "This isn't working out the way any of us thought it would, so I'm heading home. The thing is, I need a ride to Palm Springs so I can catch the red-eye to New York. From there I'll get a quick flight to D.C."

"I'll take you," Drew said quickly. "It's the least I can do."

Julie shook her head. "I don't think that's a good idea."

Drew walked toward her. "It's a great idea. Come on. You can yell at me the whole way to the airport."

"I don't want to yell at you, Drew. None of this is your fault."

"I appreciate that and I'm still taking you to Palm Springs. When do you want to leave?"

She gave him a smile. "How about right now?"

Silver managed to stay strong, right up until she got a text from a D.C. number. If she had to guess, she would say it came from Irene. She was the only person Silver knew who was horrible enough to want to break someone she barely knew.

The text simply said I thought you should know. It was followed by a forwarded message.

Julie and I are in Palm Springs. I'm taking
her to dinner before heading home.

As there was only one Julie in Silver's life,
it wasn't hard to put the pieces together. In
less than a day, Drew had moved on.

All her fears came to life. Even as her
brain said the message could be interpreted
to mean that he was leaving Julie in Palm
Springs and coming home alone, her heart
shattered into even more pieces. She lay on
the sofa, fighting tears, knowing she was
never going to be okay, never going to
recover. It was always going to hurt. She'd
finally figured out she'd been in love with
Drew all this time and now he was gone.

When the pain got too big to contain, she
called Natalie.

"Hey, you. What's up?"

The familiar, cheerful voice should have
comforted her. Instead she felt herself sink-
ing deeper into despair.

"Drew and I," she began, her voice shaking.

"I'm at the gallery," Natalie said, interrupting. "Are you at home?"

"Yes."

"I'll be there in five minutes. Maybe less.
Don't go anywhere."

Silver got up and unlocked the door, then

went into the kitchen to start a pot of tea. Before the water had boiled, she turned off the stove and got out a bottle of tequila. She cut up limes and pulled out a shaker filled with good quality salt.

She'd just finished her first shot when Natalie burst into the apartment.

"What happened?" she asked as she flew across the room and hugged Silver. "Oh, honey, was he a moron? Was it worse? Do we need to have him beat up?"

Silver hugged her back, hanging on so tight, she was afraid she would do damage. It took several minutes before she could finally let go.

"He's gone," she said, letting the tears fall. "I sent him away and he went. He's in Palm Springs with Julie. She's perfect for him. She's beautiful and smart. She speaks Chinese. I don't speak Chinese. I speak a little Spanish and that's it. She's accomplished." More tears fell. "That's the word. *Accomplished* and I'm just some blonde who owns a bar in a trailer."

Natalie pushed her into one of the kitchen chairs. She carried over the tequila, two shot glasses, the plate of lime wedges and the salt, then poured them each a big glass of water. After sitting across from Silver, she smiled.

"Technically you own three bars in trailers, so don't be selling yourself short."

The unexpected comment had Silver laughing for a couple of seconds before she began to cry. "I've lost him forever. I never had him, I know that, but now I've lost him and I don't think I can do it. I don't think I can survive this."

Natalie took a shot, then reached for her water glass. "I feel like I'm missing some stuff here. Start at the beginning and tell me what's going on."

Silver closed her eyes and wondered where the beginning was. When Drew had bought the trailers? No, it was long before that.

"It started the summer I turned eighteen," she said, and walked her friend through the intense romance that had resulted in her pregnancy. She finished with their last fight. The one where she'd sent Drew away and he'd gone without saying a word.

"You told him it was over," Natalie said, pouring her third shot. Silver was on her fourth.

"What else was I supposed to say?"

"I don't know. How about the truth? How about telling him you're wildly in love with him?"

"Then he would only feel sorry for me. I didn't want that."

Natalie looked confused. "Silver, you're the strongest person I know. This isn't like you at all. What's going on?"

"I don't want to be my mother. She gave her life over to the men she loved. I can't do that. I won't. If I tell him I love him, then he'll have power over me. I don't know what will happen. I don't know what he'll do."

Natalie's brown eyes turned sympathetic. "You're scared."

"Of course I'm scared. I just realized I've been in love with Drew for over a decade. How stupid is that? I'm a complete and total fool."

"And you're terrified."

"That, too."

"No, I'm saying you're acting out of fear. You're not being rational. You're like a wounded animal."

Not a description Silver liked at all.

Natalie leaned toward her. "You're so convinced he's going to reject you that you're pushing him away before he can hurt you more. You know how to live with the pain of unrequited love. You've been doing it forever. But the pain of being rejected is unimaginable. You're risking your future happiness because of your fear. That's kind of dumb."

Silver honest to God didn't know what to say to that. *You're wrong* was certainly an option, although not a truthful one. She had a bad feeling that Natalie had gotten it right on the first try.

"How on earth could you know all this?"

"I've been doing a lot of reading," Natalie admitted. "Ronan's still wrestling with all the crap in his family. I thought being informed would make me a better partner for him. It's really interesting and I'm finding it's influencing my art in unexpected ways. Which isn't the point."

She lowered her voice and her tone gentled. "You pushed him away on purpose."

"He wasn't supposed to go," Silver admitted, hating herself even as she acknowledged she was a wimp and a coward. "He was supposed to win me back."

"I'm sure he'll figure that out. He just needs a little time."

"I don't want to give him time. I want him punished. Julie, too."

"That's so nice." Natalie smiled. "Tell him you love him."

"Never."

"Tell him you love him. If you don't, you'll regret it for the rest of your life."

"I can't."

"You won't."

"I'm not brave, Natalie. It's all bluster. A facade. On the inside, I'm spun glass."

Her friend shook her head. "I might not have lived here that long, but I've heard stories about you. Silver, when you were a kid, you saw the life you had with your mom and you knew it wasn't good for you. You were strong enough to ask for something different. You came here when you were fifteen and you made a life. When you got pregnant, you found a great family for your daughter and you gave her a wonderful chance at a new future. You've created a successful business from nothing, you have a circle of friends who would walk through fire for you and through it all you've stayed honest and kind. That's an impressive legacy."

Silver's tears returned. "It's not like I speak Chinese."

"While that would be great, we don't have a massive Chinese-speaking population here in Happily Inc, so if you're looking for a new skill set you might want to try something different. You love Drew."

"I know."

"You're going to have to admit it. That's the only way to be free. If you're right and he dumps you, then you will feel the pain and you will move on. If, as I suspect, he loves you back, then you'll live happily ever after. Isn't that worth the risk?"

"No! It's not." Natalie was right — she was afraid she couldn't endure being spurned to her face. She didn't want to see the pity or scorn in his eyes.

Natalie's mouth dropped open. "Oh, Silver, I was wrong. I was so wrong. I'm sorry. It's *not* the pain of being rejected."

"You just said it was. I just accepted that was it. You can't change it now."

"You're not afraid he'll let you go — you're afraid he never loved you in the first place. If he loved you and got over you, that's one thing, but what if there wasn't ever love at all? What if it's all been one-sided, because that's how it was with your mom, wasn't it?"

Silver wanted to curl up in a ball and die. Instead she reached for the tequila and poured another shot. "You have got to stop whatever it is you're reading. It's not fair to the rest of us."

"He loves you," Natalie said firmly.

"Yeah, right." She downed the shot, licked salt off her hand, then sucked on a lime. "For a man in love, he sure walked away without a backward glance."

As for telling him how she felt . . . In her gut, she knew Natalie was right. At some point, she would have to come clean. If he cut her into little pieces, then she would figure out a way to put them back together and get on with her life. At least by telling him the truth, she would break the cycle. Maybe that would be enough to help her escape her mother's fate.

"After Bethany and Cade's party," she said aloud, to make it more real. "I'll confront him after the party."

"Good for you. And if I'm wrong and he's awful, I'll ask Ronan and his brothers to beat the crap out of him."

Silver managed a smile. "Thank you. You're a very good friend and I love you."

"I love you, too."

Preparation for the I Do BBQ party required all hands on deck. Silver arrived just after seven in the morning to find Renee was already working. The caterer would arrive at eleven to start setting up and Silver's trailers would be in place by noon. Keeping busy was the best antidote to a broken heart, she told herself. She was grateful to have a day full of something other than missing Drew.

Hay bales and all the decorations had arrived the previous day. While a small army of hired staff set up tables and chairs, both inside and out, Silver went to work blowing up balloons. She found the work oddly relaxing, which was both good and bad. While she enjoyed her mind finally quieting down, she hadn't slept in three days, so the downside of relaxing might be her keeling over in a dead sleep.

The florist showed up at nine. There were brightly colored arrangements in glass cowboy boot vases for the tables and sunflower kissing balls hanging down. Tall sprays of flowers flanked the entrances.

By eleven, Natalie, Carol, Wynn and Silver were setting up the lawn games.

"You sure about this?" Wynn asked as Natalie prepared to spray-paint a Twister board onto the lawn.

"It's going to be great," Natalie promised.

"I just can't see the royal crowd playing Twister," Wynn muttered.

There were His and Her beanbag toss games, horseshoes and croquet. As they worked, Silver found herself able to go minutes at a time and not think about Drew. It helped that none of her friends said anything, although the occasional arm squeeze or meaningful look told her they knew what had happened.

When the games were in place, they went inside. The tables were nearly finished.

Burlap table runners offset white table-cloths. Mason jars acted as water glasses. The promised taco bar was being set up and the grill for the s'mores had already been placed outside.

A little before one, Pallas called them to join her. Silver and her friends stood in front of Weddings Out of the Box as a long line of black SUVs pulled up.

Wynn grabbed Silver's hand. "Crap, she didn't tell us what to do. Do we curtsy? Just shake hands? I've never met royalty before."

"Renee swears a simple handshake is plenty."

"Okay. If you're sure." Wynn touched her stomach. "Why am I nervous? This is ridic-ulous."

Silver leaned close. "Because we all grew up reading about kings and queens and handsome princes."

"Yeah, look how that turned out."

The doors on the first SUV opened and three impressive-looking bodyguards stepped out. They were tall and muscled, wearing dark suits and sunglasses.

"Oh my." Wynn leaned close. "I could use me some of that."

"They're on duty."

"I can wait."

One of bodyguards moved to the second

SUV. Before he could open the door, Bethany stepped out of the third vehicle.

"I know, I know," she called with a laugh. "There's way too much pomp, right? Parents. I mean I love them but *sheesh.* Did they have to be royal?"

The passenger door to the second SUV opened and a tall, regal man stepped out. He, too, was dressed in a suit, but no one was going to mistake him for a bodyguard. Even without a crown, he managed to look kingly. A pretty woman in her late forties got out on the other side. Silver immediately saw the resemblance with her daughter.

The next few minutes were a blur of introductions. Silver shook hands with Bethany's parents. They were charming and friendly and seemed to know a bit about everyone. Bethany's younger brothers went off to inspect the games. Pallas and Renee ushered the entire royal party inside. The king and his entourage went into the groom's room while Queen Liana, Bethany and all Bethany's friends headed for the bride's room.

Once they were in the plush space, Liana kicked off her shoes and laughed. "Okay, tell me there's champagne because we have got to get this party started."

Silver had already placed champagne and

nonalcoholic sparkling cider on ice. She popped open the bottles and poured the bubbly liquid into glasses. Queen Liana smiled at all of them.

"All right. It's a test and I think I'm going to do great." She had the friends line up, then started at the left. "Pallas, Renee, Natalie, Wynn, Carol and Silver." She bit her bottom lip. "Is that right?"

"It's perfect, Mom."

"Excellent." The queen looked at her daughter. "Bethany, I love you so much and I want you to have a good time today." She turned back to her daughter's friends. "You're stuck calling her father King Malik, I'm sorry to say, but for today, I am simply Liana."

She set down her glass. "I heard about the cute outfits you have planned."

Pallas opened the large closet doors where the T-shirts and jean skirts were hanging. Cowboy boots sat below each outfit. Silver had wondered why Pallas had asked her to drop off her party outfit earlier in the week. When she saw the cute display she realized it was just one more fun touch to make the day memorable.

Liana and Pallas exchanged a glance. Pallas grinned. "So, Bethany, I hope this is okay. You're wearing the white T-shirt that says Bride and the white skirt with the fringe. The rest of us are in red Bride's Posse T-shirts and denim skirts. When I mentioned that to your mom, she wanted in on the action."

Bethany started to smile. "Mom, this is so like you. What did you do?"

Pallas reached for a pink T-shirt that said Mother of the Bride and a black denim skirt.

"I have the cutest boots to go with it," Liana said, sounding like a teenager. "I know you girls are too young to understand, but I'm getting really close to fifty and this may be my last chance to look hot, so I'm going for it." She grinned. "The skirt is just short enough to drive your father wild. I can't wait."

Bethany winced. "Um, Mom, no one wants to know about that, okay?"

"Perhaps, but he does know how to bring it."

Bethany sank onto one of the chairs and sighed. "Welcome to my world."

Silver found herself fighting unexpected tears. Not just because she missed Drew desperately but because the love between Bethany and her mom was so tangible. Family, when it worked, was the greatest gift, she thought wistfully.

CHAPTER TWENTY-ONE

Two hours with hair and makeup people working their magic, plenty of champagne and good friends went a long way to restoring Silver's mood. She knew that Drew was somewhere in the building, no doubt hanging out with Cade and waiting for the party to begin. While she wasn't looking forward to seeing him, she knew he wouldn't do or say anything today. He would never embarrass his cousin. Silver figured with a bit of planning on her part, she could easily stay out of his way. As for his parents, well, she barely knew his father and she doubted Irene wanted to spend any time with her, so it was all good.

Liana and Bethany walked out arm in arm, the Bride's Posse friends behind. There were already at least a hundred people around with more arriving. Music played and the bars were open. She made a conscious effort not to see Drew anywhere.

Perhaps an impossible task, but one she was committed to.

Silver found herself with Wynn for a while. A little later, Natalie and Ronan seemed to be shadowing her. It took her a while to figure out that her friends had a plan — for the duration of the party, someone would always be nearby. She spotted Irene and the man she assumed was Drew's father talking to the king and queen. She felt a moment of disquiet, then reminded herself whatever his parents had going on with the royal family was the least of her problems. She had to get through the rest of the party without having an emotional meltdown.

She stayed strong through the buffet. She found herself seated between Ronan and Mathias, with their respective fiancées nearby. They kept her laughing with ridiculous stories about growing up in Fool's Gold. Once she looked up and saw Drew talking with Jasper. For a second their eyes met. She felt a combination of pain and desperate longing, then quickly turned away. She didn't look up from her plate for at least a minute and by then he'd moved on.

After eating, people went outside. The games were a hit and when the band started playing, dozens of couples got up to dance.

Silver was enjoying the music, full, a little buzzed and content with the day. She'd done well, she told herself. Maybe getting over Drew wasn't going to be as hard as she —

"Silver, we have to talk."

She didn't have to turn around to know who was speaking. She recognized the voice. Her sense of being okay went poof, leaving her scared and hurting.

"This isn't the place or time," she said, refusing to look at him. She kept her attention on the dancers. King Malik and his wife were quite the couple, moving in time with the music and gazing into each other's eyes. *A love that lasted,* she thought with a sigh. That must be nice.

"Silver, please."

She made the mistake of turning around and looking into his eyes. Just being close to him was enough to make her weak. She nodded once, then braced herself for what was to come. He reached for her hand and led her inside.

They ended up in the groom's room. The smaller space had only one mirror and no big closet, but there was plenty of seating.

She chose one of the chairs rather than the sofa so he couldn't be too close, then waited while he settled across from her. He leaned toward her, his elbows on his thighs, his hands linked together.

"There's a lot going on," he began. "My parents and everything they wanted. You and me, Autumn. I've had a lot to consider."

"And Julie."

"What?"

"You left out Julie. Your dinner together in Palm Springs."

"How did you know about that?"

"Your mother forwarded your text. So how was it?"

She knew she sounded bitchy, but she couldn't help it. If Drew had some big emotional revelation, he would have started with that. He would have begun by telling her he missed her, missed them. That he loved her. But this conversation wasn't heading that way.

"She was flying home," he told her. "I drove her to the airport. Her flight wasn't for a few hours so we went to dinner."

"I'm sure it was lovely." She stood. "Drew, there's nothing to say."

He stood. "There is and you need to listen. Silver, everything is different now. We're not kids. This is real. That week with Autumn showed me what I've been missing."

She couldn't do this, she thought desperately. Couldn't hear him say he didn't want her. Yes, she was a coward and she would feel bad about that later, but for now she had to protect herself.

She ran to the door and jerked it open. "Silver, wait!"

She saw Wynn in the hallway. Her friend made a beeline for her.

"There you are. I've been looking for you all over." Wynn glanced over Silver's shoulder and saw Drew. "Stay or go?"

"Go," Silver whispered. "We have to go."

Wynn led her back to the party. Silver stayed near her friends and tried to find her happy place but it was gone. She slipped out quietly and went home. Once there, she curled up in bed and closed her eyes.

She would be fine, she told herself. Perfectly and completely fine. All she needed was time and a big enough head injury for her to lose her memory. Until then, she was going to have to fake it — even with herself.

Silver must have fallen asleep because the sound of her phone ringing woke her. She grabbed it and pushed the talk button.

"Hello?"

"Where are you?"

She recognized Renee's voice. "I'm home. What's going on?"

"Oh, something you have to see to believe. Seriously, we have a big problem here. Hurry."

With that, Renee hung up.

Silver got up and looked at her phone. It was close to midnight. The party would have ended hours ago, so what could be going on?

She grabbed her keys and made her way back to Weddings Out of the Box. The whole place was dark and there weren't any cars except . . .

She recognized Drew's car parked near the long fence line. As she got closer, her headlights swept across a man holding a spray paint can. Sloppy letters covered the fence from one end to the other: *Drew Loves Silver.* There were dozens of crooked hearts, some with arrows piercing them. There were also some stars and an animal of some kind but she wasn't sure if it was a horse or a dog or what.

She parked and got out, leaving her headlights on to illuminate the scene.

Drew turned and saw her. "Silver!" He sounded delighted — and drunk. "You're here. Look what I did. I said it all wrong before. I told Julie I loved you and she said she was the wrong person to hear the message. That I had to tell you. But when I tried, you left and it was wrong." He paused. "*Wrong* is a really funny word."

He pointed to the fence. "I love you and I want the world to know. Isn't it great?"

"It's your cousin's business and you've just defaced it. No, it's not great. You don't love me, Drew. You don't know what you want but I'm pretty sure it's not me."

"You're wrong." He grinned. "Wrong, wrong, wrong."

A car drove up. Silver groaned when she saw it belonged to the Happily Inc police department.

"Garrick," she said as a familiar officer got out of his vehicle.

"Silver." He shook his head. "You're attracting trouble these days. Want to talk about it?"

"Not really."

"He do this?"

"He's holding the paint can, Garrick. I would have thought your training covered this sort of thing."

"I would have thought you'd want to plead his case."

She was tired of all of it. Of Drew coming and going, of hearing about Julie, of the backhanded "I love you." She wanted to believe it, but come on, he told her with spray paint? How was she supposed to

438

believe that?

"Okay, then." Garrick walked over to Drew. "I guess you're with me."

"Is Silver coming, too?"

"Not this time." Garrick looked at the wall. "Pallas is not going to be happy."

"Drew's her cousin," Silver said. "She might not be happy, but she'll be understanding."

Silver waited until Garrick drove away, then returned to her truck. She would head home, send Pallas a text about what had happened, then figure out what to do with the rest her life. She was halfway back to her loft apartment when she passed the Sweet Dreams Inn. Involuntarily, she slowed as she saw what looked an awful lot like Wynn and one of the sexy bodyguards heading into the hotel.

"OMG," Silver said out loud, then started to laugh. No matter how much she hurt, she had to admit her life was never, ever boring.

Drew didn't remember being arrested, nor did he recall passing out but as he woke up in a jail cell, he was going to guess both had happened.

He lay on the cot, dealing with his headache, his lack of memory and a sense of having been not only stupid, but really stupid.

It was still dark outside. He had no watch, no cell phone and there wasn't a clock on any of the walls, but he suspected it was close to three or four in the morning. He was also alone in his cell — a fact for which he was grateful.

He sat up slowly. The world spun a couple of times, then stilled. His stomach wasn't happy and the pounding in his head was going to take a while to resolve, but he'd survived.

"You're awake."

He looked up and saw Garrick walking toward his cell. The officer had a mug in his hand.

"If that's coffee and it's for me, I will owe you forever."

Garrick passed him the mug. "I'll make a note of that. Want to throw up?"

"Not especially."

"Good. I don't want these to go to waste." He handed over two aspirin and a four-pack of crackers.

"You're prepared." Drew took a sip of the coffee.

"It's a wedding destination town. We don't have a lot of serious crime. Mostly it's party-related. People get drunk and do dumb things."

There was something in the other man's tone. As if . . .

Drew swore. "Tell me I didn't spray-paint the wall at Weddings Out of the Box."

"The fence."

His memory started to return. "Did I write Drew Loves Silver over and over again?"

"Yup. And there was some weird animal. I have no idea what it was."

"Me, either." He rubbed his temple and swore. "Silver was there, wasn't she?"

"Uh-huh. For what it's worth, she let me arrest you."

"I'm sure she thought I deserved it. Oh crap. We talked about Julie."

Garrick chuckled. "I knew there was a story. I've spoken with Pallas and she's not pressing charges."

Drew closed his eyes. "She's got to be pissed. Jeez, what was I thinking?"

"You weren't. It happens. I'm going to call someone to come get you. Odds are you're still too drunk to drive. I don't want to use a Breathalyzer to be sure, because then I'll have to write it up and I hate having to write it up." He held up Drew's phone. "You get to pick who."

Cade would be with his bride-to-be. No way Silver would want to rescue him. "Jasper," he said, motioning to the phone. "His number is in there."

"I'll tell him to hurry."

"Thanks."

Garrick left to make the call. Drew sank back on the cot and wondered how he was going to fix everything that had gone wrong. Twenty minutes later, he still didn't have a plan, but it turned out he did have a visitor. Instead of Jasper walking in, Drew saw his father. Because the night just couldn't get any worse.

Garrick escorted his father into the cell and unlocked the door. Drew looked at the officer.

"What happened to Jasper?"

Drew's father shrugged out of his jacket and sat on the only chair in the cell. "I'm old friends with the sergeant on duty. He called me when he realized you'd been brought in."

"He got here first," Garrick said with a shrug. "I've already let Jasper know you have a ride."

Drew wasn't happy to know the night could get worse. He sat on the cot and waited for what he was sure was going to be a hell of a lecture. Under other circumstances he would tell his father to go pound sand — that he wasn't in the mood to listen.

But today he thought maybe, just maybe, he'd earned a good talking-to.

"I've been thinking a lot about Autumn," his father said, surprising him with the topic. "How old is she?"

"Eleven."

"That's a good age. I meant what I said before. I want to meet her."

Drew blinked in surprise. "Ah, sure."

"I'd like that. Your mother . . ." He leaned back in the chair. "Irene is ambitious, more ambitious than I am. She has always had big dreams and she's willing to do the work to get there."

Or walk over anyone who got in her way, Drew thought, but didn't say.

"Sometimes she forgets not everyone shares her worldview," his father continued. "Sometimes she lets her determination blind her to what's important. Like the people we love. Drew, if you don't want to join the firm, then don't. You're blessed — you have enough food to eat and a roof over your head. You have options and so many people don't. Why be unhappy on purpose?"

"I know, Dad. I've told her and told her, but she won't listen."

"Maybe because she knows you're not telling the truth. Or at least not all of it. You can't just run from something — you have to also be moving toward something else. What is it you want? What's missing?"

"Silver." Drew spoke without thinking because no thought was required. She was what he wanted. Her and them together and more children and a life that made them both giddy.

"I know you love her, but —"

"No, Dad. There's not a but in that sentence. I want to be with Silver. I want to stay in this ridiculous little town. I want to be a part of local businesses and help them grow. I want to fund start-ups and turn AlcoHaul into a franchise and be a good man who is married to the woman of his dreams. That's what I want."

His father studied him for a long time. "There's a lot of your grandfather in you," he said at last. "That story we all tell about the founding of the town, how your grandfather lied to get people coming here to get married, he didn't just do it for the bank. There was enough money — the family would have been all right. He did it for the town. Without him, there would be no Happily Inc today." He smiled at Drew. "Now what?"

"I have no idea. Silver made it clear she doesn't want to be with me."

"Did she? Was this before or after you

fought for her?"

"There's no fighting when it comes to Silver."

"Son, I may not know much about women, but I know this. They want a man willing to walk through fire for them. That goes a long way. If you fight the good fight and lose, then I'll be on your side, but if you don't even try, then you deserve what you get."

He started to say he didn't have anything, only to realize that was his father's point. He hadn't fought for her. She'd even said the same thing. Spray-painted words on the side of a wall didn't count. She needed to know that he meant it, that she was the best, most important part of his world. She needed to be convinced. Which sounded great, but he genuinely had no idea how to make that happen.

"It'll come to you in the moment," his father said. "Trust me. Better yet, trust yourself."

"I'm not sure I'm a good bet. I haven't gotten it right yet."

"Oh, I don't know. I've always been proud of you, son. I still am."

The words got him a lot more than he would have expected. He had to clear his throat before he could speak. "Thanks, Dad.

Any chance you can spring me from jail?"

His father chuckled. "Let me go see what I can do."

CHAPTER TWENTY-TWO

Silver spent Sunday feeling sorry for herself. Pallas texted to say that Drew was painting over the fence himself and that all was forgiven. Silver doubted her friend had been angry in the first place. It was a stupid stunt and he was making it right. Good for Pallas. What bothered Silver a lot more was that she had no idea what it meant for her.

She'd been so angry the night of the party. So humiliated. To have him write that, say it that way, had crushed her. Worse, she didn't know if it had been a spur-of-the-moment "Hey, I'm drunk" thing or if he'd meant it. Did he love her? Was he messing with her? Or had it been the liquor talking? Was his heart involved at all?

She hated that she couldn't ask. Okay, yes, technically she could text him or call or hey, even go see him, but she wasn't going to. Not when her feelings were so raw. And it wasn't as if she was hearing from him. There hadn't been a single peep from the man, damn him.

Around five, Silver realized she was in a horrible spiral. She went to the grocery store and bought a bunch of fruits and vegetables and vowed that first thing in the morning, she would go to the gym and throw the produce into her Vitamix and drink all the nutritious goodness. She would give up booze and sugar for at least a week. Then she would make some decisions about her life.

Monday morning, she'd barely gotten home from the gym when someone knocked on her apartment door. She opened it to find Grandpa Frank on her landing.

"Good morning, Silver. I wonder if I might have the pleasure of your company for an hour or two."

The old man looked dapper in a dark suit, white shirt and striped tie. By contrast, she was in shorts, a tank top and athletic shoes. Her hair was pulled back in a ponytail, she wasn't wearing makeup and she hadn't even had time to shower after her workout.

"Now? I kind of need a few minutes to freshen up."

"I'm afraid we don't have time." He smiled and tapped his watch. "Come along."

She didn't know Grandpa Frank that well,

but she doubted he was going to kidnap her. As to why he would want her with him, she honestly had no idea, but he wasn't someone she could comfortably refuse.

"All right," she murmured, grabbing her bag and the smoothie she'd made for after her workout. "But I can't be gone long."

They walked down to his Mercedes. He held open the passenger door for her, then carefully closed it when she was seated. He walked around to the driver's side and got in next to her.

It was only when they'd pulled away from the curb that she thought to ask, "Where are we going?"

"To the bank's board meeting."

"What?" Her voice came out as a yelp. "I can't go there dressed like this."

"You look lovely."

"I'm dressed for the gym."

"You'll be fine."

He drove past Weddings Out of the Box and pointed to the freshly painted wall. "Drew did that himself. He didn't hire anyone to clean up his mess."

"Maybe he shouldn't have made the mess in the first place," she grumbled.

"He did it for you."

"Drunken spray-painting isn't exactly how a woman wants to be wooed." She didn't bother explaining that she still wasn't sure if he'd meant what he wrote or not. The fact that she hadn't heard from him since that night didn't bode well.

Grandpa Frank pulled into the bank's parking lot but instead of getting out he turned to her. "I've lived a very good life. Along the way, I've learned a few things. Choices can make all the difference in the world." He pulled an envelope out of his suit jacket pocket. "For you, my dear."

Silver opened the envelope and saw a check for a hundred thousand dollars. Her mind went blank. "I don't understand."

"It's a bank loan, if you're interested." He smiled. "I heard what happened and I went over your loan application. As far as I'm concerned, you're an excellent risk and I still have a little pull here."

"This check isn't from the bank," she said, staring at him. "It's from your personal account."

His smile broadened. "I was hoping you wouldn't notice. You're right, it is. But the loan is still real, Silver. With the same terms as the bank loan. As I said, it's important to be able to have options. Sometimes the freedom to make a decision doesn't matter at all but other times it means everything."

"If Drew isn't my business partner, then

he's free to choose," she whispered, looking between the check and Grandpa Frank. "I'll know he's really doing what he wants to do and not staying because he feels obligated to me."

"Drew has always had a powerful sense of responsibility. The man does like to do the right thing."

If he knew he wasn't her partner, then he could follow his heart, she thought, barely able to breathe. And she would know what he actually wanted. Her or something else.

"You're sure?" she asked.

"Very, but I do need an answer. Do we have a deal, my dear?"

"We do." She put the check in her bag. "We absolutely do."

They walked into the bank. Silver was very conscious of her casual attire, and the feeling of not fitting in only got worse when they entered the crowded conference room. There was a big center table with about twenty chairs around it and dozens more lining the outside of the room.

Everyone was dressed in suits and they all turned to look at her as she and Grandpa Frank walked in.

"Hello. This is Silver. She's my guest."

Silver did her best not to look as out of place as she felt. She accidentally met

Libby's frosty gaze and turned away only to stumble into Drew.

"Silver. What are you doing here?"

"Your grandfather asked me to come." She ignored the rapid beating of her heart and the love that swelled up inside of her. She knew the right thing to do. She'd known it twelve years ago when she'd first gotten pregnant and she knew it now.

She grabbed his hand and pulled him into the hallway. When the door had closed behind him, she said, "Drew, Grandpa Frank is loaning me the money to cover the costs of the trailers and the trucks and everything. I can buy you out as soon as the check is in my bank account. You don't have to do this."

"What are you talking about?"

"You don't have to stay because of me. Because of the business. I want . . ." *I want you to know I will love you forever. I want you to know you're the best man I've ever known. I want you to know I have dreamed about us being together and there is absolutely nothing in the world I want more.*

But she didn't say any of that. "I want you to be happy. I want you to follow your dreams, wherever they lead you."

"You're determined to get rid of me, aren't you?"

"I'm determined you do what's right for you."

She was proud of herself for being strong, no matter how much it was going to hurt later. She loved him enough to let him go.

"And you think you know what that is?" he asked.

"Not at all. What I don't want is you trapped by obligation. Now there isn't any."

The door opened and Irene glared at them. "Drew, get in here. Your grandfather is starting the meeting." She turned her icy gaze on Silver. "You need to leave."

"No," Drew said. "She's staying, Mom."

Silver debated taking off, but she had to know what was going to happen next. She ignored Irene and followed Drew back into the boardroom. Grandpa Frank stood at the front of the room and he gaveled the meeting into order.

Drew didn't know what to make of his grandfather's move with the money. Going into business with Silver had been his idea. He liked being a part of what she did. With the loan, she didn't need him, which, based on what she'd said, seemed to be the point.

He sat at the table. He could see his parents. Silver had taken a seat behind him, so he had no idea how she was reacting to the proceedings. There was the usual board business, then Grandpa Frank once again stood.

"We're here to select a new chairperson. Libby and Drew are the main contenders unless someone else wants to throw their hat in the ring." He waited for a second. "No? All right. You know each of the candidates, but before the board votes, I suggest Libby and Drew each make a statement."

Libby immediately rose to her feet. "Thank you," she said, looking at each of the board members in turn. "This bank is an honorable institution with a proud history. We have always been a pillar of the community. I know times are changing, but not all change is good."

She turned to Drew. "I'm worried that the other candidate isn't prepared for the responsibility of running things here. I've hoped he would grow into the role but in the past few months, he's shown me that he might never be ready."

Drew's mother sprang to her feet. "Libby, what are you doing?"

"Telling the truth." Libby slipped on her glasses and picked up a piece of paper. "Drew has a child out of wedlock, which in this day and age seems perfectly fine, except he is in no way supporting that child." She looked at him over her glasses. "He discarded his eleven-year-old daughter like a used tissue, walking away and never once trying to get in touch with her."

Everyone stared at him. Drew did his best not to respond. He would have his chance later.

"In addition, he's bought into a bar. He spends his weekends serving drinks at parties. Just this past Saturday he was arrested for drunk and disorderly conduct after using spray paint to deface a private business." She pulled off her glasses. "I ask you, is Drew really someone we want running our bank? Do we trust him with the welfare of our clients? I submit he isn't ready for the responsibility."

With that, she sat down.

Drew stood. His mother was practically frothing and his father had a death grip on her arm. His grandfather looked more amused than upset and he had no idea what anyone else was thinking, nor did he care.

"Libby makes a strong case about what I've done wrong, but no case at all for what she'll do right," he began. "So let me address both sides of that. It's true, I have an eleven-year-old daughter, but I did not abandon her. Her mother and I gave her up for adoption. Autumn has been loved and cared for since before she was born. She's a great kid and doing just fine."

He thought about what else she had accused him of. "I did buy a minority partnership in a local business. AlcoHaul is a traveling bar that is a critical part of our wedding industry and this community. As for getting arrested, I have no excuse. It was about something personal and I was an idiot. If that's enough to disqualify me, then I accept the consequences for my actions."

He thought about what Libby hadn't said. "Here's what I would do differently if I ran this bank. I would make sure we were friendlier to local businesses. I think taking a risk on our own community is important. I think we should have more financial literacy, and to that end, I'd like to offer free seminars on various aspects of banking and money management. We aren't a multinational corporation and that means we have more flexibility. Let's work for good *and* for profit. They don't have to be mutually exclusive. We should fight for what's important. We should —"

Not just the bank, he thought unexpectedly. He should be fighting for what was important. He should be fighting for Silver. He hadn't — not when they were kids and not now.

He returned his attention to the meeting. "Anyway," he said. "That's all." He stepped away from the table. "Libby and I will get out of your way so you can vote."

Libby glared at him. "You don't get to say that. You're not in charge of this meeting."

He ignored her and turned to where Silver was sitting, gaping at him.

"Could I see you outside for a moment?"

Silver was so impressed by what Drew had said that she forgot to be embarrassed by what she was wearing. He'd been forceful without being a jerk and he'd totally put Libby in her place. She was impressed and proud and just a little bit weepy.

They stepped into the hall only to have every other nonboard member join them. Drew pulled her into his office and shut the door behind him.

"Hi," he said, looking at her. "How's it going?"

She twisted her hands together. "Drew, you did really great in there. Libby's awful."

"She is, but that's not what I want to talk to you about." He stared at her. "I was going to tell you that I'm sorry I haven't fought for you. Not before and not now."

Was? He *was* going to say that? What had changed his mind?

"The thing is I realized you've never fought for me, either," he continued. "You've always let me go."

"It was for your —"

He held up his hand to stop her. "My own good. Yes, I know. That's what you've always said and a disinterested bystander might agree, but I'm wondering if that's all it was. Did you also let me go because it was less scary than asking me to stay?"

Silver felt herself flush as her heart rate increased. He'd guessed her deepest, darkest secret and she was more scared than she'd ever been in her life.

"I love you, Silver. I love your strength, your laugh, your kindness, your big heart. I love how you get stubborn and how you're independent. You're a smart businesswoman and a good friend and an amazing mother. But you're also afraid. You love me enough to let me go but do you love me enough to want to keep me?"

He smiled at her. "I ask because that's what I've had to see. I never fought for you, not the way I should have. I let you go that summer because of college. I signed away Autumn because I didn't have a clue as to what I was giving up. And I nearly lost you again today. Well, I'm not going to let that happen. I love you and I'm standing here saying I will fight as hard as I have to because I want to keep you in my life. For always."

Tears burned. Happy tears and sad tears and every other kind.

"I'm sorry," she told him. "I'm so scared that I'll be like my mother, living my life for a man who won't love me back. It was easier to let you go. I was scared to fight for you."

"And now?"

Here it was — her moment of truth. She stared into his eyes.

"I will absolutely fight for you, no matter what. If you want to go to D.C. and work with your parents, I'll go with you. I'll sell the business and find something there. If you want to stay here and run the bank, that would be even better, but whatever you decide, I'm with you. I want you to be happy and I want you to be happy with me. I love you, Drew. I've loved you since that first summer. I wanted to believe I was okay but the truth is I never got over you. Not even for a second."

He pulled her close and she hung on as tight as she could. She rested her head on his shoulder and breathed in the wonder of him. Then his mouth was on hers and the world slowly righted itself.

"Okay," he said as he pulled back. "Let's

get some things straight. I don't want to move to D.C."

"Are you sure?"

"Silver, I'm sure. I want to stay here. I want to be your business partner and your husband. I can do both."

"Technically you haven't proposed, but okay, I'll go with it. I want to stay here, too."

"Good. That's out of the way. Now, about the other part."

Before she knew what was happening, he dropped to one knee. "Silver, I love you. Will you marry me? Will you join me in promising we will always fight for each other? Marry me, love me, let me love you."

Happiness bubbled inside of her. She smiled at him. "Gee, Drew, this is so sudden."

He was still laughing as he stood, pulled her close and swung her around. "Answer me, woman!"

"Yes, of course, yes."

He set her down. "Are you going to give that check back to my grandfather? Can I still be your business partner?"

"You are my everything, but I had a thought about the check."

He raised his eyebrows. "Which is?"

"You made a very impassioned speech about helping out in the community. It seems to be something you care about. Why not do that along with working at the bank?"

"I'd like to start an angel fund and give start-ups the cash to get going."

"Don't forget the financial literacy classes. Maybe that could be some kind of a non-profit thing. Oh, you could work with the local high school." She grinned. "You know, your grandfather was willing to give me a hundred thousand dollars just because. Imagine what he would give you if you asked."

"I might have to do that."

She touched his face. "Your parents aren't going to be happy."

"I can live with that, if you're okay with it."

"I never wanted you to choose, Drew. I don't want you to lose your family."

"My mom's going to take a while to come around, but I think my dad will work on her. As for the rest of them, they love you already."

"Not Libby."

He chuckled. "I think you're going to be Libby's best friend. After all, she's about to get her heart's desire. I'm going to tell the board I'm withdrawing my name from consideration."

"What? Are you sure? You love the bank."

461

He kissed her. "I love you and I like what the bank can do for people, but I have a feeling I can do a lot more outside of the bank. Besides, I still have the franchise thing to work on."

She studied him. "Are you sure?"

"I am. Of being with you and of my future." He looked at her. "I love you, Silver."

"I love you, too."

"Ready to face the world?"

"Absolutely. As long as we're together."

They went back into the board meeting. Silver waited while Drew withdrew his name from consideration. Irene wept but Howard gave his son a thumbs-up and Grandpa Frank winked.

Later, at Drew's place, they sat on the patio, watched the giraffes and talked about their future together. There was no more looking back — just looking forward to a lifetime full of love and wonderful possibilities.

ABOUT THE AUTHOR

Bestselling author **Susan Mallery** writes heartwarming, humorous novels about the relationships that define our lives — family, friendship, romance. She's known for putting nuanced characters in emotional situations that surprise readers to laughter. Beloved by millions, her books have been translated into 28 languages. Susan lives in Washington with her husband, two cats, and a small poodle with delusions of grandeur. Visit her at SusanMallery.com.

The employees of Thorndike Press hope you have enjoyed this Large Print book. All our Thorndike, Wheeler, and Kennebec Large Print titles are designed for easy reading, and all our books are made to last. Other Thorndike Press Large Print books are available at your library, through selected bookstores, or directly from us.

For information about titles, please call:
  (800) 223-1244

or visit our website at:
  gale.com/thorndike

To share your comments, please write:
  Publisher
  Thorndike Press
  10 Water St., Suite 310
  Waterville, ME 04901